SUPER G

FANTASTIC BOOKS FOR KIDS 8-12

Diary of a
SUPER GIRL

KATRINA KAHLER & JOHN ZAKOUR

Table of Contents

Book 1 - The Ups and Downs of Being Super 5

Book 2 - The New Normal 125

Book 3 - The Power of Teamwork! 221

Book 1

The Ups and Downs
of
Being Super

The Long Day...

"I leaped across the parking lot towards this black van car. The bad guys were in it. They turned and saw me and hit the gas! I leaped again and picked up the car like it weighed nothing! I turned the car over and shook it until the bad guys fell out...They rolled to the ground, and then each ran off in opposite directions...I took off my shoe and tossed it at one of them. It hit him on the back of the head...he fell to the ground, out cold. Truthfully, I'm not sure if he was knocked out by the force or the smell of the shoe! I turned to see the other guy. No way I was letting him get away!"

I noticed my hands had clenched into fists as I told my story to Jason.

"Then what happened?" Jason asked me, a smile on his face.

"Then I woke up...," I said.

"Bummer," he said, his smile fading. "It sounded like a great dream, Lia!"

"It seemed so real!" I said with a shrug. "I blame you! You're the one always talking about superheroes and comic books!"

"Well, comics are awesome," he said.

It had been a LONG day at school. Still, no matter how terrible my school day went, I always enjoyed my walk home with my best friend, Jason. Okay, I know what you're thinking, he's a boy, and he's a friend, but he's not my boyfriend. We're more like BFFs. Mom and I moved to our new home in Starlight City when I was three. I walked out of my house and saw three-year-old Jason playing with Lego in his yard, alongside his mom. My mom and I walked over. Jason handed me a piece of Lego and said, "Play!" I smiled and said, "Yes!" Hey, we were three years old. We didn't have the biggest vocabulary back then. But we still knew, at first sight, we'd be friends forever.

Yeah, it's kind of funny to be BFF with a boy, but since that day, we have shared everything. Maybe someday it could turn into more of a crush. After all, I guess he's good-looking, and he's fun to hang out with. But like I said, I've known him forever, well, at least as long as I can remember. So, dating him might be weird. We're like brother and sister in many ways, except, of course, we get along really well.

"So. How'd you do on the science test?" Jason asked, coaxing me to the present.

"I can't believe I got a B on that," I sighed in frustration. "I thought for sure I had an A- at worst. I studied the planets in our system so well. I remembered all the moons. I knew Pluto is now a dwarf planet...Which I don't agree with, BTW." I looked at Jason in disgust. I should definitely have got at least an A-.

He smiled sympathetically. "I'm with you on that. I mean, come on, how can Pluto be a planet one day and some other day it's not. Just because a bunch of space research people said, it's not big enough to be a planet?" He paused for a second. "Oh, when I say it like that, I can kind of see why they changed their mind…I guess I'm just not big on change."

"Me either," I replied.

Then something else came to mind that I was also annoyed about. "And it's not fair that lacrosse practice is so hard. I swear Coach Blue thinks we're training for the Olympics or something. She ran us up and down the field so many times. I believe my sweat was breaking out in a sweat. I desperately need a shower. I must smell right now…."

"I haven't noticed," Jason said politely. He pointed to his nose and smiled. "Of course, I do have a head cold."

I gave him a friendly little shove. He playfully went staggering backward like I had pushed him too hard. "Be careful!" he said, fake rubbing his arm. "You are way strong!"

I shook my head, "Not according to our team captain, Miss Perfect, Wendi Long. She said that I need to work on my abs and my wrist shot… I'm surprised she didn't critique my breath and hairstyle."

Jason shrugged. "Ah, you can't blame Wendi. She's not a bad person. It's just that being perfect comes naturally to her."

I gave him another friendly little push. "You just say that because she's the best-looking girl in the school."

"Well yeah, but only if you like golden blond hair, sea-blue eyes, and perfectly clear peach complexion…." He grinned.

I sighed. "Yeah, she seems immune to zits…Unlike me. I have one on my nose that needs its own postal code."

Jason laughed. "It's not that bad. Nobody has called you Rudolph yet…." He paused for a second. "You ready for the big day tomorrow?"

"You mean the math quiz?" I said though I knew what he was getting at.

"No, you turn the big 1-3 tomorrow. You become a teen!"

"Well, *you* became a teen last week," I said. "So far, have you seen any difference between being a teen and a tween?"

Jason stopped walking. He looked up at the clear blue sky and thought for a moment. Scratching his head, he said,

"Now that you mention it, I feel older. I think my back cracks more, and I believe I might have a gray hair…"

"Ha ha!" I told him.

He gave me a friendly pat on the shoulder. "Nah, so far, 12 and 13 seem the same to me. But who knows, maybe for you, it will be different. After all, girls mature quicker than boys," he said.

I laughed. "We do mature mentally faster!"

Jason started using his fist to make noises with his armpit. "What makes you say that?" he said, squeaking away.

We laughed all the way to our houses.

Home Sweet Home...

I got home and kicked my shoes off the second I walked in the door. Shep, my ever-loyal German Shepherd, ran up to me, tail wagging away. It's great to come home to somebody who is so excited to see me. Shep licked me a few times as I bent over to pat him. Then he turned his attention to my shoes. For some reason, he always insists on sniffing my shoes when I get home.

"Ah, Shep, those things probably smell bad!" I warned. "It's been a long day."

But that didn't stop Shep. He sniffed my shoes contentedly. "Wow, you are a tough dog!" I laughed.

Walking into the living room, I plopped down on the couch. I needed a nap. The funny thing was when I was a little kid, I HATED naps. I guess I felt that I'd miss out on something if I slept. Today, after a day of tests and practice, I needed a 20-minute power nap. It wasn't just the work that got to me. Sometimes I felt the hardest part of middle school was dealing with other middle school kids who I couldn't help thinking were always rating me and comparing me to other girls. There were so many things to worry about. Right then, I had a giant zit on my nose and was sure that everyone must have noticed it. But my main worry was what Wendi Long was saying about me on Facebook and in private to her friends. I could only imagine what she said behind my back. Eventually, I fell asleep and dreamed of being an ugly duckling who turned into a beautiful swan. Weird!

I woke up a little later at the sound of the front door closing.

"Mom?" I called, half-awake from the couch. I pulled out my phone and looked at the time: 4:20 that was early for mom. "Is everything okay?"

She didn't usually leave work early. At least not since I was old enough to watch out for myself. Mom and I have been alone for as long as I can remember. In fact, I can barely recall my dad. But that's okay. Mom and I make a great team.

She walked into the living room still in her white medical scrubs. "I came home early," she said, sitting beside my feet on the couch. "Looks and smells like you had a long day." She broke into a wide grin.

"Yeah, it's been pretty big," I replied. "I'm wrecked! What are we doing for dinner?"

"How's pizza sound?" she smiled.

"Like you read my mind!" I told her, my own face breaking into a smile of its own. "But you still haven't said why you're home early?"

"My last surgery got canceled, so I figured I'd head home before they asked me to do something else." She patted me on the legs. "Spend the evening with my daughter. After all, you're going to be 13 tomorrow."

"I realize that, Mom."

She looked me in the eyes. "There's something I want to talk to you about before the big day. Prepare you...."

My eyes popped open. "Mom! I know about the *birds and the bees,* as you call it. You've already talked about that, and then they talked about it at school as well."

She laughed. "No, it's not that. It's just well, your name is Lia Strong, and you're part of the Strong family. You're also one of the Strong women. You don't know this yet, but all of us Strong women change when we hit the teen years," she was talking slowly, hoping I would understand.

"Mom, I know about puberty and the changes it brings!" I told her. I pointed to my body. "Some of them have started already!"

"That's actually not what I'm referring to." She stood up from the couch, then bent down to touch her toes and stretched upwards again. "Strong women change, differently...."

"Mom, what are you talking about?"

Without another word, she bent down and picked up the couch with me on it. Then she lifted it over her head with one hand. And when I say lift it, she did it easily, like it was a twig.

"What the...."

"Lia! Watch your language!" she scolded before I could finish.

"Yeah, this is definitely different!" I said.

"I told you," Mom replied, lowering the couch with me still on it, back to the floor. "You take a shower and change while I order the food. We'll talk over pizza and wings."

"You drop this on me and then say, we'll chat in a bit?" I looked at her in amazement and shook my head. This was too much to take in.

She put a gentle hand on my shoulder. "Believe me, honey. This is a wonderful change. But like all changes, it will take some getting used to. But I promise you'll understand it better with a full stomach."

I sat up on the couch. "There were a lot of buts in that statement," I told her.

She smiled, and I could see she was not going to say another word. Finding it hard to believe what had just happened, I got up and headed upstairs. Right then, I figured it best not to argue with a mom who could lift the couch. If what she said was true, tomorrow I would be able to do that too. I had a million questions running through my brain. But Mom was right. This would all go down better after a shower and pizza. Not sure why, but a good shower always cleared my head. And tasty pizza puts me in a good mood. Yeah! My mom was one sharp lady.

The New Rules...

Mom and I sat down at the kitchen table, pizza and wings between us. Something about the smell of a pizza puts me at ease.

"So, how was your day?" Mom asked, pouring some pepper on her pizza.

"Mom! I've been very patient so far!" I replied abruptly. Right then, I think I had the right to be frustrated.

She grinned. "Okay, okay...well...first off, being super is...well... super. We can do things other people only dream of."

I nibbled on a piece of pizza and shook my head in agreement. "Yes, I noticed you lifting a couch like nothing... How strong are we?"

"Each of us differs. You know your grandma can still whip a gator like nothing. Your great-grandma can lift over 300 pounds with one hand. Though, of course, she never does that in public. And she insists her mom could throw a tank the length of a football field easily." Mom told me all of this in her most serious voice.

"Wow!" It was the only word I could think of as a response.

"Well put," Mom said, munching on a wing. "We have other abilities too.... I'll only mention the basic ones until we see what ones show up in you. All our senses are very heightened. Our skin is very dense. Yes, it can be poked and penetrated by some sharp objects, but we heal very quickly."

"So, we're like Wolverine in the X-men movies."

Mom bobbed her head. "Kind of. Only no claws."

"Phew!" I said.

"Oh, we also have super-breath," Mom told me, apparently reminded by my sigh. "Well, technically, it's not the breath. Our lungs are just super powerful. Which means we can blow people away and toss them over and over."

I smiled. "Oh, that's so cool!"

"Except if you forget and sneeze," she told me. "That can be bad!"

I slumped back in my chair.

"You just have to be calm and relax, Lia, and you'll be fine," She spoke with a confident assurance. But it was one that I certainly didn't feel. "Mom! I'm a teenage girl! Do you remember how hard that is??"

She laughed. "Yes, I remember the days. But when you're feeling stressed, close your eyes...take a few deep gentle breaths...ease them in and ease them out. All the while, imagine you're somewhere nice and quiet...by a pond or on a cloud...then count down from ten, slowly."

I did as she said. I closed my eyes, took a few breaths, and then slowly counted backward from ten. I opened my eyes. I had to admit I felt calmer already. "Wow! That works!"

She pointed to the side of her head. "Med school, baby!"

Munching on another slice of pizza, she looked at me for a moment and then continued. "When touching, or grabbing objects or people, treat them like they are very fragile crystal...because to us they are."

"You're kidding?" I asked, my eyebrows raised in disbelief.

She picked up a thick ceramic mug that she liked to drink coffee out of. It had to be the biggest, thickest mug in the house. I watched as she closed her hand around it. The mug crumpled into ceramic dust. My mouth dropped open. "Lia, close your mouth," she shook her head at my wide-eyed expression. "Nobody wants to see what you're chewing...or, in this case, forgetting to chew."

"Oh wow!!" My mouth was still open, and I was in total shock. When I saw her frown, I closed my mouth and did as I was told. Then I thought of an important question. "Does this mean I'll never be able to hold hands with my boyfriend?"

She shook her head. "No, of course not."

"What do you mean?" I asked, a deep frown creasing my forehead. "No, of course, I won't be able to hold hands, or…no, of course, I will be able to hold hands?"

"Yes, Lia, with practice, you'll be able to hold hands. It's not that bad. You just need to be aware of your strength." Mom smiled.

"Phew!"

"One thing, though," she nervously tapped the table. "Hygiene is super-duper important."

"Mom, I'm a girl in middle school. For us, hygiene is always important."

She nodded. "True. But now you're going to have to be extra cautious. I'll give you some of my super deodorant. That is the only type that will work." A big smile crossed her face. "I actually developed it myself. It's good to know chemistry and the superhuman body so well. When I give it to you, make sure you use it on your underarms really well. You don't want to lift your arm up to ask a question and knock out half the class!"

I rolled my eyes. "Mom, I know how to use deodorant."

"And your feet!" she cut me off urgently. "That's something you must not forget. You must coat them well. And make sure you wear shoes that let your feet breathe. And of course, never ever, ever wear socks two days in a row. You want people to be able to keep breathing after you take your shoes off!"

"Mom! My feet don't smell! At least not THAT bad! Well, they're not lethal." I added, after a moment's thought.

"That's cause you're not super yet. Once it hits, look out. What you now think isn't that bad, will suddenly be able to drop a pack of charging rhinos from 30 feet away!"

"Ah, okay," I replied, though I couldn't believe that.

"Oh, and the reason why we never get pizza with onions and garlic is that it's very important for us never to eat anything that can give us gas." She stopped for a minute so I could consider what she'd said. "For some reason, our bodies are immune to certain things, but others we tend to make worse. Life's a tradeoff, I guess."

"In other words, no bean burritos," I said jokingly.

She nodded firmly, her eyes locked on mine. "Definitely not. I had one at the zoo once by accident...the smell dropped the entire lion exhibition. It was empowering and embarrassing at the same time. If you ever do need to fart."

"Mom, I never fart!"

She looked at me. "If you do need to fart, make sure you do it in a wide-open well-aired place. Legend has it that one of our ancestors farted at the Gobi forest."

"Mom, the Gobi is a desert," I said very matter of fact.

Mom nodded. "It is now!" she replied straight-faced. "Plus, in 1908, your great, great, great, great, Great-Grandma Carol farted while camping in Siberia. The damage was so bad, and scientists believe the place was devastated by an asteroid!"

"Anything else I should be aware of?" I asked, fighting back a gulp.

"Sneezing!" Mom said. "Luckily being super, we are immune to most illnesses, but pepper and some foods can still make us sneeze. Just always cover your mouth if it happens. You don't want to sneeze down a building."

I nodded. "I can see why that would be bad."

"Yeah, great-grandma once sneezed over a mountain...."

"Yikes!" I said. "These powers are kind of cool and scary at the same time!"

Mom leaned over and hugged me. "Yes, they are. Like I said, being super is wonderful, but you have to be cautious at the same time. Life always comes with tradeoffs. Plus, you have to keep the power a secret."

I leaned back in my chair and laughed. "Yeah, I guess we don't want to end up part of a secret government program!"

Mom hugged me again. She liked to hug. "Not just that, but if people found out, we could do super things they'd either be scared of us or want us to do special favors for them."

"Never thought of that," I said.

She grinned. "That's why I'm the mom!"

"So, when will this hit me?" I asked curiously.

Mom looked at her watch. "Well, you were born at 5 a.m. So anytime after that. It's not an exact science. I'm not even sure if it is a science. What I do know is that it's an amazing gift!"

"Well, this explains the dreams I've been having...about me lifting cars and battling bad guys. I blamed Jason's comics."

Mom patted me gently on the shoulder. "Nope, that's your subconscious kicking in and preparing you for what's to come!"

"Lovely," I said.

Mom looked me in the eyes. "Honey, this will be wonderful, tricky but wonderful. At times, it might be challenging, but challenges are good!" She kissed me on the forehead. "You'll be great!"

"I hope you're right!"

After dinner, I headed up to my room. To take my mind off my *problems*, I did my homework. Of course, my English just happened to be reading, The Lion, The Witch, and The Wardrobe. A story about kids learning how to deal with a strange world and their powers in that world. Kind of ironic, I guess. I went to bed that night half thrilled, half worried. I wasn't sure if I would still be me when I woke up. Mom had to be exaggerating the problems of being super. She HAD to be.

After a while, I fell asleep. First of all, I dreamed of leaping through the air, and then the dream became a nightmare when I crashed down in the middle of the city, causing a huge crater. I looked at the crater and said, "Oops, my bad."

Morning comes...

The next thing I knew, I felt something wet on my face, desperately trying to wake me up. I forced my eyes to pop open. There stood Shep licking me. I took a second to collect myself. I still felt like me. Maybe my powers hadn't kicked in yet? Maybe Mom was wrong about me? Shep persisted in licking me, hoping I would get up.

I laughed and said, "Shep, *stop!*"

Suddenly he did stop. And when I say stop, I mean he went stiff and fell to the ground with a clunk.

"MOM!" I shouted.

Mom leaped up the stairs. She was in my doorway in less than a second.

"MOM! LOOK WHAT I DID TO POOR SHEP! MOM! WHAT DID I *DO* TO POOR SHEP?"

Mom staggered back a step and covered her nose. "Super morning bad breath!" she said, shaking her head and bending down to check on our poor dog.

I stuck my hand over my nose and lips and puffed a little breath into my hand. I crinkled my nose. "Sure, my breath is a kind of bad, but not bad enough to drop a 120-pound guard dog in his tracks...."

"Not to you or me, because we're super, but to non-supers," she nodded to Shep with her head, "It's a different story."

I sat up in bed. "Is he dead?" I gasped.

Mom shook her head. She gave Shep a few quick pats to his chest, and he sprang back to life. I breathed a huge sigh of relief. My breath hit Shep, and he passed out again. Mom rolled her eyes. "Honey, you have to be careful!" she started patting his chest once more.

"Right!" I said, covering my mouth. "Oh no! Does this mean I'll never be able to kiss my husband good morning without killing him?"

21

Mom smiled. "You'll learn to control it, especially by the time you get married...many, many years from now."

I could only hope Mom was right about this.

She picked Shep up like he was a little puppy then motioned to the bathroom with her head. "Now go wash up. And don't forget your super deodorant. We'll go over the do's and don'ts again during breakfast."

"Right," I said. I got up and walked to my bathroom door. I grabbed the doorknob and pulled the door off the hinges like it weighed nothing. Yep, this would take some getting used to. "Ah, Mom, maybe I should take a sick day today!"

Mom smiled and shook her head. "Nonsense. The best way for you to learn to control your powers is to be out in the world. It will force you to concentrate on being careful." She walked out of the room but called over her shoulder. "I'm making your favorite for breakfast, pancakes with blueberries."

I could only hope Mom was right. After all, Middle School came with enough problems already, without me having to worry about farts that were silent but deadly.

Breakfast Time...

I hurried into my now door-less bathroom, ready to hit the showers. First, though, I stopped and looked in the mirror over the sink. Yep, I still looked like me, brown hair, blue eyes…a nose that had a zit on it. But then I noticed the zit was gone. Okay, so I guess something good had come from being super.

I got in the shower and scrubbed and cleaned like I had never done before. Oh, don't get me wrong, I take my showering very seriously. If you're a girl in middle school and you smell, you are marked for life. But today, I made extra certain that I didn't miss a spot.

After the shower, I used generous portions of mom's super deodorant on any part of me that might sweat. I tossed on my school uniform. It's a perfect drab white shirt with brown shorts. In a way, I like having a school uniform. It cuts down some of the drama of what to wear each school day. Of course, we still get to accessorize, though. Today I decided to go with a nice pendant my great-great-grandma had given me.

By then, the smell of pancakes had worked its way up to my room. That smell called me down to breakfast.

I felt relieved to see that Mom had prepared my favorite breakfast of blueberry pancakes, wheat toast with fruit, and a glass of fresh orange juice. I needed something normal to start this far from a normal day.

As I ate, Mom lectured.

"Okay, controlling your strength is easy as pie."

"Is that a medical term, Mom?"

"Ha! Just when squeezing or grabbing a person or thing, take a deep breath and mentally think they are made of fine crystal."

"Got it, breathe and take it easy," I said.

"Foods to avoid: onions, garlic, beans, anything that could give you bad breath or gas."

"Luckily, I'm a girl in middle school, so I normally avoid those anyhow."

"You used my special deodorant, right?" Mom asked proudly.

"Yep!"

"You packed it in your school bag just in case, right?"

"Yes. Mom."

She leaned over and gave me a kiss. "Well, I think you're ready for the world!"

"Let's just hope the world is ready for me!" I sighed.

With that, I heard a knock at the door. "Wait, is that Jason?"

Mom sniffed the air. "Yes, I can smell his brand of hair gel from here," Mom pointed to her nose. "Super sense of smell," she smiled.

I sniffed the air. Now that Mom mentioned it, I could smell it too. "Wow, I had no idea that stuff had such a strong scent," I pulled out my phone and looked at the time. I had to get moving.

Leaping up, I grabbed my book bag, took one last sip of juice, and kissed Mom goodbye.

"Are you sure I'm ready for this?"

She put both her hands on my shoulders and looked at me in the eyes. "Lia, nobody is ever ready for this. But you are as ready as you can be. When you get out there in the world with your friends, you will learn and adapt." She smiled. "I'm sure of it!" Kissing me on the forehead, she waved me out of the kitchen.

I took a deep breath and turned towards the door.

Same Walk, Different Me...

Jason rang the doorbell again. My phone buzzed. It was a text from him.

JASON> I'm here! ☺

LIA> Yep, figured it out :-) Coming!

JASON> OK

Funny how HE seemed extra anxious today. I opened the door, and there stood Jason, a smile on his dimpled cheeks and holding a blueberry muffin with a candle on it.

"Happy Birthday!" he shouted, handing me the muffin. "Blow out the candle!" he coaxed.

Okay, now this could be tricky. I took the muffin and turned it away from him in case I hit it with too much power. I puffed my lips and concentrated on letting out just a little whiff of air. My breath hit the candle. The candle fizzled out and then fell to the ground. I guess it could have been worse.

"Wow, I see you're extra pumped today!" Jason said, hugging me.

I hugged him back, concentrating on being gentle. He didn't yelp in pain, so I think I succeeded. "Thanks!" I said, smiling at him. The muffin and candle had been such a sweet thing to do.

I bent down and picked up the candle.

"Now that you're a full teen, do you feel different?" Jason asked.

I nodded and smiled. "You'd be surprised!"

My walk to school with Jason was always the calm before the storm of the day. I liked the fact that we still walked. It gave us time to talk, and it dragged out the start of each day at school.

"Read any good comic books lately?" I asked.

Jason's face lit up. "What really? Do you really want to know? Usually, when I talk about comic books, your face goes kind of blank. I know you're trying to be polite, but comics and superheroes aren't your favorite things. You always say, I like to stay grounded in what's *real*," he said that last part badly, imitating my voice.

"Wow, that was horrible," I said, giving him a little shove.

He went flying much farther to the side than I had intended. He staggered to a stop and said, "Impressive!"

"I've been working out. Remember that captain Wendi Long said I need to pump up," I told him. "Now, how about those comics?"

His face lit up. "I've been rereading the Death of Superman!" he said, almost popping out of his socks with excitement.

"Wait. Superman dies??"

Jason nodded. "Yeah, he sacrifices himself to save Earth from an evil clone of himself...the comic is kind of like the movie but better." Jason must have noticed the look of concern on my face. "But Superman does come back."

"Phew," I said, though really, I had no idea why that made me feel better.

Suddenly we heard loud, angry barking. The barking got louder and louder. Both Jason and I knew who the culprit was. We turned to see, Cuddles, the meanest, nastiest Doberman pincher on Earth, running towards us, fangs out. Cuddles' owner, a sweet old blue-haired lady named Ms. Jewel, ran after him, desperately trying to stop him.

"Cuddles! Stop! Stop!" she ordered.

Cuddles continued to race towards us and the open gate to his lawn.

"Sorry, kids! He got away from me again!" Ms. Jewel called, puffing after her dog.

Jason and I both froze in our places. We had been through this drill before. Cuddles would approach us. Sniff us. Growl at us. And then decide we were no threat as long as we stayed off of his yard. And you can bet that was our plan.

This time though, when Cuddles got within sniffing range, he jammed to a sudden stop. He looked me in the eyes. He rolled over and whimpered.

"Now, that's different!" Jason said.

"I guess he knows we're mostly harmless," I replied, giving myself a quick whiff of my underarms to make sure I still smelled fresh. Thankfully, I did.

Jason shrugged. We continued on our way to school. I pulled out my phone and sent a fast text to my mom.

LIA> OK, that was weird. Cuddles, the world's worst-named dog, stopped charging and rolled over when he got a whiff of me, and I don't smell bad at all!

MOM> That's because animals can sense our power

LIA> Good 2 no

MOM> Honey, I know this is a txt but still use the right words, please!

LIA> Good 2 know

MOM> The u! ☺

Locker Talk...

Jason and I stood at our lockers, pulling out the books we'd need for the first and second period while putting away the stuff we wouldn't need. I like morning locker time. It gives me a chance to catch up on what's going on. I even kind of liked the bright green barf color of the halls. Something about them mixed with the orange lockers made the school look like a colorblind clown had designed it. Somehow it was a look that clicked with my tastes.

One of my friends, Krista Johnson, raced across the hallway towards me. Krista is beautiful, with long wavy blond hair and huge blue eyes. She's just...how can I say this politely? Forgetful. As usual, I was sure she needed something from me.

"Hey! Lia! Happy, happy, happy BIRTHDAY!" she squealed, bubbling with excitement. She hugged me. I hugged her back as gently as I could. She didn't scream. I took that as another good sign. I was catching on to this super-strength stuff. "You smell different," she said, a curious expression on her face.

"Ah, new deodorant," I replied slowly.

Krista smiled. "Wow, it's a nice one!"

"Thanks," I replied, relieved. I only hoped it kept working as the day dragged on.

Krista stood there looking at me, tapping her foot.

"Do you need something, Krista?" Jason asked. Jason wasn't as patient as I am with her.

"Not from you, silly, but from Lia!" Krista looked at me. It kind of reminded me of how a doe looks when it's confused. "Ah, we have lacrosse practice today. Right?"

I nodded. "It's a weekday, so yes, yes we do," I told her.

Krista put her arms behind her back and started wobbling back and forth. "Ah, do you like possibly maybe have an extra stick for me to use...I left mine at home. I could run home after practice, but then I'll be late, and Wendi will yell at me. I don't want that!"

I turned to my locker. Luckily, I always kept an extra lacrosse stick in there, just in case. I pulled out the stick and handed it to Krista.

"Is that a yes?" Krista asked me.

"Yes!" Jason and I both answered together.

Krista took the stick and hugged me again. Of course, she poked Jason and me with the stick. Jason staggered back a step. I didn't even feel it. "Thank you! Thank you! Thank you!" she said. "I'll return it once I remember to bring mine!"

Krista walked away humming.

"You might not ever see that stick again," Jason said.

Tim Dobbs, a short, stocky kid with a brush cut, rushed up to his locker. Tim almost always had on headphones and was always running late. Still, he was a good guy. "Hey, Lia, Happy Birthday!" he told me, actually taking his headphones off.

"Thanks, Tim!" I said.

Tim gave Jason a nod. "Hey!"

"Hey!" Jason responded.

When it comes to male communication, I swear boys aren't much more advanced than cavemen.

"Wow, everybody knows it's your b-day," Jason said, nudging me. "You must be famous."

"Nah, but I do have Facebook!"

From behind me, I heard. "Oh, Lia!"

I knew that perfect lyrical voice. It belonged to our lacrosse captain and homecoming queen, Wendi Long. I turned and saw Wendi strutting towards me. She had long blond hair that seemed to dance on her shoulders, bright blue eyes, a perfect nose, perfect teeth, and the most beautiful skin that I was sure had never seen a zit. Seeing such perfection walk towards me, I sighed.

My sigh drove her back a few steps. I'd have to be careful with that. I'd also have to be careful that I enjoyed doing that.

"What's up, Wendi?" I asked.

The second that Wendi reached us, I swear Jason's IQ was cut in half. "Ah, ah, hi, Wendi..." he stuttered.

Wendi stood there, arms crossed, looking me in the eyes. "Remember, we're starting practice at 2:45 today!" she announced.

"Yes, like we do every day!" I answered.

"I just wanted to make sure you're on time today. We're scrimmaging, and you'll be leading the squad that's playing against my squad. I want to make sure you are at your best to give us as much of a test as possible." Wendi's mouth was a firm line. She took her job as team captain very seriously.

I nodded. "Don't worry. I look forward to playing against you."

Looking over Wendi's shoulder, I spotted Brandon Gold coming towards us. Brandon is captain of all the sports teams, class president, and top student in the class. Plus, if he wanted to be, he could be a male model, as he was so good-looking. His only flaw was that he went out with Wendi.

"Hey, Lia! Happy Birthday!" Brandon smiled. I swear his teeth glistened.

"Ah, thanks," I said as calmly as possible. While my insides were saying, "HOLY COW!!! BRANDON KNOWS WHO I AM!! HE KNOWS IT'S MY BIRTHDAY! HE SPOKE TO ME!"

"Hey, how do you know it's her birthday?" Wendi demanded.

"It's on Facebook!" Brandon told her.

"And you're friends with Lia?" Wendi asked as if she were talking about the king greeting a peasant.

"Yeah," Brandon answered simply as if it was no big deal.

Wendi pulled Brandon away. "Come on, we'll be late for class!" she frowned at him and grabbed his arm.

"Bye, guys!" Brandon waved as Wendi dragged him down the hall.

"What does a guy like Brandon see in Wendi anyhow?" I asked, louder than I intended to.

"Maybe because she's so good-looking," Jason replied.

"Oh, plus she's rich!" he added.

"Okay, I get the point. I just think Brandon can do better."

Jason grinned. "You may be a bit biased. After all, you and Wendi have been rivals for a while now."

I shook my head. "Not sure how we're rivals. She wins all the time."

Jason patted me on the shoulder. "Nah, you're too hard on yourself." He stopped talking. "Oh no, speaking of rivals, here comes Tony Wall."

I turned to see Tony walking steadily towards us. Tony had just finished "borrowing" lunch money from some younger kids. Now he had his sights set on Jason. Tony was a classic bully, he wasn't very smart, but when you're bigger than everybody else, there's not a lot of need for brains. I might have had to deal with Wendi, but no way I would let Tony bully my best friend. We only had a minute until the morning bell, so I just needed to delay him.

I inhaled and then softly exhaled in Tony's direction. He went staggering back and hit the lockers behind him. A couple of the smaller kids also blew backward, but they were too amused by Tony smacking into the lockers to care. A bunch of kids (including the smaller ones) began to laugh.

"Quit laughing!" Tony ordered, fists curled.

"Hey, Tony? What happened?" Brandon called to him. Brandon happened to be one of the few kids in the school Tony didn't try to bully.

Tony shook his head. "I don't know…some sort of crazy draft in the school today."

"I felt it too!" Wendi said.

I had to confess a part of me enjoyed using super-breath on Tony. Yeah, I pushed back a few innocent kids too, but it was all for the greater good. Now I knew Mom wasn't joking when she said no onions or garlic. That could have been dangerous. Well, fun for me but dangerous for everybody else. I didn't need that. Right? I had to use this power for good. I mean, that had to be the reason I had this power? To help the world? Of course, there's nothing wrong with having fun too. Is there? Before I could think too long, the morning bell rang. I snapped back to reality. Of course, my reality was different now. It would be challenging on all sorts of levels, but I knew I could handle it.
I had to!

Class Time...

My morning classes were three of my most challenging: Science, Math, and English. But the good news is, I enjoy a challenge. The bad news is, Mr. Ohm, our Science (and Math due to budget cuts) teacher, was handing back our science quizzes from yesterday. Mr. Ohm handed me my test. I like Mr. Ohm. I believe he's a good guy. Sometimes, since he's single and decent-looking (for a teacher), I think he could be a good match for my mom.

Other times, I think having a teacher around all the time would not be good at all. Mr. Ohm looked directly at me when he gave me my paper. It had a score of 85 on it.

"Not bad," he told me. "It was a hard quiz."

"I didn't think it was THAT hard," Wendi said.

"Oh man, I thought it was way hard!" Krista added.

I knew from the tone of his voice Mr. Ohm was disappointed in me. But not nearly as disappointed as I was in myself. I had studied so hard. But when I glanced through the test, I saw where I'd gone wrong. Somehow, I thought Pan and Narvi were moons of Jupiter, and Thebe was a Saturn moon. I was so annoyed with myself for getting those three wrong.

Mr. O must have noticed the look of disappointment on my face. "Cheer up!" he encouraged. "You can do a paper for extra credit if you want." He looked up at the class. "You all can if you wish."

Some of the kids sighed in relief, others groaned, others sat there still trying to wake up. I had to say I felt better.

Next was Math class once again with Mr. Ohm. I usually enjoy Math. It can be tricky, but it always makes sense. It follows a pattern. Patterns are comforting. That day though, in fact, all week, we were studying units of measure and practicing converting metric to non-metric and Celsius to Fahrenheit.

I mumbled under my breath, "Why can't the whole world just use the same systems! After all, it's just different ways of labeling the same stuff!"

Apparently, I said it louder than I had intended because several kids stared in my direction. Mr. Ohm looked at me and nodded. "Good point, Lia. Maybe when you're older, you can work on uniting the world."

I heard somebody laugh. I knew it was Wendi.

"Maybe I will," I said. "Maybe I will!"

My final morning class was English with Ms. Bliss. The name doesn't describe her well at all. Ms. Bliss is OLD. I mean, she taught my mom English. She always wears her glowing white hair up in a bun. I also believe she thinks of her English class as the most important class in the school, if not the country, the world, and the Universe. She gives so much homework, it's unbelievable. She likes to say, "Kids today

36

have it too easy. It's my job to toughen them up for the real world...."

Yesterday, for homework, she told us to read the first three chapters of The Lion, the Witch, and the Wardrobe. Fair enough. I guess she is the teacher. But she gave us a pop quiz on it this morning. The quiz covered the first four chapters, and it was going to be added to our final grade!! Ms. Bliss said she did it because - "A good student will do more than what they are told!"

I didn't know how I went. I just knew I only read the first three chapters. And, of course, it was an essay test. I couldn't have been happier when the bell rang for lunch so I could get out of there.

Lunch Break...

Lunchtime was my favorite part of the day, the part where I could hang out with my friends. Plus, while the cafeteria was painted the most disgusting shade of green, the food was surprisingly tasty. Jason, Tim, Krista, and I were sitting at a table together, talking about nothing and everything all at once.

"Emily looks so pretty with her hair like that," Krista commented.

I chewed on my mouthful of pasta. It wasn't quite as good as my mom's, but it came close. I nodded to Krista. "Yeah, I love it short on her as well. It suits her so much!"

Jason and Tim talked about action movies. Funny to see Jason get so excited as they disagreed about the greatest movie ever.

"Diehard, man," Tim said.

"Nope, Princess Bride!" Jason insisted.

Lunch wouldn't be complete without Wendi strolling by our table; Brandon on one side and her best friend, Lori, on the other. Lori plays defense on our team, and she may be the toughest girl in the world.

Wendi looked down at my plate. "Good to see you chose the veggie salad with your pasta. You'll need the energy for our game this afternoon."

"Right!" Lori grunted.

"Nice to see you guys again," Brandon said with his usual perfect smile.

Wendi pulled him along to their cool kids' table.

Now Tony was challenging kids to arm wrestling for a dollar. After dominating one table, he set his sights on us.

"Hey, either of you loser dudes feeling strong and lucky today?" he smirked.

Tim took a deep breath, I knew he was getting ready to stand, but I spoke up, "Tony, Jason will take you on."

38

"He will?"

"I will?" Jason replied.

I nodded to Jason. "You can do this; you've been studying judo under Sensei Joe."

"Yes, but Judo isn't arm wrestling," Jason argued.

"Plus, you play lacrosse every day!"

"Yeah, but it's not arm wrestling!"

I shrugged. "It's all about leverage."

I stood up and gave Tony my seat across from Jason. Tony plopped into my seat, put down his elbow, and opened up a meaty hand.

Jason shot me a look that said, *are you crazy?*

I gave him my look that said, *you can do this!*

He reluctantly put his elbow on the table and locked hands with Tony. Tony's hand engulfed Jason's.

I bent over. "I'll start you guys on three…. One, Two…" I reached down and gently pushed on Tony's arm right behind his bicep, between the elbow and shoulder. I'd taken enough martial arts in my day to know there was a pressure point there. If I gave that spot the right amount of super pressure, it should totally weaken Tony's arm. "Three!" I said quickly.

Tony gritted his teeth and tried pushing Jason's arm down. To pretty much everybody's surprise (most of all Jason's), Jason's arm didn't move back at all. Instead, his arm pushed forward, driving the arm of a very shocked Tony to the table.

"I win!" Jason shouted, tossing his arms up in the air.

Tony sat there, mouth wide open.

"Careful, Tony, you don't want to swallow a fly," Tim joked.

We'd caught the attention of almost the entire café, and just about everyone laughed.

Tony got up, an irritated smirk on his face. "Oh, whatever!" He ducked his head and hurriedly scurried away.

I almost felt sorry for Tony. Almost. But I felt so good about myself that I chomped hungrily on my veggie salad. "Man, this salad is great!" I beamed.

"Yeah, it is good," Krista said. "Only I have to avoid it because the raw cabbage and broccoli can give me gas," she whispered in my ear.

Oh, I had forgotten about that. Still, maybe raw cabbage and broccoli wouldn't affect me. We talked for a few more minutes. And then suddenly, I felt an all too familiar urge in my stomach. Uh oh, I knew I needed to get out of that room and outside. Fast.

The Fart...

I rushed up to the supervising teacher, Mr. Khrone, who sat at a table next to the double doors leading in and out of the cafeteria. Mr. K was a big bald man with a softly spoken voice.

"Mr. K, I have to get to the bathroom fast!" I said in a rush. "Personal lady problems," I added, blushing.

Mr. K turned redder than my face felt. He handed me the hall slip. "That's okay, take your time," he replied.

I knew if I went directly outside, that would cause suspicion. I took the slip and headed towards the girl's bathroom. There were two things that I'd always noticed when I went to that bathroom. It was painted a pretty shade of light blue, which was so much better than the ugly green that the rest of the school was coated with. Also, and more importantly, each of the stalls had a little window cut into the wall. I assume it was for ventilation, but today, those windows would most likely save the school.

I raced inside, my heart pumping furiously in my chest. Breathing a quick sigh of relief, I realized I was lucky (for once) as the place was empty. I decided on the middle stall and locked the door behind me. Turning towards the wall, I looked at the window just above the toilet. It wasn't a big window, but it would work. I leaped up onto the toilet and reached for the handle. It happened to be one of those windows that pulls open just to let some air in or out. I pulled the window, and it dropped open about a quarter of the way. But I was definitely not going to fit through that space. The window may have been built to only open part way, but it wasn't built to stand up to super strength. I grabbed the handle and yanked it down. The window's metal framework fought me for a second and then gave in. I pulled the window completely out of the frame and fell to the floor, the window in my hand. It could have been worse; I could have fallen into

41

the toilet. Or I could have let my gas out right then and there, and somehow, I didn't think that would be a good idea at all. It was just lucky that so far, I'd managed to hold it in.

I jumped back up on the toilet, held my breath and my stomach, and slid out the window, once again being careful to hold back my gas. Being outside was good, but I knew I needed to get as far away from the school as possible. Glancing urgently around the school's backyard, I noticed the lacrosse practice field was empty. That would have to do. I jumped up in the air and leaped a good hundred feet with that jump. "Wow!" I exclaimed loudly to myself. "That was pretty cool!"

A couple more super jumps, and I found myself in the middle of the empty field — time for my release. I turned away from the school just to be safe. That was when I noticed a herd of cows maybe 100 yards away. They looked at me and began to moo. "Sorry, cows!" I said. "I have no choice."

Then I let out my fart. It felt good. The fart made just a little PUT sound. If I'd stayed in the cafeteria, most people probably wouldn't have even noticed. Sniffing the air, I noticed it didn't seem that bad at all. Maybe Mom was exaggerating. Then I realized I could no longer hear the cows behind me. When I turned around, I saw the entire herd lying on the ground, legs up in the air. Using my supervision (which I just found out I had), I saw they were still breathing. But man, I had clobbered them, "Oops!" I said. "Yeah, people would definitely have noticed that!"

I leaped back to the school and climbed through the space where the bathroom window had been. I returned the window back into the frame. Next would come the hard part, going back out and interacting with my classmates, knowing one fart and I could drop them all. It was a kind of weird feeling of power tinged with total embarrassment.

Just as I left the bathroom, I ran into Krista.

"Phew, you're okay!" Krista said. "We were starting to worry. Usually, you don't take that long!"

"Oh, I'm fine," I assured her. "That broccoli and cabbage just got to me!"

She put her arm around me, and we headed back to the cafeteria.

"See Lia, I told you, that's a dangerous combination!"

"You have no idea!" I replied.

The second half of school day...

After the craziest lunch period in the history of lunch periods, I had a history class with Mr. Paradise. Mr. Paradise was one of those teachers who loved to talk and talk and talk. He would practically glow when lecturing about history, always telling us, "You need to know history, so history doesn't repeat itself."

He went on and on about the people in history who abuse power. He told us how "power can corrupt...." It was the kind of talk that hit home, especially now that I knew I could fart and be the only one left standing in the classroom. Mr. Paradise must have seen me staring off into space, thinking about how I can't let this power get to me.

"Lia, you look like you're giving this a lot of thought," Mr. Paradise commented.

I snapped back to the moment. "Ah, yes, actually I am."

Mr. Paradise smiled. "Good, you should. You all should. You all have your own power and skills. At this age, you are just coming to learn what your powers and gifts are. After all, you need to understand your own unique powers before you can use them wisely in the world!" Mr. Paradise tended to get a bit poetic. A lot of kids thought it was weird to talk that way. Usually, I did too, but today his words hit home.

Art with Mrs. Brown went smoothly. It was a day for oil paintings on canvas. Mrs. Brown put an apple and an orange on a table in front of the class.

Our assignment was to simply draw those and have fun. Mine looked like a red blob alongside an orange blob. The two, kind of smudged together to a reddish-orange blob. There are some things that superpowers just don't help with. When I looked over at Jason's, I saw that his painting looked like a real-life apple and a real-life orange.

"You have incredible talent," I told him.

"Thanks," he smiled.

Mrs. Brown appeared and looked over our shoulders. She took in Jason's near-masterpiece and said, "Miss Strong is correct. You do have talent!"

Jason beamed.

Mrs. Brown turned her attention to my painting. "Art is about enjoyment," she said. "Did you enjoy this?"

I nodded. "Yeah, I kind of did."

Mrs. Brown grinned. "Then good job."

Computer class with Mr. Swimmer happened to be another class that Jason stood out in. I swear he could make a computer sing – literally! He wrote a program where you could type in a phrase, and the computer would sing it. Mr. Swimmer was amazed. In fact, even Tony Wall walked over, put his hand on Jason's shoulder, and said, "Good job, dude!" I smiled at that. Apparently, Tony, like most bullies, would respect strength. I felt a little better about using Jason to humiliate him during lunch. As Mr. Paradise would say in history, "Throughout history, people have believed the end justifies the means." In this case, it might have.

My school day ended with yet another humbling experience, French class with Madame Broch. I have no idea why, but whenever I attempt to speak French, my tongue gets tied up in knots. I thought maybe having a super tongue, and super coordination would help. But no such luck!

"Bonjour, comment allez-vous?" Madame Broch asked me as I entered the room.

"Be end, Mercy," I answered, my tongue-twisting over the easiest words.

Madame Broch rolled her eyes just a bit. "Nice try, dear," she sighed in English.

Yep, it was now official. I may have superpowers, but I was still just an average kid who happened to be really strong.

At the end of the school day, Jason and I met at our lockers to collect our gear for practice. Jason played on the boy's lacrosse team. It certainly wasn't a love for him, but like he would say, "the running is good."

Plus, it gave us a chance to hang out and walk home together after school.

As we collected our sticks and pads, Ms. Janet, the janitor, walked by, sweeping the floor. I like Ms. Janet a lot. She's a retired army sergeant who now cleans the school in the afternoons.

"Hope you kids have a good afternoon!" Ms. Janet smiled.

"You too!" Jason and I both replied together.

"After I leave here, I get to go clean a few more houses," she added with another smile.

"Ms. Janet, why don't you enjoy your retirement more?" Jason asked.

She grinned. "I enjoy working. It makes me feel useful. Besides, these days any extra cash I get goes to help my grandkids in college." She shrugged. "Well, nice talking to you kids. Have a good practice. These floors won't sweep themselves, so I'd better get to it."

I thought for a second about using my super-breath to blow all the dust out of the school, but I didn't. I wasn't sure I could control my power enough to do that. Besides, Ms. Janet seemed to enjoy her work. So, I guessed I should leave her to it.

Boy, I was tempted, though!

Practice Make Perfect...

After school, I met Krista on the lacrosse field for practice. I enjoy our practice sessions. I liked working out with the team and how we learned to cooperate and work as one. I even love doing drills. Wendi, being the star of the team, hated drills. She just loved to scrimmage. So, of course, she managed to talk Coach Blue into an all-practice scrimmage session.

And of course, before we started, I got a text from Mom.

MOM> Remember to be careful at practice!

I knew this would be a test of both my abilities and my patience.

Coach Blue broke us up into two squads. The first was basically Wendi and Lori, and all the biggest girls against Me, Krista, Marie, and all the smaller, quicker girls.

"They definitely have a size advantage on us!" Krista whispered to me as we lined up to start.

"Don't worry. We have speed and brains on our side!" I told her.

"Okay, ladies, I want this to be minimum contact!" Coach Blue warned. "After all, you are all on the same team, so we don't need you beating each other up."

Lori snickered.

"So, what we're going to do is…each team will take a turn with the ball. If they score or miss, the other team brings the ball up the field." Coach pointed to Wendi. "Wendi's team will get the ball first!"

Coach Blue blew her whistle with all her might. I swear she loved the harsh sound it made. Wendi grabbed the ball, ran down the field, dodged a couple of our defenders then quickly shot the ball into the back of the net. She raised her arms in victory! Lori came over and gave her a high five and a chest bump.

Shannon, our goalie, tossed the ball to me. I started running up the field. A couple of Wendi's teammates lunged at me. I dodged them easily as they seemed to move in slow motion. I darted up the field. I'd never felt so sure and confident. I just knew I was going to score. I ran past two more defenders as Wendi shouted. "Somebody stop her!"

Too late, I had already closed in on the goal. I flicked my wrist and rocketed a shot over the goalie's right shoulder. I smiled. I shot that just hard enough to get past her without it being so hard. It was dangerous. I felt I was catching on to my powers.

"Wow, I barely saw that!" Michelle gasped. "Nice shot, Lia!"

Wendi picked up the ball and grumbled something about luck and even how a blind squirrel finds a nut now and then. Wendi passed the ball to Lori. Lori passed back to Wendi. The next thing we knew, they had scored again.

Shannon tossed the ball to Krista. Krista threw a long pass to Marie. Marie noticed I was open and hit me with a perfect pass. I caught the ball and tossed it in the goal in one fluid motion.

Krista and Marie ran up and patted me on the back.

"Wow, you're playing so amazing today!" Marie grinned.

"You are on FIRE!" Krista shouted.

"It's just the great teamwork," I insisted. Deep down, I had to say I felt amazing, like nothing in this world could stop me.

Wendi walked by, intentionally hitting me in the shoulder. I barely felt it, but I still moved my shoulder like she had affected me. Wendi hit the ball out of the goal and glared at Michelle.

"Can't you stop anything, girl?"

Michelle shrugged. "Hey, I'm a good goalie, but that was just a better shot."

Wendi looked at Lori. Lori nodded. I didn't like the look or the nod.

Wendi took the ball and headed back up the field. She flicked the ball into the net, but this time she didn't celebrate. She reached into the goal, grabbed the ball with her stick, and tossed it to me.

"Okay, Strong, let's see how strong you are!" she said.

"I like a challenge," I replied.

I made my move up the field. Wendi ran behind me. I wasn't running full speed, but neither was she. I didn't know what she had planned. Still, I kept my eye focused on the goal. I also knew I didn't want to score this goal. Okay, I did want to score this goal. I wanted to score so bad. Then I could taunt Wendi. But I knew I needed to pass the ball around. Not only was that being a good teammate, but it also didn't make me look too suspicious.

I snapped a quick pass to Krista. Hearing footsteps coming at me from the side, I turned to see Lori closing in on me full speed, stick up. I lowered my shoulder just as Lori rammed into me. Lori went flying over me and then crashed to the ground out cold. I fell to the ground, too, even though I barely felt the hit.

Coach Blue blew her whistle. "Timeout! Timeout!" She ran out onto the field. "You girls alright?"

I sat up. "I'm fine, coach."

Lori laid there on the ground. Marie tapped her gently on the arm. "Lori, Lori…"

Lori lifted her head. "Anybody get the number of that truck that hit me?"

"That was a dirty hit by Lia!" Wendi insisted, jumping up and down.

"Looked clean to me," Coach Blue said. "One of the rare times she didn't agree with her star."

Lori sat up. "Coach is right. It was a clean hit." Lori gave me a thumbs up.

I walked over and helped her to her feet.

For the rest of the practice, we ran drills. I learned that my power is certainly fun to use, but I always had to be on my guard!

That was something I had to watch out for!

Snack Break...

After practice, Jason, Krista, Tim, and I headed to Mr. T's Donuts & More. Mr. T's was the big hangout for middle school kids. The place had everything we needed, comfy couches, free wifi, yummy snacks, and the best milkshakes in the world. It even had an old-school retro-type pinball machine. Everyone loved the place!

The four of us sat on a couch munching on our food. I had a strawberry donut that I was washing down with chocolate milk. The smooth taste of the milk made me so glad that I wasn't lactose intolerant. I knew some people who were, and they couldn't have any dairy products whatsoever. I would have hated not enjoying milk without releasing a fart that would drop the entire room.

"Man, it looked like you had a great practice," Tim said.

Jason chimed in. "I would have loved to see the look on Wendi's face when you tossed in all those goals."

"Oh, she was so not happy!" Krista added.

"I just got lucky, guys," I said with a smile.

No sooner did we mention her name than Wendi appeared at the door with Brandon and Lori in tow.

They walked by our couch. Wendi stuck her nose in the air like she hadn't noticed us. But Lori looked at me and at least gave me a nod. I took it as a gesture of respect. Brandon actually smiled and stopped to talk. My heart skipped a beat when he said, "Lia, I saw you from our practice field. You were playing so well. Keep it up!"

Wendi stopped and acknowledged we existed with a, "Oh hi." She pulled Brandon along, "Come on, Brandon, let's go to our couch."

Before I had time to think about what just happened, something weird hit me. I got a funny feeling in my stomach. No, this wasn't going to be another super fart (thank the stars). This was something else. Like I just knew something bad was going to happen. Looking out the big windows that lined the wall at the front of Mr. T's, I scanned downtown Starlight City. We were right across from the SLC Bank. Sure enough, I saw two men in hoodies getting out of a big black car parked right in front of the bank. In a hoodie, a third man sat in the driver's seat with the car running. They were going to rob the bank! Nope, that was not happening, not on my watch.

I got up and grabbed my book bag. "Sorry guys, I need to go to the bathroom."

"Want me to come?" Krista asked, starting to rise.

I smiled and shook my head. "Nah, it might be safer if you don't."

"Got it," Krista said, dropping back to her seat.

I moved to the bathroom as quickly as I could without moving at super speed. My heart pounded away in my chest like a beating bass drum. I couldn't tell if it was because I was nervous or excited. Probably a little of both.

I went into the middle stall and closed the door. Somehow, I had the feeling there were going to be a lot of bathroom visits in my life from now on. I looked up to see a window at the back of the stall. Not a huge window but one I could fit through. Now I needed a disguise.

Rummaging through my book bag, I found an old black tutu from a dance recital I did at the start of the year. I also pulled out a white ski mask. For once, the fact that I never cleaned out my book bag was a good thing. I quickly changed into my new outfit. Sure, I didn't look stylish, but nobody would be able to identify me. Or at least, I hoped not because that was the important thing right then.

I jumped up on the toilet (after making sure it was closed) and popped open the window. I slipped out the window and promptly fell into a big garbage can in a side alley. Yep, I really should have looked before I leaped or dropped in this case. Feeling the squishy goo under my feet, I decided I didn't want to know whatever the heck I was on top of. I pulled myself out of the trash bin and spun around as fast as I could, causing most of the slime and trash to spin off me. I took a deep breath. It was Go Time! I only hoped I could handle it. For a brief moment, I considered texting my mom. But no, there was no point in worrying her. I knew I could handle this. I was a Strong woman – literally and figuratively. I had taken enough karate lessons that I knew how to fight. I just needed a plan. Not to leap in feet first this time because that's how people get hurt.

I surveyed the scene. The driver was tilting backward and forwards nervously in his seat. I noticed smoke billowing out of the tailpipe. I smiled. I had my plan.

Not on my watch!

I leaped across the street, landing right behind the old black smoking sedan. I bent down not only to hide but to cripple the car. I grabbed the exhaust pipe in my hand. I couldn't tell if it was hot. If it was, the heat didn't bother me. I pinched the pipe closed like it was made of putty. No way this car would go far at all.

I leaned back and ducked behind the car. Now I just had to wait for the other two guys to come out. From the chaos I could hear inside the bank, it wouldn't be long.

Seconds later, the two masked men burst outside the front doors of the bank. One of them, a bigger man, turned back into the bank and shouted, "If nobody follows us, nobody gets hurt."

He leaped into the front seat of the car. The other man jumped into the back seat.

"Drive, drive!" The bigger man ordered, waving his gun around like it was a conductor wand.

From the spot where I'd been hiding, I had a clear view as the car pulled away from the curb. It sputtered and jerked forward. Then it coughed a stream of black soot out the back.

"Drive faster!" the big man ordered the driver.

With my super hearing, I could hear every word that the men said. Their voices were a mixture of frustration, anger, and fear.

"I'm hitting the gas as hard as I can!" the driver said, shaking and panicked, "I've got no idea why this car is moving so slow."

The car stammered and sputtered to a stop.

"What the?" the big man said.

"Maybe we don't have gas?" the man in the back offered helplessly.

"I put ten bucks' worth of fuel in before we came here!" the driver said.

I reacted fast. Jumping forward, I grabbed the front and back passenger doors. I pulled them off the car like they were made of plywood.

"What the?" the big guy repeated once more.

I leaned into the car and grabbed him, then rammed his head up into the roof of the car. He went limp. I pulled him out of the car and dropped him to the curb. The guy in the back seat aimed his gun at me. I shot forward and grabbed the gun's nozzle. Pulling the gun out of his hand, I crushed it into a ball of metal. The man lunged forward in desperation and punched me in the nose.

He pulled his hand back, wincing in pain.

"Now that was rude!" I said, changing my voice to sound very official. "Plus, kind of stupid since I bent your gun like nothing." I leaned over the back seat and pinched him on the shoulder. He crumbled over.

Turning my attention to the driver, I stared at him as he stood there with his arms up in the air, shaking. He handed me his gun. "I give up!" he gulped.

I took the gun and squished it. "Smart man!" I told him. "Still, I need to make sure you don't run away!"

"I won't! I promise!" he said, crossing his heart with his fingers.

As if I could believe a guy who was perfectly willing to rob a bank just seconds ago. I reached forward and tapped him on the forehead. His head rocked back, his eyes rolled to the back of his head, then dropped shut. He plopped back in his seat, out cold.

Reaching for the ignition, I turned off the car. I then backed out of the car and leaped up into the air towards the alley.

The New Normal...

When I returned to the restaurant's dining area, everybody was still gathered around the front window. By then, the police had come and were taking away the battered bad guys. Jason's dad, who was chief of police, talked to the local press.

Jason was bursting at the seams when he saw me. "OMG! You missed it! You missed the most awesome thing!"

"It wasn't that awesome!" Wendi insisted.

"What did I miss?" I asked, pretending to be completely ignorant of what had just gone on.

"Some super girl stopped the robbery!" Brandon gushed. "She totally clobbered those three bad dudes. I wonder if she's good-looking?"

"If she was pretty, why would she wear a mask?" Wendi asked.

"Probably to hide her identity," I answered, far more defensively than I would have liked.

"Could you please turn on the TV, Mr. T?" Jason called out. "My dad is speaking now."

The TV in the corner of the room popped on. Mr. T flicked a switch to the local station, and there stood Jason's dad, looking all tough and official in his best and bluest uniform. "These men are three of the five Hanson brothers," Jason's dad said. "The other two are still at large, but we will get them."

"What about the news that some sort of supergirl overpowered these three and saved the day?" the reporter asked.

The chief hesitated for a second. He drew a deep breath. "Well, while we do appreciate the help of ANY citizen to make our town a better, safer place…. I can't condone the actions of a vigilante."

"But she did save the day!" the reporter insisted.

I fought back the urge to say, you go girl.

The chief nodded again. "Yes, she did, and we appreciate it. But one of the Hanson's, the oldest named Bart, is threatening to sue the city. He says she used excessive force, plus he is demanding to be reimbursed for the price of the guns she destroyed."

"That's ridiculous!" I said under my breath.

Jason heard me and agreed.

Krista, Tim, and a few others also nodded in agreement.

"That is a good point," Wendi admitted. "The girl might be strong…but she certainly isn't that smart and definitely, has no sense of style!"

Brandon shook his head. "I still gotta wonder if she's cute..."

Wendi elbowed him in the stomach, an annoyed expression on her face.

Brandon bent over then straighten himself up. "I'm sure she's not as cute as you."

I considered saying; I bet she's way cuter. But then decided I had enough going on right now. No need to start upsetting Wendi. Besides, she was my teammate and captain, and we needed to work together. Not only would that be better for the team, but it would make my life easier. Having super strength didn't protect me from the mean comments of other girls. My skin might have been tough as steel, but I still had emotions, normal kid emotions. I needed all the friends I could get. And while Wendi might not ever be a friend, I certainly didn't need her as an enemy.

Suddenly my train of thought was broken by my stomach rumbling. And by rumbling, I mean really rumbling. It sounded so loud it actually shook the couch we were sitting on. I threw my hand over my stomach and felt my face turn bright red. "Oops, sorry!" I apologized, slinking down a bit. "I'm just so hungry."

"You had a long hard practice," Jason told me. "Let's get you some food." Jason signaled for Mr. T to come over. Mr. T, a small bald man, was not only the owner but also the waiter and chef at the restaurant. He and Mrs. T, his tall, redheaded wife, pretty much ran the entire place themselves.

"What can I get for you kids, now?" Mr. T asked.

"I'll have another shake, a triple burger, and a mega order of fries," I grinned.

Mr. T smiled. "Long practice, or are you excited about seeing that Starlight City now has a superhero?"

"A little of both," I replied.

"I'll just have fries and onion rings," Jason said. "Don't want to ruin my dinner."

"Chilly dog for me with extra onions!" Tim beamed. "I'm starving as well."

Mr. T. smiled. "I guess you don't have a date tonight."

"If he keeps eating like that, he's never going to have a date!" Jason chuckled.

Mr. T. turned to Krista. "And for you?"

"Just a salad and a glass of water," Krista said. "I need to watch the calories."

Mr. T. took our order and walked off.

I turned to Krista. "Krista, your weight is fine. You look great!"

Krista looked away from me. "Yeah, well, I felt a little slow on the field today. Watching you, I was in awe. You moved so fast like you were a totally different speed to me." She sighed. "Maybe Wendi's right? Maybe I do need to shed a few pounds."

Now, this was a side-effect of being super that I hadn't thought about. I hadn't considered that my performance might make my friends feel bad. Wow, this super stuff could be super complicated. I put my hand on Krista's shoulder and looked her in the eyes. "Krista, you're perfect just how you are!"

"Do you two need to get a room?" Tim kidded.

I shot Tim a look. He dropped back in his seat. "Sorry, bad time to make a joke." He gulped. He looked at Krista. "But she's right, you know. You look good."

Jason nodded in agreement. "Yeah, Krista, Wendi is just jealous of you cause you're so naturally pretty."

Krista smiled. Her face blushed a deep shade of pink. "Thanks, guys... you guys are the best friends a girl could have."

"Want to share my fries?" I asked.

"Deal!" she replied, the wide smile returning to her face.

A few minutes later, the food arrived at our table. Never had food smelled or looked so good. I guessed it was due to my new super senses. Plus, my stomach hadn't stopped quietly rumbling. I could see that using my super strength was demanding. I dove into the food, eating as fast as possible while still trying to have some manners.

"I'm impressed," Tim said, watching me eat a triple-decker hamburger in a few bites.

"I've never seen you eat like this," Jason frowned, a curious expression on his face. "And I've known you forever."

"Must be low blood sugar from practice!" I told him. I picked up the shake. My instinct was to guzzle it down in one gulp. But I had to fight that instinct back. Instead, I took a small sip. My taste buds jumped for joy, and it took all my willpower to put the shake back down on the table. *Breathe in between bites and gulps*, I reminded myself. Being super doesn't mean being a super hog. My stomach still craved more food. I had an urge to open my mouth and eat all the fries with one gulp. But no, I could control this. I had to control this.

Reaching over, I grabbed one fry only and popped it into my mouth. I savored the flavor and the texture. Sure, I was hungry, but no need to rush into quenching this hunger. I was a Strong woman mentally and physically. I finished my snack at a leisurely pace, enjoying both my friends and my food.

Yes, I could do this super thing! At least I was pretty sure I could do this super thing. I just needed to be careful. I could be careful. All I had to remember was to breathe and think before I leaped.

Cat in tree...

After our rest stop at Mr. T.'s, Jason and I walked home. By then, Jason was practically bursting at the seams.

"Too bad you missed that super girl! She was awesome!" he was shaking his head in amazement.

I nodded. "I'm sure she was…but why are you so happy about it?"

Jason stopped walking and looked at me. "I thought you knew me better than anybody."

"I thought so too," I said. I stopped to think for a moment. My eyes popped. "Oh, you're happy that Starlight City has a superhero just like in the comics!" I replied quickly.

Jason grinned. "Yep! It's so good! The way she took care of those three Hanson Brothers like that. Wow! My dad tells me those Hansons are nasty dudes."

"Can't imagine your dad saying, *dudes*," I said in return.

Jason shook his head. "Well, no, not in those exact words. But they are bad guys! Bad to the bone, he says. He also says they're not to be messed with. According to him, they aren't very bright, but that makes them even more dangerous."

"Yeah, I can see that," I nodded in agreement. That was something that had stood out clearly.

"But here's the amazing thing. This girl, this super-strong girl, took them out like they were nothing. And she ripped the doors off the car like they were toy doors."

"Well, remember, Wendi thinks this is all some sort of reality show trick or a commercial," I looked at him, trying to be convincing.

Jason shook his head again. "Nope. No way my dad would be involved with anything like that. This girl is legit!" He looked up into space. "I wonder if she has a boyfriend?"

I nudged him (extra gently) to move forward. "Come on, let's get home."

"Yeah, okay," he said, moving again. "Why would a girl like that ever be interested in me anyhow?"

"Because you're smart and caring!" I answered sincerely.

He smiled at me. "Thanks. But smart and caring isn't cool. How about way, way handsome?"

I shrugged. "You're okay. Though you may want to work on your modesty some," I teased.

Before Jason could say another word, I heard a muffled sobbing from across the street. Turning towards the sound, I saw our little neighbor, a cute blond seven-year-old named Felipe, sitting on his porch steps crying. I pointed him out to Jason.

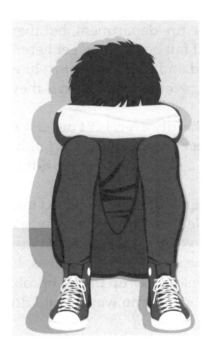

"Now that's not normal. Felipe's the happiest kid I've ever seen!" Jason said, a look of concern crossing his face.

I started across the street. "Come on, let's go see what's wrong." Hearing Felipe sobbing like that broke my heart. I had to fight back the urge to move at super speed to see what was bothering him so much.

Felipe saw us coming and wiped his tears. He didn't want us to know that he'd been crying. I guess boys are macho from an early age.

"What's going on, Felipe?" I asked, bending down to him.

He glanced at me and shook his head, but I gave him an encouraging smile, and he spoke. "I'm worried." His sad face was streaked with tears.

"About what?" Jason asked.

Without taking his tear-soaked eyes off us, he pointed to a big oak tree in the yard. "My cat, Bella, is stuck up in the tree. Way up in the tree. And she's too scared to come down. My mom called the fire department, but they can't come yet. I'm so scared she'll fall before they get here."

Jason smiled and tried to comfort him. "Don't worry, Felipe. Cats hardly ever fall, and even if they do they land on their feet."

"Yeah, but hardly ever, isn't never," Felipe said. "Plus, landing on their feet doesn't mean it wouldn't really hurt!" he added. Felipe was a sharp kid. I had to admit that he had a point.

Looking over at the tree, I noticed it was big and thick and covered with leaves. The tree had to be over a hundred years old. Using my super-vision to zero in, I saw Bella the cat sitting on one of the upper outer branches. How had she managed to get herself way up there? I probably could have leaped up to grab her, but no way I could do that without giving myself away.

Part of me wanted to wait and let the fire department handle it. But a bigger part of me said that helping a crying seven-year-old was just as important as stopping a gang of crazy robbers. This might have even been more important. I mean, come on, what's better than making a little kid happy?

I started walking towards the tree. "Don't worry, Mr. Felipe, I will get the cat down for you!" I said confidently.

"You will?" Felipe and Jason both said at once. I'm not sure which one of them sounded more amazed.

Felipe stood up to follow me. Jason followed Felipe.

"How?" Felipe asked.

"Yeah, how?" Jason asked.

I reached the base of the tree and looked up. "I've been studying trees…." I said.

"You have?" Felipe asked.

"When?" Jason added.

I looked at both boys. "I like to read about different things on the internet sometimes. Usually on my phone," I replied vaguely.

"Oh, she means when she's in the bathroom, trying to get out of class!" Felipe concluded.

Yep, like I said, Felipe was a sharp kid.

Jason looked up, shading his eyes from the sun. "That cat has to be at least twenty feet up. How are you going to get him down?"

Putting my hand on the tree, I told them both. "It's a little-known fact that if you hit a tree in the right spot, the tree will vibrate just enough to shake its branches. I can make the branches shake, so Bella drops from the tree."

Felipe gulped.

I touched Felipe gently on the shoulder. "Don't worry, when she drops, I'll catch her before she hits the ground. She'll be fine, I promise!"

Jason stood there, arms crossed, eyes squinting. "So, you're going to make a giant tree shake and then catch a falling cat?" his eyebrows were raised in disbelief.

"Yep," I answered.

He leaned in and whispered to me. "You know, even if you somehow manage to shake a big, thick, sturdy tree like this, it would still be tough to catch a falling cat from that height."

I nodded. "Don't worry, I can do this," I assured him.

"You do realize that even if you manage to catch this cat, this cat is going to be very scared and lash out with its sharp claws!"

I nodded again. "I'm aware of that." I looked at Felipe's hopeful face. "But it's a risk I am willing to take."

Jason stared at me for a moment or two. He sighed. "If you actually think you can do this, then I believe you. What can I do to help?"

"Just you and Felipe stand back by the house, so I have room to move," I replied.

"Okay," Jason agreed. He hesitated for a moment before ushering Felipe back to the porch.

I looked at the tree. I looked up at Bella. I knew shaking the tree wouldn't be the problem. The trick would be shaking the tree just enough so I didn't knock the tree out of its roots. Plus, I wanted Bella to drop but not go flying. This would take some knowledge of physics and a lot of luck.

I slowly approached the tree. I looked up at Bella. Yes, she was still way up there. I peeked back over my shoulder at Felipe and Jason. Felipe was biting his nails, and Jason had his arm around him. That was sweet. I told myself to concentrate. I could do this. I just worried that hitting the tree would cause a lot of damage. Then, like a lightning bolt, the answer flashed into my head. I didn't need to hit this tree. I just needed to puff a bit of super-breath upwards into the tree. I could direct that force much more easily.

First, I puffed a breath into my hand, just to make sure I didn't have super bad breath. After all, I wanted to knock Bella from the tree, not knock her dead. My breath smelled of salt and French fries. I smirked. No way, that would be dangerous.

Next, I put on the show for Jason and Felipe. I very, very gently tapped the tree while looking upwards. But then I inhaled and then exhaled up towards Bella. The force of my breath knocked some leaves flying and jarred a surprised

66

Bella up and over the tree. She went flying towards the house, paws clawing away in fear and shock.

I shot past the tree hoping Felipe and Jason were paying more attention to the now flying cat rather than me. Positioning myself between the tree and the house, I stood right beneath the falling Bella. Reaching up, I caught Bella with two hands. I breathed in, making sure I closed my hands softly. Bella scratched and clawed through my school uniform. I couldn't blame her. She was scared and in shock. I cradled her in my arms.

"Calm down, Bella," I whispered. "You're fine now."

Bella suddenly stopped struggling. She started to purr. Nestling her head under my arm, she fell asleep with what appeared to be a contented smile on her face. She then began to snore.

Jason and Felipe rushed over to me.

"Thank you! Thank you!" Felipe said, hugging me.

"It was nothing," I told him. I handed him his sleeping cat. "I guess the experience tired her out. She'll be fine in a couple of hours!"

"Thank you! Thank you so much!" Felipe repeated. "I'd better get Bella back into her bed, so she's nice and safe." He turned and headed into his house, humming happily all the way.

"That was amazing!" Jason said with an astonished look on his face.

"Ah, it was nothing," I insisted.

The Big Reveal...

Jason looked at me, his face flushed with color. I could hear his heart racing. "Seriously! That was incredible!"

I shrugged. "Ah, just luck."

Jason shook his head in denial. "No way! Those were some crazy skills. How the heck did you know that about trees? And how in the multiverse did you catch a falling cat?" Jason noticed my sleeves had rips in them from Bella's claws. "Oh, that had to hurt."

He reached for my arm. Without thinking, I let him check it. He rolled back my ragged sleeve. It felt so nice to have Jason care about me like this. "Your sleeves are ripped to shreds."

"Yep, cat claws will do that," I said proudly, still not getting it.

"But...but...your arms... they're perfectly smooth. Not a cut or scratch on them!"

That's when I got it. I pulled my arm quickly away. "Just lucky again, I guess." My heart was hammering. Did he suspect something?

Jason's mouth dropped open. "OMG!"

"OMG, what?" I coaxed, my stomach churning anxiously.

"You are her!" Jason said, his face a mask of shock.

"Her who?"

Jason pointed at me and started walking slowly backward. Not out of fear, but out of amazement. "You're the super strong girl!"

I laughed. "Don't be so silly!"

Jason kept walking backward and going over the events in his mind. "It all makes sense...first, you have the amazing practice, Lori plows into you and gets annihilated, then you disappear when Super Girl comes out... you come back when she disappears...then you eat a super amount of food." He was piecing it all together, one event at a time. This was not supposed to happen!

"Jason, you're ridiculous," I giggled nervously. "You've been reading too many comics!"

He stopped walking and stood stock-still in the middle of the road, locked in thought. "My best friend is super!" he exclaimed loudly. "This is soo cool."

I shook my head. "Jason, I wish I was super, but I'm not..." Before completing the sentence, I spotted a car speeding down the road directly in Jason's path.

The driver, a kid not much older than Jason and me, had his eyes downcast, probably looking at his phone rather than the road. No way could I let Jason pay for the driver's mistake.

Suddenly Jason heard the car rushing towards him. He turned to the car and froze in his tracks. I leaped through the air and landed between Jason and the oncoming car. I held Jason back with my left arm and extended my right towards the speeding vehicle. By then, the driver had seen us and jammed on the brakes. The car started skidding to a stop, but it was still going way too fast. I leaned forward with my right arm and jammed it into the hood of the car, forcing the car to a dead stop. The airbag popped out. My hand left an impression in the hood of the car. The car attempted to push forward, but I didn't allow it to budge.

"Put the car in park!" I ordered the driver, who stared at me, his mouth open wide in terror.

I felt the car stop trying to resist me.

I then reached over and pulled the handprint impression out of the metal of the car. All the while, Jason stood there, stunned with disbelief. "Jason, get across the street!" I told him, my voice full of authority.

"Right!" he said, and without hesitating, did as he was told.

I walked up to the driver. He sat there rigid and speechless. The airbag had deflated, but he didn't move an inch. He looked up at me. "I, I don't know what happened. I just looked away for a second."

"Yeah, that was way dangerous!" I told him.

He lowered his head. "I know. I'll never look at my phone while I'm driving again." He shivered with fear. His face was ghostly white. "Are you two alright?"

I nodded. "Yeah, we got lucky!"

The kid shook his head. "I have no idea how I ever stopped the car in time. You sure you guys are okay?"

"Yes, we're fine," I nodded.

"Wonder why the airbag went off?" he asked.

I shrugged. "Probably just some sort of safety precaution."

He frowned with confusion and then agreed, "Yes, probably a safety precaution!"

"We won't tell anybody this happened if you don't tell anybody this happened," I stared directly at him.

He looked up at me, his face filling with relief. "Believe me, I don't want anybody to know I screwed up like this. My parents would have a massive fit!"

"You promise you'll keep your eyes on the road from now on?" I asked. I made it sound like a question, but it was more of an order.

He nodded. "Oh, I so promise! I never ever want to be scared like that again."

I trusted him. I had certainly made an impression. "Okay, just be careful. There are a lot of small kids in this neighborhood!"

"Right, got it!" he agreed, nodding his head, his face still a pasty white.

He waited for me to join Jason on the other side of the street. Then he started up the car and drove off, giving us both a small wave.

I looked at Jason and saw that his expression was full of pride. It was not the face of a guy who had almost been hit by a car.

"Why are you smiling like that?" I asked. "Weren't you scared?"

"No, of course not, you're my best friend, and I know you've got my back!" he answered confidently.

I shook my head. "Jason, you almost got run over by a car. You have to be more careful. Only dumb luck kept you from getting killed."

"It's not luck," Jason insisted. "It's amazing! My best friend is super! This is the coolest thing ever!"

Between friends...

"Holy cow!" Jason continued, "I can't believe you're the girl who stopped the bank robbers. And then you just saved my life!"

I lifted a finger. "One, I can't believe you just said, *holy cow.*" I put up another finger. "And two, you can't really believe that I'm super."

Jason looked me in the eyes. "Lia, you just stopped a speeding car with one arm! And you put a dent in the car. A big dent! You can't deny being super. Cause seriously, that ain't normal!"

"Don't say ain't!" I told him.

"Just making a point," he grinned.

I sighed. My sigh knocked him backward.

I lunged forward, holding him up, "Oh Jason, I'm so sorry."

He laughed as I steadied him. "Look! You just breathed on me, and I went flying!"

"Well, not FLYING," I insisted. I couldn't stop a smile from appearing on my face.

"Girl, you are super!!" he began jumping up and down.

I rolled my eyes. "Don't call me girl!" I insisted.

He steadied himself. "Okay, okay. I got a bit carried away. After years of comic reading, I am actually best friends with a super being. This has got to be the best day of my life!"

In a way, I couldn't help but feel relieved that Jason had figured it out. Not only was he my best friend in the world, but he was also a comic and superhero expert. He could help me understand all of this better. He could help me find my new place in this world. Plus, maybe he could help cover for me if I needed an excuse. After all, in the movies, all superheroes had confidants, people they could rely on, to help them. Jason had always been mine. So, it was perfect that he could be a part of this.

72

I nodded, finally admitting the truth. "Yes, I am super."

He leaped into the air. "I knew it! I knew it!!"

I gently put a hand on his shoulder to calm him. "Remember, it's a secret. Right? I don't want anybody else to know. Mom says if I tell people, they would want me to do things for them."

"That makes sense," Jason agreed. "So, your mom is super too?"

I nodded. "Yep, afraid so!"

He beamed. "Well, that explains why your grandma and great-grandma are so fit. They must be super as well?"

I nodded again. "That's what mom tells me. I guess all the Strong women are, well, way strong."

"Why didn't you tell me this sooner?" Jason asked, eager as could be.

I lifted my hands up. "I didn't know until yesterday."

He looked at me. "You kept this from me for an entire day!" He turned away, a hurt expression on his face. "I thought we were friends!"

My heart started to race. I couldn't bear the thought of losing Jason over this. Touching him gently on the shoulder, I said, "Jason....I...."

He turned to me, grinning widely, and waved me off. "Just teasing you, Lia! I totally get the idea of keeping a secret identity."

I breathed a sigh of relief. Once again, sending Jason staggering back a little.

"Oops, I still don't know my own strength."

"That will take some getting used to," Jason realized the obvious.

"Just be glad I didn't have onions or garlic for lunch," I told him.

He laughed. "So, exactly how strong and tough are you?"

I shrugged my shoulders. "No idea," I paused. "Mom seems to want me to learn by doing. I know I could squish a gun like it was nothing. It felt like putty in my hands. And I knocked out those Hansons with a tap."

"Plus, you have really powerful breath," Jason added. Then a sly smirk passed over his face. He pointed to his garage. "Let's say we give you a test or two."

"Sounds like fun!" I told him. I was so glad that he'd found out. I knew my mom wouldn't be thrilled, but I also knew she would understand and trust Jason, just like I did.

Testing...

Jason's garage was filled with weights, exercise machines, punching bags, and dummies. His dad, the chief, happened to be very big on staying in tip-top shape. He always told Jason and me that a good cop's best weapons were his mind and his body, in that order. Guns were messy, and a good cop never had to use one.

First, Jason set up a weight bar for me. "How strong do you think you are?" he asked.

"No idea," I replied honestly. "Strong enough to stop a car and pull doors off a car. I also pulled one of the Hanson guys out of his car like he was nothing."

Jason grabbed a couple of big weights and put them on the bar. "My dad only has 500 pounds of weight. We'll start with that," he grinned. "If it turns out to be too heavy, which I am guessing it won't be, then I'll remove a few plates."

"Plates? They look like weights, not something you eat off." I said, kind of joking.

"We're going to have to work on your witty comments. They're not that funny!" He chuckled anyway.

Standing up on a concrete platform, Jason made sure the weights were steady. After locking in the right and left sides, he walked to the middle of the weight bar and tried to lift it. It didn't budge. "I can't even begin to lift this weight. So, I can't help you."

I hopped up on the platform. Something inside me, I don't know what, told me I wouldn't need Jason's help. "That's okay," I assured him. "Just to be on the safe side, though, you'd better stand back in case I lose control."

I knew I was being extra cautious because I could tell this was going to be very easy once again. I also somehow knew it would be safer for Jason to stand back.

He reluctantly moved back to the other side of the garage.

When I figured he was safe, I reached over and grabbed the bar with my left hand, then hoisted it over my head like it weighed nothing. I smiled proudly. I also smelled something, something like two-day-old cheese mixed with a skunk. That odor emanated from my left armpit. It definitely had a kick to it, but surely it wasn't that bad? I looked over at Jason. His eyes rolled to the back of his head, and he dropped down as stiff as a board. I lowered my arm down and locked my arms to my sides. I guessed that the thought of Jason getting hit by the car had caused me to burn through my deodorant.

"OMG! I just killed my best friend with super B.O!" I thought. Now that was a phrase I'd never expected to be saying to myself!

I stared at Jason and saw his left foot begin to twitch. His chest began to rise up and down. I hadn't killed him after all. He was probably lucky I'd only lifted one arm. My first thought was to run right to him. But then I figured if I did that, a whiff of me from up close might REALLY kill him. I jumped off the platform and grabbed my bag. Ripping open the bag, I pulled out my special deodorant. Before applying it, though, I blew on each of my underarms, hoping to force the sweat and stink off. I coated my skin with deodorant.

Then I raced to Jason's side. Kneeling down beside him, I gently shook his arm. "Jason, Jason!" I coaxed.

His eyes slowly opened. "Wow, did you get the number of that train that clobbered me?"

I shook my head in dismay.

He sat up. "That was crazy! I've never been hit that hard in judo or lacrosse. My head is still spinning." He hesitated for a moment and then smiled with realization. "So, that's what they mean by seeing stars."

"See! This power of mine is too dangerous!! You got knocked silly by one whiff of my armpit from across the room! If I lifted both arms, you might have died. Nope, no more power for me!"

Jason laughed. "You're so cute when you panic." He grinned at me encouragingly. "Look, Lia, you have this power for a reason. Sure, you're going to have to learn to control it. But I know you can do it."

"What makes you so sure?" I asked.

"Because I know you, you can do whatever you put your mind to!" He patted me on the shoulder. "It's obvious you're way super strong. And I don't have nearly enough weights to test you. So, let's try the treadmill and punching bags instead."

"You sure you want to keep doing this?" I asked, frowning.

He stood up with my help. "Of course, I do! I was born to do this kind of thing. I've been waiting my whole life!"

I reluctantly agreed but made sure to take care this time and continued training under Jason's watchful eyes. First, he asked me to run on the treadmill. After hooking me up to the heart monitor, he set the tread to move at the highest speed and resistance. I started moving my legs in rhythm. In less than a minute, I had the treadmill churning faster than the speedometer could measure. The bottom of the treadmill began to ooze smoke.

"Stop! Stop!" Jason shouted, waving his hands in front of me.

I slammed my legs down through the pad of the treadmill, and the tread stopped moving. But the machine kept smoking. "Oops!" I said, hopping off the machine.

Jason grabbed a fire extinguisher and sprayed it down. "I think I can fix this. Luckily, my dad never uses this machine, so it should be okay. Meanwhile, I think we can determine that you are way fast."

I nodded. "Yeah, I guess that's a safe bet."

Next, we moved to a big heavy punching bag dangling from the ceiling. Jason pointed to the bag. "This is the heavy bag. Be careful."

I curled my hand into a fist and gave the bag a light tap. It went flying off the hinges and crashed into the far wall.

"Oops!" I said for the second time.

"OMG!" Jason's face was a mixture of surprise and shock.

Looking over my shoulder, I explained to him. "Yeah, that's why I only tap people to knock them out."

He shook his head adamantly up and down. "Yep, that's smart."

I walked across the room and picked up the punching bag. Hoisting it up on the hinge, I patted it down, smoothing it out. It didn't seem that beat up and looked like it had barely been used.

Jason gave me a solid metal bar which he actually had trouble lifting.

"So, what do you want me to do with this?" I asked. "It's not heavy at all."

"Twist it!" Jason ordered.

I promptly went and tied the bar into a knot and then another knot. I displayed it for Jason by balancing it on one finger and popping it up and down.

"Okay, stop showing off!" he laughed. "Now, please put it back to how it was."

I untangled the bar and put it back on the floor. Then I looked at my phone. "This has been fun, Jason, but it's getting a bit late, and I have homework to do. I'd also like to clean up a bit before Mom gets home. She's going to want to talk about my day. I'm sure she won't be thrilled to hear you know about my powers."

"But I'm cool!" Jason said.

"Yeah, let's hope my mom agrees!" I answered with a smile, but a worried feeling was creeping into the pit of my stomach.

"Oh, BTW, you better start thinking of a name for your alter-ego. Super Girl is what everyone is familiar with in the DC comics. Is that what you want to be called?"

"Okay," I replied with a nod. I hadn't even thought of that. But I figured sooner rather than later, the media would name me.

Heading home...

On my way home, I noticed a heap of birds on the ground, in the area around Jason's garage. They appeared to be shaking. After a closer look, I quickly figured that they must have been blasted when I blew the smell off my underarms. I really did have to be careful with my powers and just hoped that the birds would survive!

I heard a familiar voice shouting, "Hold the bus. Hold the bus!!"

Looking down the street with super-vision, I saw Jan, the janitor running towards a city bus. The bus had started its engines and was getting ready to take off.

I couldn't let that happen. I knew Jan had not only served our country in the past, but she had worked way hard today. I needed to hold that bus. I just had to do it carefully, without being super if I could. I was quite certain I could hold the bus in place, but I had to be more subtle-like. I needed to use my head here.

I leaped forward to the bus, but instead of grabbing it, I walked up the stairs towards the driver, a short skinny woman.

"Swipe your bus pass, please," she said, pointing to a scanner next to her.

"Okay," I replied, reaching into my book bag. "I'm sure it's here somewhere!" Looking over my shoulder, I saw Jan closing in on the bus, but I still needed more time. I dropped my bag on the floor. The bus driver rolled her eyes as I began to search through my pockets. First, I pulled out my side pockets. Then I pulled my wallet out of my back pocket. I slowly started going through each item. "Will my school ID help?" I queried slowly.

The bus driver shook her head impatiently.

I thought about searching in my shoes for a second, but then I got worried I might have super stinky feet that would knock out the entire bus. While it would keep the bus in place, it would also defeat (or defeet) the purpose of holding it for Janitor Jan.

"Girl, do you have a bus pass or not?" the driver demanded.

"Must have left it at home," I apologized. "Can you wait?"

"No!" the driver said firmly.

I heard Janitor Jan's footsteps on the road nearby. I nodded to the driver and hopped off the bus. Just to be safe, I put my hand on the door so the driver couldn't close it.

Janitor Jan reached the bus door. "Lia, what are you doing here?" she asked me, panting.

"Just holding the bus," I explained.

"Thanks, Lia!" I could hear the gratitude in her voice. "It's been such a crazy long day. I'm so glad I didn't have to walk home."

I smiled as I watched Janitor Jan get on the bus. The door closed, and the bus drove away. I felt good about myself. I had solved a problem without using superpowers. Well, without really relying on them.
Feeling more pleased than ever, I headed for my house.

Home Sweet Home...

I got home and dropped my book bag on the floor. Plopping down on the couch, I pulled out my phone. Shep came over and licked me, tail wagging. He could sense I'd had a long day.

"Thanks, Shep. Nice to know I can always count on you!"

I had to admit I was dying to see what my social media feed had to say about the supergirl or whatever they were going to call me. It turned out most people were calling me Super Teen. Not sure how they could tell I was a teen, but I kind of liked the name.

As for the comments, they were mostly positive.

Super Teen is way cool.

She took out those bad Hanson Brothers like they were nothing.

Man, I wish I could rip doors off cars.

If I were her, I'd use my powers to rob the bank. Well, okay, I'd be tempted.

There was already a hashtag #SuperTeenRocks

I had to admit that made me feel awfully good. I was becoming famous. Sure, I was becoming famous in disguise, but that was okay. I knew they were talking about me. Plus, I was doing my thing to help make the world better. As well, I could still live a normal life. Well, at least as normal as I could, being super.

Then there were the questions asking who the girl was, and of course, negative stuff that mostly came from Wendi. In the previous hour, Wendi had tweeted or posted:

I think she's fake.

She must be ugly because she doesn't show her face.

It's easy doing good when you have superpowers.

Let's talk about something real. How about our practice? That cheap hit Lia put on poor Lori!

83

That last comment got to me a bit. Wendi just couldn't admit that somebody else was good at something. But I felt my anger drop when I saw Lori's comment.

Wendi, cut it out! That was a clean hit by Lia. Stop talking bad about one of our teammates!!!

Then there was another comment…

Seriously, it's great that both you and Lia played so well. Your team is going to dominate!

I beamed as I read that one, as it was from Brandon. It was so cool that Brandon not only noticed me but also thought I'd played well. Brandon, the best-looking boy in school, if not the world, had defended me. I felt so good, and I could have floated off the couch. But then a couple of city warnings popped into my newsfeed, bringing me back down to earth.

"Two Hanson Brothers remain at large!"

"Citizens who spot either of the two should IMMEDIATELY contact the police. Captain Michaels."

"These men should be considered armed and dangerous. Their capture should be left to the professionals."

I knew that the last comment was aimed at me. Speaking of comments aimed at me! A text popped in from my mom.

MOM> Just got out of surgery. I saw what you did. Part of me, the Strong part is proud. The Mom part in me says, Be careful! Love Mom.

I texted her back.

LIA> Don't worry, I'm always careful!

A fly started buzzing around my face. The fly darted back and forth, first to my face then around my feet. It seemed to be circling me, kind of taunting me. Even its buzz, buzz appeared to be a challenge.

When it hovered around my feet, I kicked my shoes off. They had been on all day, and I was dying to get them off. I just didn't dare do it when there were any other humans around.

The fly instantly stopped buzzing, and it nosedived to the floor.

"That's what you get for messing with me!" I told the fly. Looking down at Shep, who was now sleeping, I thought, *Oops! Lucky he didn't get a direct hit!*

I stood up, picked up the fly off the floor, and headed to a window. Mom's plants in the window sill had wilted. One of them was a cactus. *Oh my gosh*, I thought as I opened the window and tossed the fly out. *My smelly feet can wilt a cactus.* I knew three things: this would get me a speech from Mom about using my power wisely. I needed a shower badly. And lastly, it was definitely a good thing I hadn't taken my shoes off in public.

Heading up the stairs, I decided I should take a very long shower.

Shower interrupted...

When the water from the shower hit me, somehow, it felt better than any shower I had ever taken. I finally understood what Mom meant when she talked about water washing away any tension. I made a concerted effort to make sure I really scrubbed my underarms, feet, and toes and between each toe. If it could smell, I washed it well. From now on, that would be my motto:

If it can smell, wash it well....

Okay, it wasn't exactly "Up and away!" or "To infinity and beyond!" This would be more of a private motto. I'd work on the more flashing one later.

I heard a weird ringing sound coming from the sink outside the shower. I kind of recognized that ring. Moving the shower curtain aside, I glanced across the steaming room to see my phone flashing. Somebody was calling me! Not texting, not snap chatting, not tweeting me. Somebody wanted to talk to me the old-fashioned way. This had to be important.

I jumped out of the shower, wrapped a towel around myself, and grabbed the phone. When I saw Jason's name and image with the wording, incoming call, I hit the speaker button.

"Jason, what's up?" I asked.

"Turn on your TV, put it on channel 13 news," Jason had a sense of urgency in his voice. He was usually calm and cool. (Except, of course, when talking about comics.) So, this had to be important.

Walking into my room, I grabbed the remote and flipped my TV on. I punched in channel 13. A local reporter appeared on the screen. She was at the Starlight City city zoo. Yeah, the name was a bit silly, but that wasn't what mattered right then.

"Breaking news from Starlight City city zoo! There is a seven-year-old boy who has somehow fallen into the gorilla

86

pit. The boy has been approached by the zoo's pride and joy, a 20-year-old male gorilla name Henry. Zoo officials and police are trying to determine the best way to handle the situation. They can't tranquilize the gorilla because the sedative will anger him before it relaxes him. They are afraid to shoot Henry because he has the young boy in his arms."

The camera zoomed in. There was my neighbor, sweet little Felipe, in the arms of a massive gorilla.

"Oh, this is so bad!" I said to Jason over the phone.

"You gotta get him out of there!" Jason pleaded. "My dad and his men are there, but I'm afraid they could do more harm than good. I'm betting you could free Felipe from Henry without Henry *or* Felipe getting hurt."

I thought for a split second while looking at the screen. Felipe was staying surprisingly calm. It looked like he was talking to Henry. Henry, for his part, seemed fascinated by Felipe. I knew that Henry could crush Felipe by accident. Gorillas had to be extra careful around humans. I could relate, but I was pretty sure Henry didn't quite grasp that concept.

"Okay, I'll put on a disguise and get there asap!" I told Jason.

"Thanks, Lia!" Jason said, sounding relieved. "I'll bike there."

"Jason…"

"Don't worry, Lia. I'm not going to try to be a superhero. I'll be there so I can run interference for you if you need it!"

"Thank you, Jason!" he truly was a sweet, great friend.

I spun around really fast to spin dry myself. It worked so well. But I needed some sort of costume. I went into my closet and pulled out a red pair of tights that I'd worn to a dance recital the previous year. When I tried them on, I found that they still fitted. Ripping through my drawers, I found an old pink mask that I'd used when trick or treating as a kid. I popped it on. It also still fitted. I then tossed on an oversized white t-shirt that came almost to my knees and a pair of white canvas sneakers. Costume complete. It wasn't fancy, but it worked.

I needed a way to get to the zoo without anybody seeing me. The good news was...our house was centrally located, so nothing in this city was far away. The tricky news was...I couldn't just walk or run or jump there without attracting attention. I went to my window and looked out at the neat houses lining our street. I had it!

I pried open my window and jumped from the window to our neighbor's roof. From there on, I jumped onto the next roof and then the next and the next, until I came to the end of the street. Luckily, I had a good sense of direction. Even from the rooftops, I knew where the zoo was and what my next jump should be. On the roof of the house at the end of the block, I needed to leap across the street to head off in the other direction. This would be a tricky leap. I needed to leap far and land without doing damage to the house.

Bending my knees, I pushed forward and leaped up into the air higher than I thought I ever could. I flapped my arms a bit, not sure why I did that. In mid flap, I figured I had a better chance to glide than to fly. Duh. I held my arms out straight. I overshot one house but landed face-first on the house after my target. The distance was impressive, even if the landing wasn't. I stood and leaped again and again from roof to roof.

The zoo soon came into sight. I had to say that was quite an amazing way to travel. Of course, now came the tricky part, getting into the gorilla pit unnoticed and without scaring Henry. I may not have been an expert on gorillas. In fact, all I knew was from a TV show I'd watched a while back. But I did know that scaring a giant 400-pound gorilla wouldn't be a good thing at all.

I jumped into the zoo's parking lot. From there, I could hear all the commotion coming from the pit. I coiled and jumped over the zoo's fence. I then landed on the ground right near the gorilla pit and leaped again. This time, I landed in the back end of the pit and had a clear view of Henry. He had put Felipe down but still had one giant hairy hand wrapped around Felipe's arm.

Felipe remained relatively calm as he spoke to the ape. "Ah, Mr. Henry the ape, I didn't mean to come down here. Sorry. Some big ugly guy pushed me. Now, if you let me go, I'll leave." I could sense Felipe fighting back the tears.

Slowly, I made my way towards Henry and Felipe. I had hoped Henry would be able to sense my power like other animals.

Felipe noticed me before Henry did.

"Are you here to help me?" he asked.

I nodded.

He smiled happily. "Wow, Super Teen is here to save me!"

Okay, news of my name sure traveled fast.

"How did you know that?" I asked Felipe. "This is my new outfit, and I thought I wouldn't have been recognized."

He smiled. "Who else would come down into a gorilla house to save me?"

"Great point," I replied, slowly walking towards Henry.

Henry turned his massive hairy head towards me.

He, like most of the human onlookers above us, really had no idea what to make of me. I showed Henry my open hands.

"Henry, I am here to help," I said slowly and surely. "I know you only want to take care of Felipe since he fell into your home. That's very nice of you. But I am here to take Felipe back to his mother and father so they can take care of him." I used my most calming, soothing voice.

"I don't think he speaks English," Felipe told me.

"Yep, I know that, but I'm hoping he can feel my emotions and feelings," I told Felipe.

"You big kids can be weird sometimes," Felipe said with a shrug.

I drew to within an arm's reach of Henry. Henry pulled back and put both arms around Felipe possessively. The crowd above gasped.

My super-hearing picked up Chief Michaels' voice. "Great! We finally had a shot, but now we've lost it. This is what happens when amateurs take matters into their own hands."

I also heard Jason defend me by saying, "Give her a chance Dad, I know she can save Felipe without hurting the gorilla."

"Come on, Henry," I said slowly. "Let the boy go. His Mom and Dad need him." I held open my arms. "You can take me, instead. I could use a big gorilla hug."

Henry looked over his shoulder at me, thick bushy eyebrows raised. He seemed to be taking in my words. Well, if not my words, then my sentiments.

"Let the little boy go, Henry." I coaxed with my words and my eyes.

Henry released Felipe from his grip. I jumped forward and hugged Henry tightly. I needed to make sure he didn't grab Felipe again, so I tightened the bear hug I had locked on him.

"You okay?" I asked Felipe, turning towards him.

He nodded. "Yes. Thank you, Super Teen!" He gave me a huge grateful grin. Now that was sweet.

I lifted Henry off the ground. "I'll take him back to his home area now. You wait here for the people to come and get you."

"Okay!" Felipe agreed, the smile on his face faltering as he watched me begin to move away.

Then something Felipe had said to Henry jumped into my mind. "You said you were pushed in here?" I asked.

Felipe nodded. "Yeah, by a couple of huge men. One was talking to my mom, and the other pushed me in. I heard them say they needed a distraction."

OMG! It had to be the Hansons. They were going to rob the zoo. Listening with my super hearing, I somehow managed to pick two far-off voices out of the crowd. They were talking about getting to their car and making a smooth getaway.

First things first, though. I needed to get Henry nice and safe into his cage. I patted him on the back and started carrying him slowly to the end of the pit area. There were a couple of handlers in the enclosure who had been unsuccessfully trying to coax Henry back.

Henry started to fight me, but I tightened my grip. "Just relax, Henry!" I ordered. "You may be strong, but you're going to lose this if you fight me."

Henry instinctively became calm. I guess he finally felt my power. I carried him over to his handler and put him down gently in the cage. The people above clapped.

Through the noise, I heard Jason say, "See, Dad, I told you she could do it!"

"You were right, son!" he replied.

It made me so happy to hear their words. Still, there was no time to bask in the glory. I had two Hansons to catch. And I was angry. How dare they risk a young boy's life so they could rob a zoo!

I leaped out of the pit over the crowd. I realized that this was just like the dream I'd had. One super leap, and I was in the parking lot. I saw a black van starting to speed away. Nope, not going to happen. Those nasty Hansons had gone way too far. Time for me to put a stop to them once and for all!

The Bad Guys...

Using my super-vision, I spotted two men in the front seat of the black van racing out of the parking lot. They were laughing and seemed quite proud of themselves. Only total jerks would be pleased about putting a young boy in an enclosure with a real-life gorilla, just so they could make a few bucks.

I leaped across the parking lot. I dropped in front of the speeding van and held out both arms. "You bad boys better stop if you know what's good for you!"

"Hit her!" the Hanson in the passenger's seat ordered.

The driver slammed the brakes. "No! We're thieves, not killers!"

Hitting the brake had slowed the car down some but not much. It still slammed into my outstretched arms. The car crashed to a stop, and the hood crinkled up like tin foil.

The two brothers popped open their doors and headed off in different directions. I sighed and pushed the broken car away from my body. It went tumbling across the parking lot towards a bunch of parked cars. Oh, rats! I didn't take into account how strong I really was, especially when angry. Not wanting to let the flying escape car damage innocent peoples' cars, I jumped back into the air and over the ruined van. Landing just beside it, I caught the van a mere few inches before it hit the row of parked cars.

Just then, I heard something behind me. I turned to see one of the Hansons charging at me with a big lead pipe. I shook my head as he rushed at me, screaming, "ARRRG!" at the top of his lungs.

He smashed the pipe over my head. When he pulled it back, it had a head-shaped dent in it. He looked at the pipe. Then he looked back at me. Tossing the pipe over his shoulder, he took a boxing position.

"You aren't smart at all. Are you?" I said to him.

I held out my jaw, and as I expected, he foolishly punched me in the chin with an uppercut. When he pulled back his hand, it was throbbing red. "You broke my freaking hand!" he shouted at me.

Shaking my head, I told him. "No, YOU broke your hand, you idiot!"

He pointed at me with his good hand. "I'm going sue!"

I shook my head. "No, you're not! First of all, you're a mean, nasty crook. Second, I hate to break this to you, but you have no idea who I am."   I tapped him on the head with my pinky, and he crumbled to the ground. Looking down at him, I added. "Third, when you're conscious again, you might not even remember what hit you!"

I turned my attention towards the last Hanson brother as he ran out of the zoo. Pulling off my left shoe, I tossed it across the parking lot. It flew through the zoo entranceway and hit the fleeing Hanson in the back of the neck. He fell to the ground face first. I couldn't help but smile as I leaped across the parking lot towards him. It was important to make sure he'd stay down, and I also needed to get my shoe back. That shoe could be a public hazard. Even before I was super, those shoes could stink up a room.

In a couple of bounds, I was behind the last of the Hansons. My shoe hitting him in the back of his head had stunned him, but it hadn't knocked him out. I bent down and picked it up. He was a big burly bear of a man. He was unshaven and had to weigh over 300 pounds. I walked up to him. "Stay down and be nice and quiet for the police."

He started to push himself up off the ground.

"I figured you wouldn't be smart enough to do as you were told!" I shook my head at him.

"The police aren't taking me!" he bellowed. "No..."

I held my foot under his nose, and he instantly stopped talking. Wriggling my toes, I gave him a nice whiff of my foot. After a mere half-hour in my canvas shoes, it was enough to make his eyes roll to the back of his head. He then turned blue, and I heard him mutter the words, "Wow, what power...."

His head plopped straight down in the dirt. He'd be no problem for the police. It looked like he'd be out cold for days.

I popped my shoe back onto my foot and leaped up into the air to bounce back home.

A long day done...

Climbing through my bedroom window, I found my mom sitting on my bed watching TV. It was still tuned in to channel 13 news.

"And there you have it, folks! Super Teen not only saved seven-year-old Felipe Moore from the zoo's star attraction, Henry the Ape, she also carried Henry into his cage unharmed. Then the super teen somehow figured out the last of the Hanson brothers had robbed the zoo. This powerful teen easily overpowered two dangerous thugs. One of them is still unconscious, and as one of the medics put it, 'he's in dreamland.' I, for one, am happy we have this super team looking out for our interests in Starlight City."

Mom flicked off the TV. "Busy first day, I see?" She patted the bed.

I sat down next to her. "You mad?" I asked her.

Mom smiled and put her hand on my shoulder. "How could I be mad about you helping people and an ape?" She took a deep breath. "I'm proud and worried... mostly proud. It does seem like you're doing a good job with your powers. I know it can be tricky!"

I shook my head. "Tell me about it. I had some nervous sweat when Jason almost got run over by a car. It burnt through my deodorant like nothing. Then I thought I'd killed him when I lifted my arms while he was testing me on his dad's sports equipment."

"Wait, Jason knows you're super?"

I nodded anxiously, not sure how she was going to take that news. "Yeah, he figured it out, Mom. He's so smart." I tried to gauge her reaction before trying to explain further. "But I'm glad he knows! It gives me somebody to talk to that's my age. Plus, I hate keeping things from him. Plus, he's the one who told me Felipe needed my help. Plus, he stood up for me when his dad was complaining about me. Plus, he knows a ton about comics and superheroes, so he's a great resource."

Mom smiled weakly. "That's a lot of pluses, Lia. It sounds like your powers are developing quickly. But then I guess you are the 20th Strong woman to be born. Legend has it you could grow to be the strongest of us all."

"Wow!!" I exclaimed. "Really?"

She nodded. "Not sure how reliable the legend is, but you are certainly off to a great start. We all get super strength and durability, but some of us develop other powers. Like my mom has heat vision, especially when she's angry. I have x-ray vision that comes in handy as a doctor."

"Okay, x-ray sounds weird but creepy," I told her.

She laughed, "It's handy once you get used to it." She paused for a moment before continuing. "How about super pheromones? Have those popped up yet?"

"Not entirely sure what those are?"

"Your scent has a way of making people like you a lot. It makes them more willing to do what you say. I don't have that power, but your great-grandma does."

"Ah, that's why all the men are always giving her their jello."

Mom laughed. "Yes, she does love her jello."

I thought for a moment. "Jason did act weird after I accidentally knocked him out with my underarm odor. Plus, the last Hanson mumbled some freaky stuff after I waved my stinky toes under his nose. So maybe…"

"Well, that's another tricky power, but one I'm sure you can handle."

I smiled at the idea of being able to make people do my bidding. Now that could come in all sorts of handy.

Mom put one hand on my shoulder and looked me in the eyes. "I recognize that look. Your great-grandma looks like that before making people cluck like chickens."

My smile grew. "Yeah, now I understand how she does that cool trick. It's like hypnosis."

"No, it's way more powerful than hypnosis. A hypnotized person won't do anything against their will. A person under pheromones' influence will do pretty much anything to please. You have to promise to be careful IF that develops more."

I nodded. "Check! Got it, Mom! You can count on me. What other powers can I get?"

She looked at me. "The list is pretty long and extensive. There's the basic freeze breath. Some of our great grandmothers could move things with their minds and even make themselves fly. One could scream and shatter rock. One even had acid burps."

"Gross," I said. "I wish there was a manual."

Mom stood up. "Actually, I have something better." She darted away at super speed. Less than a second later, she sat by my side, holding a book. "It's nice to finally be able to show you my true self," Mom said. She handed me an old leather-bound book. I opened it up. The title page said: A History of the Strong Women.

"Each of the last 19 Strong women has left notes in this book. It's a history of us."

I started flipping through the pages. The first ones were dated 1650. I knew from doing a genealogy paper at school that's when our first ancestors arrived here, not only in this country but in Starlight City. My great, great, great, great, great, great, great, great, great, great, great, great, great, great, great, great, great, Great-Grandma was one of the original founders of this city. Even though I'd hardly ever bragged about it, I still felt proud of it. Wendi told everyone how her family had been here for 300 years. I knew she'd have a fit if she learned mine had been here longer. Either that or she'd call us all losers for not being able to get out of this city. With Wendi, you can never win. That's why I never brought it up. I was just happy to know we'd been a part of this city from the start. Now holding this book in my hand, I felt closer to my ancestors and prouder than ever.

Mom stood up. "Okay, today is a very special occasion, so I'm cooking your favorite meal tonight!"

I sniffed myself. I did have a bit of nervous odor about me. "Should I take another shower?"

She shook her head. "Nah, it's just us Super Strongs tonight. Right? Much rather have you spent the time hitting the books, or maybe even have a night off!"

"That sounds good!" I grinned.

Just as she left my room, my phone vibrated. It was a text from Jason.

JASON> Man, you were AWESOME!

LIA> Thanks, Jason.

JASON> I knew you could do it! I knew you could!

LIA> I'm glad one of us did :-)

JASON> Lia! U were super b4 U were super!

LIA> UR dad doesn't seem to think so....

JASON> He thinks Lia is great. It's just he's not used to the other part of you. Don't worry, he'll come around.

LIA> I hope so!

JASON> Trust me. C U tomorrow for our walk to school. ☺

LIA> Wouldn't miss it for anything! If you need any help with your French homework let me know :-)

JASON> Oui Oui (that means yes yes…)

LIA> Ha! Ha!

A wonderful day...

Mom cooked my favorite chicken casserole with broccoli on the side. Some kids found it weird, but I loved broccoli, especially smothered with my mom's cheese sauce. Mom assured me that when cooked, broccoli wouldn't make either of us lethal. I told her about my fart and how I clobbered a herd of cattle. "You should have seen them, Mom. They dropped like they were fleas. And then I had to double-check they were still breathing. Thank goodness they were okay. I'd hate to be responsible for harming a herd of cattle!"

She laughed and told me, all in all, I had handled everything well. She also said that as I matured, I would learn more control. Mom explained that she could hold her gas in now and only risked letting it escape when she was in a safe zone on her own somewhere. She said she'd also used it once at the cinema. A bunch of people in the theater wouldn't stop talking, so she released a silent fart. She put the entire place to sleep for the duration of the movie.

I laughed so hard at that story. It was the funniest one she'd told me so far! After that, though, we talked about normal things: school, work, friends, boys. Although, I changed the subject back to school when she asked if I had any crushes. That was just too embarrassing. But like mom said, we may be superhuman, but we're human first.

Because it was a special day, Mom let me off having to clean up the dishes. So, I went to my bedroom to check my Facebook news feed. There were many comments about Super Teen from kids at school and lots of people I didn't know. Most of them were positive...

Wow, she's amazing.
To think we have a superhero here in our town!
Nice to see her saving the day.
I wish I had her powers.
Glad she saved Henry and the boy!

101

Man, she is fast.
Did you see how high she can jump?
Her disguises are cool!

I especially liked that one. Of course, there were some negative comments as well, and Wendi's name was attached to a couple of those.

That girl is so over-rated! And besides, she seems dangerous!
A couple of other people were also unimpressed…

Kids these days shouldn't take the law into their own hands.

One of the Hansons claims she beat him with super foot odor – gross.

But that was what some people thought was the best superpower of all. A few even wished they had super foot odor themselves because they could have so much fun with it. Krista commented that she'd love to have the shoe store all to herself! Hmm, that was a good idea.

I went to bed fairly pleased with myself. It had been a crazy day. It may very well have been the best day of my life. I learned I could make a difference in the world. A BIG difference. Sure, it might be tempting some time to knock out the mall and go on a wonderful shopping spree. But I knew I could fight back those temptations and do the right thing. Well, at least do the right thing more often than not.

I drifted off to sleep. I dreamed of leaping up into space and looking down on Earth. I noticed a big green asteroid heading towards our planet. I flew to it and caught it, stopping it in its path. Then I pushed the giant green rock back out into space. I flew back down to Earth to be greeted by a huge parade. Everybody loved me.

Suddenly I woke up and smiled. Now that was a cool dream. I wondered if I could ever get that powerful, able to fly in space and stop asteroids. Wow! Before I could ponder the question for too long, I heard a noise coming from downstairs. Looking over at my phone, the time was 2:22 am. I sat up and listened.

Pat, Pat, Pat…it was the sound of footsteps coming downstairs. They weren't mom's footsteps. Too heavy. Not Shep, because he was asleep on the floor by my bed. The person was trying to be quiet, but they couldn't muffle their steps from my super hearing. I stood up, tossed on a robe, and headed down the stairs.

There in the living room, stood a man holding a flashlight.

"Dude, you picked the wrong house to break into!" I said.

The man turned his flashlight on me. "No, wait!" he said. "This isn't what it seems…I'm a friend!"

The man did look sort of familiar. I leaped towards him. I landed right in front of him. "Sorry, friends don't break into their friend's houses."

The man smiled. "My, you truly are amazing!"

I grabbed his big flashlight and squished it in my hands. "Talk, or you're next!" I growled.

The man's smile grew. The smile somehow made me feel at ease, like I had seen it before.

"Look, buddy. I don't know what games you're playing, but you're not going to get me to like you!"

"But…" he said, holding up a hand. "You're needed…"

I tapped him on the forehead, and he crumbled to the ground. "Sure, I am, buddy!"

The lights in the living room popped on. I turned, ready for anything. I saw Mom coming down the stairs. "What's going on here?"

I lifted up the man's unconscious body. I showed him to mom. "I caught this jerk breaking into our house!"

Mom walked slowly towards me. Her eyes popped open. She knew this man. She smiled at me. "I can't believe it…" she said.

"What?" I asked, shaking him like a rag doll. "You know this creep? I can tell you know him!"

Mom nodded. "I do know him. I used to know him quite well. You do too, in fact."

She bent down and gently touched him on the forehead. "He has aged, but that's to be expected."

"Is he a bad guy?" I asked, even though Mom didn't seem to be treating him like one. "He made me feel some emotions. It was weird."

"No, he's not a bad guy. I believe these days he works for the government," she explained.

"Mom, who is this guy?" I asked.

She looked at me and spoke. But never in a million years did I expect the words that came from her mouth.

"Lia, this is your father."

***

Want to read about some strong women in history?

The history of and words from the Strong Women...

Born in 1650: Alice

Talents: **super strength**

Accomplishments: The first

Words to Those Who Follow: **Be true...**

Thoughts: My parents wanted a boy, what they got was a girl stronger than any five boys. I had to keep my strength secret so people would not think of me as a witch. Perhaps I am a witch of sorts. But I take pride in knowing in my heart I am good.

When I married, I took my husband's name as that was the way in our time. Hopefully, it will not always be the way, but I always will be a Strong woman. When my Constance was born, it was the happiest moment of my life.

Born in 1675: Constance

Talents: **super breath**

Accomplishments: Used breath to put out fire

Words to Those Who Follow: **Love your parents...**

Thoughts: I am forever grateful that my mother was here to help me understand my powers. I cannot imagine what life must have been like for her growing up without having somebody to mentor and teach her.

My father is also an amazing man. Not many blacksmiths would readily accept having a woman that is far stronger than they are. I only hope my husband will be as understanding.

Sadly, while being a good man, my husband would never understand a woman who is stronger than he. Yet I must marry so I can have a child as I wish to be a mother.

Born in 1694: Joan

Talents: **see-through vision**

Accomplishments: Worked with healing herbs

Words to Those Who Follow: **We must live on…**

Thoughts: These powers of mine! I'm never sure if they are a curse or a blessing. I can see into people… I can see-through walls… I fear I may be a demon sometimes.

But then I find a person under a heavy tree branch, and I save them, and I understand these powers can bring good into the world.

My husband is a doctor and a good man. He is fascinated by my abilities. That's what he calls them not powers. He tells me I can help people. I believe he is right. It is the turn of the century — such an amazing time for my daughter to be born.

My heart is broken… my dear husband has passed away, taken by the sickness that has taken so many others. My daughter, Desire, and I seem unaffected. That means we can help the sick without fear. I guess that is good. We must witness so much sadness.

Our powers are a blessing and a curse.

Born in 1713: Desire

Talents: **Moving objects with thought...**

Accomplishments: Worked as a nurse

Words to Those Who Follow: **Passion and compassion go hand in hand...**

Thoughts: I decided I could best help the world as a nurse. I wish I could be a doctor, but this world is not ready for a female doctor.

If this world knew what I could do, they would be terrified of me. I am blessed with my mother's see-through vision.

That, along with my other ability, is a great tool in aiding the wounded and sick.

My voice also seems to bring comfort to people. I'm gladdened by that.

Born in 1732: Mary

Talents: **Acid breath**

Accomplishments: Studied the law on her own

Words to Those Who Follow: **Without Law, there is chaos...**

Thoughts: My mother and Grandmother have been such a wondrous help to me. Without their guidance, I do not know where I would be today.

I decided to help defend the poor and the defenseless as they are the ones who need me most.

But since I cannot display my abilities in public, I use the rules of law to defend them. I love the law; it is fair to all.

I cannot call myself a lawyer, but I am happy in the knowledge that I grasp the law as well as any man.

Oh, the acid burps are such a nuisance. Hopefully, none of my daughters will get those.

Born in 1751: Rose

Talents: **Super leap**

Accomplishments: Freedom Fighter

Words to Those Who Follow: **Freedom is everything...**

Thoughts: What an exciting time as our country fights for independence from the Brits.

I must fight as male and in disguise, but the expressions on the redcoats' faces when I bend their weapons are priceless.

I say boo, and they run like little children.

I am glad my daughter, Remember, will grow up in an independent country.

Born in 1770: Remember

Talents: **Super intelligent**

Accomplishments: Inventor

Words to Those Who Follow: **Your brain is as powerful as your brawn...**

Thoughts: I work with an amazing man named Franklin. He is a fantastic inventor and has a mind almost as sharp as mine.

The great thing is, he takes my ideas seriously. Though I cannot receive public credit for my accomplishments, Ben gives me much credit in private. He wishes he could tell the world about me.

I tell him most of the world does not think like him.

The day Ben passed from this Earth was one of the saddest of my life. I gladdened that he did get to meet my precious Sarah.

I continue my work... I live for my Sarah and my work.

Born in 1789: Sarah

Talents: **Super breathing**

Accomplishments: Helped bring yoga to the United States

Words to Those Who Follow: **Grow your mind and body...**

Thoughts: Though we live in a new century, I do not find it much different from the old. Great Grandmother Mary says she sees changes, changes for the better. But changes take time.

Time is one thing my mother and I and all the other women in our line do have. We do have trains that take us from place to place. I know that is progress.

I have not yet turned this book over to my daughter as I am still a young woman. Yet I have bared the passing of two husbands. One, because of war, the other due to infection. Part of me longs to fight the tyrant Napoleon.

With my abilities, I know I could crush his army. Of course, I would expose myself to the world. Is that such a bad thing? Mother insists it is.

The world is not ready for us. It may never be. Still, my daughter, Katherine needs me.

Born in 1808: Katherine

Talents: **Heat Vision**

Accomplishments: Taught meditation

Words to Those Who Follow: **Think before you act...**

Thoughts: I sadly take this book far too soon.

My mother passed away saving people in a massive fire. While the fire did not burn her skin, her lungs still ran out of air to breathe.

Grandmother says even we must breathe.

Born in 1827: Humility

Talents: **Super fart**

Accomplishments: Writer

Words to Those Who Follow: **Words have power...**

Thoughts: My mother gave me this book and told me she hopes I will do more with our gifts than she did. I told my mother it is never too late to give to the world. Mother smiled. She told me she was a thinker, not a doer.

I read the book, Frankenstein today. I read the entire manuscript in one sitting. Funny, I felt sorry for the monster.

Reading that story has caused me to want to share my words and views with the world.

I am glad many find my stories of interest and amusement.

Oh, and beans and super strength are not a good mix!

Born in 1846: Becky

Talents: **Super charm**

Accomplishments: Artist

Words to Those Who Follow: **Look for the best in people while preparing for the worst...**

Thoughts: I joked with my mother about joining the Naval Academy. I do love the water. I could certainly outdo any of the males there.

My mother told me that would not be wise. I married a naval officer instead. He is a good man, a kind man. Though I am not sure he would ever accept my abilities.

A large log fell onto my husband's leg today. I removed it with ease.

He passed away knowing the real me.

He told me he wished I had shared my gifts with him sooner.

Men, they can surprise you. My art helps me cope.

Born in 1865: Damarus

Talents: **Super sight**

Accomplishments: War Hero

Words to Those Who Follow: **Even we have limits...**

Thoughts: Funny, how I take over this book at such an amazing yet hectic time. A great war has ended. I did my part fighting in disguise as a man, like others of my kind before myself, have also done.

I only wish I could have been by the president's side when he went to the theater. I could have saved him. I know I could have.

I have done my share of fighting, now I will be the woman the world expects. I will marry and bear a child.

Born in 1884: Carol

Talents: **Most power super fart**

Accomplishments: Saved town from stampeding herd with fart

Words to Those Who Follow: **Be calm...**

Thoughts: I love living in the 1900s, such an amazing time.

Yes, I know future generations reading, this will look back at me and laugh, but we have subways, we have machines that clean our floors. We even have flying machines!

I am reluctant to use my abilities. I do not wish to stand out.

Oh in 1908, I made a visit to Siberia. After eating much raw cabbage I got a case of the winds! The destruction I caused was epic.

I am glad I was camping alone at the time, but it showed me what my powers could do.

Born in 1903: Bella

Talents: **Super-fast hands**

Accomplishments: Sports star

Words to Those Who Follow: **Be kind...**

Thoughts: Sadly, I never knew my mother. My grandmother told me she was a quiet but amazing fun-loving woman. Apparently, my mother never liked to show her abilities, yet she died saving others in a massive fire.

Reading this book, I see another of our line also passed this way. As powerful as we are, we still need to breathe.

I'm still not sure how fast I can run but I know I can run much faster than automobiles.

Grandmother and I went to something called a movie today. I told her soon the world would be ready for us. She just smiled at me.

I chose to be a cook in a soup kitchen. There I cannot only feed people, but I can learn of their problems and perhaps help them with my abilities.

This world at war is terrible. Even I feel powerless to stop it.

Born in 1935: Ann

Talents: **Voice of calm**

Accomplishments: Professor

Words to Those Who Follow: **Never give up!**

Thoughts: The world fights another war to end all wars as my mother hands this book to me.

I tell Mother that together we can fight the Nazis. We have the power!

Mother convinced me the best way to fight is to be educated. I became a college professor.

Today I read the comic, Superman.

Perhaps, soon the world will be ready for a real superwoman!

Born in 1950: Ellen

Talents: **Figured out scent could control people**

Accomplishments: Kept the Strong name
Words to Those Who Follow: **Women hold the true power...**

Thoughts: I decided to change my last name back to my ancestor's name of Strong.

After all, it was the time of women's liberation.

What better way to honor that concept than to be a Strong woman?

Born in 1968: Elizabeth (Beth)

Talents: **Worked on perfecting many powers**

Accomplishments: first to get a divorce – but stayed friends.

Words to Those Who Follow: **You can change people's minds at times...**

Thoughts: While I am grateful to all the Strong women who came before me, I am more grateful for being a powerful woman in the 80s.

Finally, we can move up the corporate ladder to success.

Using my strength and my abilities to influence people has allowed me much influence.

I find influence works better than raw strength. It is more lasting and far-reaching.

I'm using my PR company to make the world a better place.

Born in 1985: Isabelle

Talents: **Great science talent**

Accomplishments: First medical doctor and PH.D.

Words to Those Who Follow: **Science is discovering, and knowledge is power...**

Thoughts: My daughter, I am more of a woman of action than words. I am giving you this book early because I can sense greatness in you.

I chose to use my powers in a subtle way, to heal. I am the first of the Strong women to become a medical doctor. My gifts have been a great aid to me in my profession.

Your path may be very different to mine. The world is becoming a more accepting place. Who knows? Maybe they will be ready for a real superhero!

If so. I can't think of a greater hero than you. I know I will be proud of you, whatever direction you choose.

I am glad our genes mean I will be around for a long time to see you blossom.

Born in 2002: Lia

Story to be told...

Book 2

The New Normal

Dad...

This was the ending to one of the weirdest times of my life. First, I discovered that I have super powers. In fact, all my female ancestors before me had these powers. I am so strong that one of my farts can instantly drop a herd of cows. I can knock people out with a tap or with a whiff of my armpit. My breath can toss people around like a hurricane. I can leap tall buildings. I have a bunch of powers that I don't even understand yet. In other words, I'm super.

Of course, I love to use my powers to help people. I have saved a cute kid from a gorilla in the zoo, a cat from a tree, and stopped a bunch of bad guys from robbing people. (Naturally, it's tempting to think about knocking out the mall with super foot odor and having the place to myself. But that's something I would never do.) The press calls me Super Teen, and I kind of like that. But as strange as it may be to have super powers, nothing in my life was nearly as strange as seeing my father standing before me.

"Marcus! What are you doing here?" my mom demanded.

"Isabella, you look lovely as ever," he replied.

"Answer the question, Marcus!" Mom was not impressed. I swear I could see steam coming off her body.

Dad held up two hands. "When I saw Super Teen on TV, I knew it had to be Lia. I wanted to tell her how proud I am of her. Finally, one of you Strong women is willing to use her powers in the open."

Mom shook her head. "Okay, so why didn't you call and set up a time to come visit?"

"Would you have taken my call?" Dad asked.

"No, probably not," Mom admitted. "But why break into our house in the middle of the night?"

Dad smiled. "I wanted to test Lia's senses and reflexes to see how fast she responded."

"How'd I do?" I asked, more eager than I thought I'd be.

He grinned at me. "Your senses are quite good. I snuck in here very quietly, yet you still reacted in…" he looked at his watch. "Less than 10 seconds." He paused. "Now, let's try out your reflexes."
He pushed a button on his watch, and a small floating disc hovered into the room.

"Neat drone!" I grinned.

Mom shook her head. "Marcus, this is our DAUGHTER, not a test subject!" She put her hands on her hips in protest.

Glancing over at Mom, I saw that her face was creased into a deep frown. She knew where this was heading and didn't seem happy at all.

"Exactly," Dad said. "Just going to have the drone put her through her paces so I can see what she can do." He looked at my mom. "I don't suppose you've trained her?"

"I've given her suggestions and ways to keep her power under control. But I'm a big believer in learning by experience," Mom said slowly, one eye on Dad, the other on the drone.

"Does anyone want to explain to me what's going on here?" I asked.

Dad turned to me. "I'm working for a new company, the one that has the huge facility outside of town. They're called Big Massive Science. I'm head of research which gives me access to all the newest and coolest gadgets." Dad pointed at the floating drone. "This is a self-operating security drone. A few of these babies can protect a building far better than a squad of humans."

Mom crossed her arms. "And what do these have to do with your daughter? The daughter you haven't seen in over a decade," she added.

Dad locked eyes with her. "I took this job with BM Science so I could be closer!"

"And get your hands on the latest gadgets," Mom sighed.

Dad nodded. "Yep, win-win."

The entire time Mom and Dad were talking, the drone hovered above Dad's head. It made a freaky low-pitched buzzing sound. I didn't know if regular human ears could hear it, but I certainly could. I heard the sound increase in speed. A red light lit up in the middle of the drone. Something inside of me said, move now. I shot to the left. A beam of energy fired from that red dot, burning a hole in the floor — a hole right where my foot had been just a second earlier.

"What the...?" I shouted.

Dad clapped his hands excitedly. "Excellent move, my daughter!"

"Marcus!" Mom screamed. "This is your daughter you're attacking here!"

Dad shook his head. "Not attacking! Testing. If I were attacking, I would have brought more than one. Besides, I'm sure she can handle it!"

Yeah, now I could see why Mom didn't last all that long with Dad. He had kind of complete tunnel vision.

"Honey, do you want me to take this thing out?" Mom asked, looking at me.

I locked my eyes on the drone. I hated to admit it, but I wanted my dad to be pleased with me. "I've got this!" I said confidently.

Dad clapped again. "I've never been prouder of my own flesh and blood."

"You'd better hope you don't see any of her blood," Mom said, fist-shaking at Dad.

I was pretty sure he didn't hear her as his concentration was locked on the drone and me. It hovered closer to me. Still out of my reach, but closer. I swatted at it just to see how it would react. It darted back and then fired a beam of energy at my midsection. I jumped over the beam. It left a burn mark on the wall.

"I'll have the company pay for any damages!" Dad said, ignoring Mom's shocked reaction at the sight of her living room being destroyed.

The drone began dropping and then rising very quickly. It fired at me again. I saw the blast and leaned to the side, but the beam still hit me in the arm, burning through my robe.

"Hey! This is my favorite robe!" I shouted at the drone. I lunged at it. It darted to the side. I fell on my face. I swear the drone laughed at me. It then dived for my behind, hitting me with another laser sting.

"Ouch!" I screamed, jumping to my feet and rubbing my butt at the same time. I spun at the drone, trying to bat it down with my hands. It darted away, and at the same time, fired another bolt of energy at me. This one was hitting me in the knee. It stung!

I lunged at the drone again. It dodged me once more. But this time, as I fell to the ground, I forced out a fart. Not a silent one either. This fart made the room shake. The power from my fart shattered the drone into millions of tiny drone pieces. I smiled as I watched the pieces crumble to the ground. I heard another clunk. My dad laid there on the floor, stiff as a board.

Mom ran up to me and put her arm around me. "Great use of pressure and gas!" she said.

I looked over at dad. "I feel bad about him, though!"

Mom shook her head. "Don't! He brought this upon himself. I don't know what I ever saw in the man." She knelt down beside him to take his pulse. "He didn't take a direct hit, so he should be fine."

She grabbed a vase from a table. The flowers in it had wilted.

Mom showed me the wilted flowers.

"This is why we can't have nice things," she kidded.

She then tossed the water from the vase into my dad's face. He shivered, his eyes popping open. "Wow, what amazing power!" he said, gazing at the shattered drone. "More amazing…that thing is bulletproof!" He sat up and took hold of my arm that the drone had shot. He looked at it carefully. "Fascinating! You don't have a burn mark or even a scratch!"

Mom pulled Dad up to his feet. "Yeah, but you didn't know she was that durable when you brought your attack drone here!" she complained angrily, putting a fist under his chin.

Grabbing Mom's arm, I pulled it away from Dad's face. "Mom, he's a scientist like you. He had to test me!" I tried to convince her, but it wasn't working.

She shook her head. "I heal people. I don't hurt them." She leaned into my dad and growled, "Not unless they attack my baby girl!"

Dad lifted his hands up again. "Not an attack, just a test. And she's no baby. She's grown into quite the woman. Smart and powerful!"

"First thing you said that I agree with," Mom told him. "Next time you want to see our daughter, I expect a phone call. I also expect you to come without test droids, robots, clones, or anything else that might harm her. She's your DAUGHTER, not a test subject!"

Dad nodded in agreement. "I have an area with small living quarters in the basement of the lab. If you need me, you can find me there." He looked again at the dust that was the drone. "Man, they are going to dock my pay for this."

Mom lifted him off the ground. "You didn't tell anybody else about Lia? Did you?"

Dad smiled at her. "No, of course not. I'm fully aware that many of my colleagues wouldn't understand her like I do.

I also understand the need for secrecy and privacy. I'm here solely as a father and a scientist."

Mom dropped him to the ground. "Fine."

He turned towards the window, but Mom grabbed him firmly by the shoulder, stopping him in his tracks. "If you ever come again unannounced, I will have you arrested."

Dad nodded. "Understood."

He started to climb out the window. He then paused for a moment and looked back at me. "Nice seeing you again, honey. It's amazing what you've become." He blew me a kiss. That felt better than I thought it would.

I watched him drop out the window. Yep, I have a bizarre life now, I thought.

Mom shook her head and repeated once more. "I don't know what I ever saw in that man!"

"I do!" I told her. "He's smart and dedicated, just like you!" I gave her a hug.

"Yeah, I guess he does have some good points!" she agreed, hugging me back tightly. "Plus, he is kind of cute with that brown hair and green eyes." Sighing, she shook her head. "Of course, if he ever comes here unannounced again, I'll squish him like a bug!"

She broke away from our hug, then put an arm around me and started leading me towards the stairs. "We need to get some sleep. Both of us have a busy day tomorrow."

"Yep, I don't believe life is ever going to return to normal," Sighing loudly, I climbed the stairs alongside her.

She grinned at me. "Of course, it will. It will be a new normal. From now on, super is your normal. Yes, it is a lot of responsibility, but I'm sure you can handle it. You're far more mature at your age than I was."

She kissed me on the forehead, and I went to my room.

But I laid awake for a while in bed. I'd seen my dad for the first time in years! Sure, he broke into our house and brought a security drone to test me. Yeah, he had me attacked, and yes, those energy blasts did sting. And yep, he seemed more interested in what I could do than who I was. But I still felt good that I had finally seen him again and that he wanted to be a part of my life. Plus, he blew me a kiss and said he was proud of me and even impressed me. Seriously, the man took a job here just to be near Mom and me. That takes some guts, especially knowing that if he made Mom mad, she'd pretty much pound him down.

I dozed off, thinking how nice it was to have my father back in my life. Sure, these weren't the most ideal situations. But things in life are hardly ever perfect. I mean, look at me. I'm way strong and have all these cool powers, which is neat, yet one slip-up, one mistimed fart, and every person around me is out cold on the ground; my reputation ruined forever. I felt pretty certain that a whiff of my feet on a hot day could drop a squad of navy seals, the toughest Navy men alive – even if they had gas masks on. So yeah, life was not perfect. But you take the cool with the not so cool. There is always a tradeoff. That's just how the universe works.

I was super!! I had a mom who loved me. I had a Grandma and a Great-Grandma who loved me. I had awesome friends! And now my dad was back in my life. I'll take it!

Dear Diary: This is my very first official written entry as a super teen. And…Wow! Wow! Wow! Not only am I super, but I have my dad back in my life. Not sure what is cooler. I guess the superpowers. But it is nice having my dad around, even if it might be just to study me. Regardless of his flaws, he is a dedicated scientist and much like Mom. Sure, Mom heals people, but Dad's inventions could help the entire world. So, he is trying to better the world in his own way. He's just like Mom and me. That's what Mom loved about him in the first place. At least, that's my guess.

I could be wrong. After all, I'm just a teen. I haven't even had a real relationship yet. Not a boyfriend-girlfriend type of relationship. However, I do enjoy how Jason and I get along, even though we're just friends. At least for now, maybe forever. Maybe not. I guess time will tell.

Schooling...

I'm happy (and a little shocked) that the rest of the school week went fairly smoothly. Mr. P, our history teacher, assigned us a report, on our family history. In a way, that could be kind of fun. I had the neat advantage of having my grandma and my great-grandma around to talk to. The bad thing was that it had to be an oral presentation. I would need to talk for 10 minutes in front of the class. My heart pounded and raced just thinking about it. But I could deal with that. It was a normal kid problem.

Of course, it wouldn't be my life if a few unique events didn't happen. One of them involved a new girl in school. Mr. Ohm told us her name was Jessie when he introduced her in homeroom. She was tall with long wavy reddish-brown hair and creamy white skin.

Krista saw her and said, "Wow! She could be a model and probably a dancer as well."

The new girl had a cool vibe going on, and we were sure she'd fit straight in with the cool group in our grade. But our mouths fell open (especially Jason's and Tim's) when she passed on sitting at the cool kids' table at lunch and chose ours instead.

"Can I sit with you guys?" she asked with a friendly smile.

"Sure!" I said.

"Of course!" Krista added.

Jason and Tim just nodded, their mouths wide open and still in shock. Not a good look on them.

Jessie sat down and began to eat.

"We thought you'd want to sit with them," Krista indicated to the group sitting behind us.

"Ah, no," Jessie replied.

"Why is that?" Krista prodded.

"They don't look like a group I'd fit into," Jessie replied, nibbling on a carrot. She pulled a book out of her bag and began to read it.

"Where you from?" I asked.

"Sun City," she said, looking at me before turning back to her book.

"Ah, what do you like to do?" Krista coaxed.

"Dancing and reading," Jessie added. "Now, if you don't mind, I'd like to get back to this book. I'm right in the middle of a really good part." She turned all her attention to the book she had open in front of her.

That's how our meeting with Jessie continued. She sat and read while Krista and I talked, and Jason and Tim stared at her.

When Jessie finished her food, she stood up and said, "Thanks for letting me sit with you. It was nice chatting." Picking up her tray, she walked away.

"Wow!" Krista and I both said in disbelief.

"Wow!" Jason and Tim said in awe.

Krista turned to the guys. "She hardly said a thing!"

"Sure, she did!" Tim said, coming out of his Jess-inspired daze. "She answered all your questions!"

"But she didn't offer any conversation of her own!" I glanced at him with a shake of my head.

Jason shrugged. "She's probably shy." He sighed, "Wow! Good looking and shy. What a combo!"

"But, but..." Krista stammered.

Patting Krista on the back, I told her, "Let it go, girl. These guys aren't thinking straight right now."

"I admit she is gorgeous!" Krista commented.

"Sure is!" Jason agreed.

"Understatement of the year!" Tim added.

"Besides, you guys get the same way whenever Brandon comes around!" Jason insisted. He finished his statement by batting his eyes and pretending to faint.

"That's so true!" Tim said, nodding his head firmly.

"But that's different!" Krista said.

"How?" Jason asked.

"Yeah, how?" Tim mimicked.

Krista looked at me pleadingly for help.

I shrugged. "Sorry, girlfriend, you are on your own here," I told her.

"Okay, it's not different," Krista sighed.

"So, the boys' lacrosse team is playing well," I said, keen to change the subject.

"Not as well as the girls' team," Tim answered. "Man, you girls have been lighting it up in practice!"

Krista nodded. "Yes, my girl, Lia has been extra hot."
Jason just smiled at me.

Speaking of lacrosse, it seemed to be progressing well for my new normal. Sure, Wendi gave me hard times about it and said that I needed to lose a pound or two. She also said my wrist shot needed work. But even so, it was nothing I couldn't handle. Every once in a while, Lori would put her stick in my face to try to get into my head. I was half tempted to run by her and drop her with a silent fart. But that wouldn't be right. Plus, I didn't have too much control of that particular power. I'd probably drop the whole team. So, I decided that would not be cool. Instead, I dealt with it like any normal girl. I pretty much ignored it.

After each practice, Coach Blue would come over to me and let me know I was playing very well. She wanted to put me on the first line with Wendi. I could feel Wendi's eyes on mine whenever the coach talked to me. I let the coach know that I'd be more comfortable staying on the second line for now. I told her my knee was sore and thought extra playing time would make it worse.

Truthfully, not only did I not want to play on Wendi's line, I wasn't sure if using my powers was cheating. Technically I guess it wasn't. It was just me being me. I also worked hard not to use my powers during practice or games. The problem was, it was an unfair advantage over the others, and I still didn't know how to deal with that. But I figured I'd figure it out.

I walked home with Jason after practice, and we chatted the way we usually do. The talk started off all normal. Like how Jason didn't love lacrosse, but he enjoyed the running and the friendships he'd made on the team. Plus, with him playing on the team, it allowed us to continue the tradition we'd had since grade school of walking home together. I talked about how I still needed to find a way to balance my powers with my playing. While I had to admit I loved showing up Wendi and rushing through Lori, I didn't want to win games that way. I just didn't know how to go about it all. Jason said he had faith in me. He knew I'd figure out the proper course of action. Yes, those were the exact words he used. He could be such a geek sometimes.

Which brought us to this weird conversation we had...

"So, I've been thinking about ways for you to maximize the use of your powers!" Jason told me.

"Okay, I'm always open to ideas."

He hesitated, walking slower. "I thought you could use another long-distance weapon. Something more controllable and less devastating than your farts or foot sweat."

"I'm a lady," I said, pretending to act all dignified. "I don't fart, and I have wind. I don't sweat. I glow."

"Yeah, well, your wind and glow can drop an army," Jason said.

"Sadly, that's true," I laughed.

"You told me that when your dad made a drone attack you, you destroyed it with a fa- I mean wind."

"Yeah, I did."

"But your wind also clobbered your dad and killed all the plants?"

"What are you getting at, Jason?"

He stopped walking, his eyes open wide. "What if instead of farting, you pulled a booger from your nose and flicked it at the drone?"

"Oh gross!" I said, sticking my tongue out. "Girls don't have boogers!"

"I think it would work and be way less lethal," Jason insisted.

I stopped walking. All of a sudden, I understood exactly what he was attempting to do. It made perfect sense in a gross way. But I was still unsure because it was so disgusting.

"I'm not sure I like the image of me picking my nose and firing what I find at a target," I told him. "Not ladylike at all. Plus, if you really must know, I don't have any boogers!" I insisted.

Jason rubbed his chin. "Hmm, that could be true. You might process air and dust differently to regular people."

"Yeah, I guess," I said.

"Toe jam?" Jason asked.

I stuck my tongue out. "If I did have toe jam, I'd have to take my shoes off to collect it, which would defeat the entire purpose of finding a long-range weapon for me that wouldn't clobber everything around me. Plus, my toe jam might end up being a weapon of mass destruction!"

Jason nodded. "Very good point." He rubbed his head. His eyes flashed wide open. "Your spit!"

"Excuse me!"

Jason rubbed his hands together. "Your spit. You could use that as a controlled weapon."

I shook my head. "Girls don't spit!"

He held up a finger. "But they could. They just don't. And I bet your spit could take down a fighter jet. If you needed it to."

I considered what Jason had said. It made sense in a weird sort of gross way. It would be handy to have some sort of long-range stealth attack that I could control. One that wasn't potentially lethal to everybody around me.

"Okay, say I wanted to test this super spit out. How could I do it without hurting anybody or destroying anything useful?" I asked.

Jason smirked. I could tell he'd been thinking about this. "The old abandoned quarry. Lots of rocks you could blow up with nobody around. We could go home, get our bikes and ride there in like 10 minutes." He was shaking with excitement.

For a brief moment, I considered jumping us there. But then I figured that might be noticed by some people. Plus, I

140

had never jumped while holding another person. That might hurt Jason. Instead, I nodded in agreement, and we raced home to get our bikes.

When we reached the quarry, we found that a large metal fence with sharp edges on the top surrounded it.

Jason looked at the fence and commented, "It's obvious they don't want anybody in there. But you could jump over that fence easily. I won't be able to get over it, though." His eyes popped open again. "Unless you carried me over it?"

"It might not be safe," I warned.

He waved a hand at me. "I trust you."

Okay, this would take a little planning on the best way to jump a metal fence while carrying another person. Apparently, though, Jason had been thinking about this since learning about my powers.

"You can just give me a piggyback jump!" he told me.

I turned and let him grab onto my back. He lifted his legs up, and I grabbed hold of them, then gave him a piggyback ride to the fence. Once there, I bent down. "Are you sure about this?" I asked over my shoulder.

"Yeppers!" he said.

I leaped upwards and forward. We easily cleared the fence. I landed face-first in the dirt. Jason bounced off me the second my face made contact with the ground. He went rolling forward maybe ten feet, maybe more. I pushed myself up, spat dirt out of my mouth, and rushed over to him. He was on the ground face first. He got to his feet, laughing. Breathing a sigh of relief, I watched as my sigh knocked him back down.

"Sorry," I grinned, extending him my hand.

He took it, and I pulled him to a standing position. After dusting himself off, he grinned back. "That's the price I have to pay for having a super best friend!"

We headed over to the quarry, a big massive hole of hard rock. Standing on the edge and looking down, all we could see was lots of brown rock. Across the pit were a few big boulders lining the edge of the crater.

Jason pointed at one of them. "Okay, that's your target!"

I had to admit, collecting a bunch of spit in my mouth felt weird. I rolled my tongue around my cheek until I thought I had a decent amount of spit collected. I puffed my lips and blew the spit out. It went flying across the quarry but didn't come close to where I had aimed. Instead, it hit a spot much lower on the opposite side. But the force left a large hole in the wall. Debris from that hole crumbled down deeper into the quarry.

"Wow!" Jason said, leaping up and down. "That's got more firepower than a cannon!"

"Yeah, but my aim is terrible," I complained.

He patted me on the shoulder. "We'll work on that!"

I spent the next thirty minutes or so practicing aiming my spit. Now, that's something I never thought I'd say. Jason worked with me to get my super eyesight to lock on the target. Finally, after I don't know how many shots and even more destruction, I hit the boulder, I had aimed at. My spit shattered the boulder into dust.

Jason patted me on the back. "I knew you could do it!"

"Glad one of us did," I laughed.

Jason and I stayed at the quarry practicing until we both got hungry. When my rumbling stomach began to shake the walls of the quarry, we headed back home. But instead of leaping the fence this time, I used my hands to break it apart. Once Jason had walked through, I tied it back together.

When I finally arrived home, Mom asked me where I'd been.

"Destroying rocks with my spit," I explained.

She laughed.

Yeah, my new normal was certainly not all that normal.

Dear Diary: I'm not sure what to make of this Jessie girl. She's so perfect-looking, yet strange acting. Yeah, she might just be shy, but a strange feeling in my gut tells me there's something else going on with her. The way Jason and Tim (and the other boys and some of the girls) look at her doesn't seem natural. Maybe I'm silly, but just because I'm super doesn't mean I can't be jealous.

When I checked out what was being posted on my social media pages, I saw that everybody in the school was talking about Jessie. The amazing thing seemed to be that she didn't seem to have Facebook, Instagram, Twitter, or Snapchat. Well, there were no accounts that anyone could find. Wendi thought that was weird. Wendi also couldn't believe that Jessie would choose not to sit at her table.

In the end, Wendi decided that Jessie had to be a freak, a sort of pretty freak. For once, I kind of agreed with Wendi (though not publicly....) Jessie was different. But that's really something coming from ME — the girl whose spit can knock holes in the sides of mountains. Surely, there could be no one as different as that!

Elephant on the run....

    Ah, how l love my Saturday mornings. I just get to lay in bed and sleep and take it easy. It is so good to relax after a long school week. This week had not only seemed extra-long, but it was mega crazy. Lying in bed gave me a chance to recharge.

    My phone started vibrating and beeping from the nightstand next to my bed.

I knew that beep means an incoming social media post. Then I got another and another and another. Yeah, that was way too much action for so early on a Saturday morning. Most of my friends should still be sleeping right then. Even Jason liked to sleep until at least 9 on Saturdays.

Another beep. This was a different sound, and I knew it meant a text from Jason. I picked up my phone. It was 9:15. JASON> Turn on TV – Channel 13...Zoo again!

I grabbed the remote, which I also kept on my nightstand. Clicking the TV, I scrolled impatiently through the channels to number 13, looking for the local news segment. When I finally found it, I saw a man in a suit reporting into the camera, "This is Oscar Oranga for Channel 13, Live Witness News. We bring you the news faster and better than the others! We are reporting from the zoo for the second time in a week! This time one of the elephants, a 10-year-old male named Bumbo, has broken free of its home. Bumbo is now running amok in the zoo! We can only hope Super Teen is awake and watching!"

Well, Super Teen wasn't quite awake, but she was certainly watching. Surely the zoo staff could handle this. Another text popped onto my phone.

JASON>You're going to help, right?

LIA>OMW

I hopped out of bed, picking up a shirt lying on the floor beside my laundry basket. It was one I'd worn recently at the gym, so I sniffed the underarm area just to be sure. OMG! That had some kick to it. I needed a different outfit with more style and less odor. I pulled out a cute pink top with long sleeves and the face of a teddy bear stitched onto the front. It was one I'd never worn but thought it would be a great disguise. At least it was something that no one had ever seen me wear before. Then I grabbed a pair of green skinny jeans covered in a cool star pattern. They were new ones that Mom had recently bought for me. I pulled the tags off and threaded a pink studded belt through the loops to complete the outfit. Taking a quick check in the mirror, I grinned, pleased with the result. It actually looked quite good. If I was going to be in the media, at least I could look reasonably decent. Grabbing my mask, I pushed it firmly onto my head and pulled up the window. Within seconds, I was roof-hopping to the zoo.

Having done this before helped to make my journey to the zoo grounds fairly quick. I was kind of proud of how smoothly it all went. As I headed in the direction that people were fleeing from, I saw that the elephant had left a long trail of destruction.

I didn't need my super-vision to spot the large animal running down the zoo concourse. The poor thing seemed scared. I knew it didn't want to hurt anybody, and I certainly didn't want to hurt it. I ran towards it, unsure how I would handle the issue, but figured I'd work it out when I got there.

However, standing right in front of the charging elephant, I spotted a very familiar little blond boy, my neighbor, Felipe.

"Calm down, Bumbo, calm down!" Felipe coaxed, trying to stay calm himself.

Of course, the Channel 13 film crew stood there filming and not doing much else.

I leaped between Felipe and Bumbo.

Facing Felipe, I told him, "Don't worry, everything will be okay!"

Not even a second later, I was run over by the elephant. He must have hit me with his head and then trampled over me with his legs. The only thing it hurt, though, was my ego. Yeah, not a bright move turning my back on a charging elephant.

Pushing up off the ground, I leaped onto Bumbo's back. I knew that trying to reason with a frightened charging elephant wouldn't work. No use even trying. Instead, I tightened my legs around Bumbo's back and squeezed. I certainly didn't want to hurt the big guy, but I had to put him down before he ran over Felipe.

The elephant staggered forward a few more steps. By his hesitant movements, I could tell that he felt some pain. I squeezed my legs a little harder. I didn't want to kill him, but I knew he must be stopped. Weird how I had to worry about being so strong I could accidentally squish an elephant.

The second squeeze worked. Bumbo crumbled to the ground. Listening with super hearing, I picked up the sound of his heart still beating. Breathing a sigh of relief, I realized I'd just squeezed the wind out of him. Pulling my leg out from underneath, I stood up, my clothes covered with dirt. I could only guess that my hair looked a mess as well. So, of course, that was when Oscar Oranga stuck a microphone in my face.

"Super Teen! Do you have anything to say about saving the day?" he asked with far more excitement in his voice than was normal.

"Just helping," I said, trying to sound as grown-up and adult-like as possible.

Felipe ran over and hugged me.

"Wow, this is golden for the camera!" Oscar said, almost giddy with delight.

"Thanks for saving me again!" Felipe said.

"You certainly spend a lot of time at the zoo!" I told him.

"My dad is a veterinarian here!" Felipe announced proudly. "He works with the big cats." Taking a step back from me, he smiled, his eyes alight with excitement.

Felipe's dad ran up to him and hugged him. "Son, that was brave of you to try to calm Bumbo, but you could have been badly hurt!"

"Don't worry, Dad. I knew Super Teen would come and save us both!" Felipe replied with a grin.

Another zoo doctor appeared and placed a stethoscope on Bumbo to check him out.

"Thank you," Felipe's dad turned to me gratefully. "I'm so glad you arrived in time!"

The other vet looked up, smiled, and gave us a thumb up. "Bumbo is fine. Strangely enough, he seems to be sleeping."

The huge crowd of onlookers began to clap.

"Do you want me to put him back where he belongs?" I asked.

"If you could manage it, that would be great!" Felipe's dad replied.

I gently picked Bumbo up and hoisted him over my shoulder. Then I walked him back to the elephant area like a regular person would carry a loaf of bread. As I walked, the doctors and the camera crew followed my every step. I felt good and weird at the same time. Reaching the elephant area, I laid Bumbo down gently on a grassy spot near the water and patted him. When I felt assured he was okay, I leaped up into the air and bounded away!

Dear Diary: OMG! That was soo fun!! I love using my strength to help people like that. It's such a good feeling! Plus, it's so great to know I can knock out an elephant by just loosely tightening my legs around its belly. I mean, it was crazy. I actually had to concentrate and be careful when dealing with a fully-grown massive elephant so that I wouldn't cause any serious injuries. I also have to admit it was pretty cool to be able to carry an elephant on my shoulder like a peanut. All the while, the TV cameras filmed it for the world and my friends to see. That sure felt good getting some nice positive press. Woot!

When I checked my social media pages, I found they were blowing up with people saying how amazing Super Teen was. A few, actually more than a few, commented on how much they liked my outfit. I think that felt as good as being known for carrying around an elephant. Of course, Wendi insisted that Super Teen had to be some sort of trick or publicity stunt for a TV show or something. No matter what, Wendi said she knew for a fact, Super Teen wasn't that super. One thing that was always consistent in my life was Wendi being Wendi.

Oh, side note, the way Felipe looked at me after I saved him…I got the feeling that he knew who I was. But nah, no way a seven-year-old boy could figure that out. None of the media or my classmates had come close. Even Krista and Tim were wondering yesterday who the heck this mystery girl was. Could she go to our school? Was she homeschooled? Ha ha! I guess Felipe just looked at everybody like he knew them. He was just a friendly, outspoken little kid. Nothing wrong with that.

I was also relieved to find Mom understood me going to the zoo and saving the day. She understood that I wanted to help make the world a better place with my powers. She told me she was worried (cause she is a mom) but proud of me. My grandma and my great-grandma also sent me texts telling me how cool it was.

So awesome!

Dinner...

For dinner, Mom and I headed to my favorite hibachi restaurant: A Taste of Japan. Okay, not the best name, but the food there is excellent. I just love hibachi. There's something about watching a guy with sharp knives cut and toss around your food in front of you while he cooks it that just makes the food feel fresher. It kind of makes me feel like one with the meal. I also loved sushi appetizers. Nothing better than the way raw fish feels in the mouth, kind of a nice gooey squish. Of course, Mom and I were careful to be careful with the garlic and onions. Mom joked about the fact that neither of us had dates so that we could indulge a little. She ate a few more than me since she had perfected the art of not gassing the room.

I felt like a nice regular girl again. Yeah, being super is cool, but it's great to do normal things as well.

"What on earth is this!" we heard a man yell way louder than was necessary.

Turning towards the sound, I saw a huge man at the bar. He pounded on the counter and scolded the waitress, Lee Tang, "This stuff is raw!"

"Sir, you ordered eel...." Lee said, stepping back.

I know Lee, she's a big sister to Mia, who's in my class. They're both nice quiet girls. They are friendly and smart. Mia was also in the restaurant cleaning tables with a big towel.

The man pounded his fist on the sushi bar again.

"Yeah, but I thought you'd toss it on the fire!" He shook his fist, and his face had turned bright red with anger.

This got the chef to come to Lee's aid.

"Sir, sushi is uncooked, raw!" the chef explained.

"I don't even eat my veggies raw!" the man spat. "I'm not a bird!"

150

"Sir, birds, don't eat a lot of veggies," Lee said, poking her head out from behind the chef.

The man crossed his arms. "I'm not paying!!" He pounded the bar again.

Now all eyes in the restaurant were on the man.

Mom groaned. "I know that man. He's George Banks, a guy from my class when I was at school, and he's always been a jerk."

"We have to do something about him!" I said.

Mom shook her head. "We have to pick out battles. Lee's dad can handle him."

I knew mom had a good point. I felt a little embarrassed that I hadn't figured out the chef was Lee's dad. Still, I didn't appreciate this man being so rude. I glared at him. A beam of energy shot from my eyes and hit the man in the butt. His pants burst into flame!

George stood there frantically trying to blow the fire on his butt out.

"Oops! Looks like you have heat ray vision when you're angry," Mom whispered to me.

Yep, I had just figured that out.

The smoke detectors started beeping. Mom jumped up and raced over to George. "Drop and roll, George. Drop and roll...."

He looked at her. "Wait! Aren't you Isabelle Strong from my class at school?"

"Now it's Doctor Isabelle Strong... drop and roll." Mom pointed to the ground and spun her finger around.

George dropped to the ground and started rolling as instructed. Mom took a towel from Mia and dropped it over George's big backside. "Call 911!" Mom ordered. She turned to George and patted him gently on the shoulder. "You're going to be alright.... You won't be able to sit on your behind for a day or two, but you will live."

"It hurts," George groaned. "Their fire made me catch on fire. I'll sue!"

"There's no fire going on in the restaurant right now, George," Mom told him. She showed him a burnt lighter. "I removed this from your pocket before I covered you. It looks like your back pocket caught on fire because of the lighter."

"Oh…" George looked at it in confusion.

"Another reason to not smoke," Mom added, just as the paramedics arrived.

"Wait, your name is still Strong? Did you never get married?"

"Got married but kept the name."

"Bummer! I was hoping I'd have a shot with you."

"The EMTs are here to take you to the ER. Don't worry, just first-degree burns. You'll be fine."

"Hopefully, there won't be any brain damage," Mom mumbled as they took George away.

"Why didn't you tell him you were divorced?" I kidded.

"Quiet and eat your food," she scolded with a smile.

"Heat ray vision is so cool," I said. "Well, actually hot, but a cool power to have!"

Mom nodded. "We're going to have to work on training you to stay calm. Don't want you drilling holes in people or melting them when you get angry."

I nodded. "That's a good idea! Otherwise, some of my teachers and also Wendi could soon become dust!"

Dear Diary: Wow, I can fire flames of fire from my eyes. Mom says it's not technically fire. It's a beam of intense heat that can cause anything it comes in contact with to burn. My mom is such a science geek. But I get it. It's a cool but dangerous weapon that I have to be careful with. It may not have the mass effect of a super fart or super foot odor, but it can still be quite hazardous.

Part of me loves the idea of having heat vision. I don't need the microwave to warm up my food or do popcorn. Well, with practice, I won't. But another part of me realizes I have to stay calm, so this doesn't just blast out of me.

As we walked home, Mom and I worked on my breathing and meditation exercises to quieten my mind and anger, as Mom put it. Whenever I feel angry or upset, I need to close my eyes, take deep breaths and let them out. I need to count backward from 10 and keep breathing until I feel calm again. Of course, I also have to be careful not to clobber things with my breath.

Being super can definitely be super tricky!

Sunday Trip to the Mall…

Sunday was usually the day I hung out with Tim, Jason, and Krista. Today though, instead of just hanging out with the guys, playing video games, and tossing LAX balls around, Krista asked me if I would go to the mall with her to help choose some new shoes.

As it was such a beautiful day, Krista and I decided to walk. Jason told me to take my mask and a change of clothes just in case, so I did. Luckily, my new Super Teen outfit had been washed since my episode at the zoo. I wasn't sure why Jason thought Super Teen would be needed at the mall, but I trusted his gut feelings.

"So, have you started your genealogy report for history yet?" Krista asked me as we walked.

I shook my head. "Mom wanted me to talk with my grandma and my great-grandma today, but the weather is so great. I just couldn't do it. Maybe later."

"Your grandmas look so young still! They look like they could be sisters!" Krista said. "Have they had any work done on their skin?"

I shook my head. "Nope, just good genes," I said. I didn't tell her she'd be shocked if she met my great-great-grandma, who now poses as my great-grandma's sister. Yep, whatever makes us super causes us to age slowly. The good news is we are young for a long time. The sad news is every Strong woman has outlived their husbands by a good deal. Like Grandma would always tell me, life has tradeoffs. But I tried not to think of that as Krista, and I entered the mall. I certainly didn't want to focus on the negatives.

We headed right to our favorite store: Shoes! Shoes! Shoes!

154

Okay, the name wasn't original, but the shoes were reasonably priced and so lovely. I was wearing some black canvas sneakers and had sprayed my feet well with Mom's super deodorant. I was certain I could take my shoes off without worrying about knocking out the store. We were there for Krista's shopping spree, but I wanted to be prepared just in case.

Before reaching the store, we noticed a crowd gathered in the concourse. There in the middle of the crowd, stood a tall man in a lab coat. He stood next to what I could only describe as a white, life-like, crash-test dummy. The man in the lab coat pointed at the crash-test dummy.

"This, my friends, is BM Science's prototype home health aide robot, HAR!" the man said. The man turned to the robot. "HAR, take a bow."

HAR bowed. "So glad to meet you all!" he or it said.

"HAR is very strong!" the man said.

HAR walked over and picked the scientist up in his arms. The crowd clapped. "We believe HAR is the future of home health aide. He can handle almost any situation."

Krista nudged me. "This is cool. But I want shoes."

I grinned. "Let's head to the store."

In Shoes! Shoes! Shoes! Krista and I could barely contain ourselves. She tried on a cool pair of red converse high tops and then decided to try some other colors. We both looked at the heels but knew there was no way our moms would approve. Just as I picked up another pair of shoes, I heard a scream, "Help! This thing is crazy!"

The store manager ran out towards the scream, but a split second later came rolling back into the store. Right behind him was HAR, the not so helpful robot.

"I'm going to clean you up!" HAR shouted.

The scientist guy ran behind HAR, desperately trying to slow him down. "HAR! Stop! Stop!" He demanded. HAR ignored the scientist and picked up the manager with one arm.

HAR turned to the scientist. "I'm cleaning them because dirt causes disease!"

"But why are you hurting people?" the scientist yelled.

HAR locked his head on him. "Must destroy anything that is dirty!" he insisted.

I tugged on Krista. "Let's get out of here," I coaxed.

Krista shook her head. "Nah, I want to see how this plays out!"

I slipped out of the store, telling Krista I had to go to the bathroom. Moving at super speed, I headed quickly off and looked for the nearest facility. Jumping into a stall, I put on my change of clothes and my mask. Then I tossed the clothes I'd been wearing into my canvas carry bag and stashed it up high out of sight.

Rushing back towards the shoe store, my heart started to race. I felt it pounding in my chest. I had sweat forming on my forehead. My palms were clammy. I had no idea how strong this freaky bot was. But I knew I had to stop it.

When I ran back into the store, I saw the HAR holding the store manager and his scientist handler up in the air. He held them over his head like they weighed nothing.

"Hey, why not pick on somebody your own strength?" I asked in my most mocking voice.

HAR spun his head around to look at me without moving his body. It gave me the shivers. He dropped the two men to the ground. HAR turned towards me and started rubbing his hands together anxiously.

"Finally, I get to clean up the mess that is Super Teen!" he shouted. He pointed at me with a plastic white finger. "That pink t-shirt you're wearing doesn't go well with green skinny jeans and white shoes! Where's your sense of color?"

I stomped towards him. "I'm not dressed for a fashion parade!" I told HAR. "But this outfit is still pretty cool!"

HAR bent over and laughed while pointing at me. "Ha! Simple human... You're so funny!"

"You going to stop this craziness?" I asked.

HAR bent his robotic knee joints and raised his fists in front of his plastic face. "Hardly."

"You're an aide robot, not a fighter!" I said.

"I know how to adapt!" He shouted, lunging forward and punching me in the nose.

I gave him credit. I felt that punch, but my head didn't flinch at all. HAR pulled back his fist and looked at it, taking in the dented metal that was the size and shape of my nose.

"Nice try!" I said. I reached up and grabbed HAR by the top of his head. I pushed down hard. HAR's body buckled under the pressure like a collapsing spring. Maintaining the same level of force, I acted like a human trash compactor

157

reducing HAR to the size of a lunch box. He'd be no more trouble now.

The people in the store began to applaud!

The store manager ran up to me. "That was amazing!" he said as he breathed a huge sigh of relief.

"It was nothing!" I replied. Although I'd been super nervous, it had turned out to be very easy.

"That crazy mad robot was right about something, though!" The manager said and pointed at my feet. "Those blah canvas shoes don't go well with that outfit. What size are you?"

"Ah, six...."

"Perfect!" he turned to one of the shelves of shoes and grabbed a box. He showed me a brand-new pair of pink converse sneaks. "I think you'll enjoy wearing these."

"I couldn't!" I told him.

Just then, the police arrived. The scientist guy ran up to them. "Our robot had a little malfunction."

"Please accept the shoes!" the manager insisted.

"Okay," I said. After all, they were great shoes and the pair I'd secretly been wanting to buy.

He pointed to my feet. "Try them on. I want to make sure they fit perfectly!"

Without even thinking about it, I agreed. After all, I had taken out the robot without much of a fight, so I thought my feet would still be fresh. I popped my heel out of my shoe. I popped my toes out. I wiggled them some. I heard a gasp, and then another and another. Then a plop, plop, plop. Within a second, I was the only one left standing in the store and in that entire area of the mall! I picked up my shoe and sniffed it. Oops! I had forgotten about nervous sweat! I slipped my foot into the pink converse. On the bright side, it fit perfectly.

I sighed. Rushing back to the bathroom at super speed so no security cameras would notice me. I changed into my regular outfit, then headed back to the store and helped revive the people.

By then, Oscar Oranga and the press had arrived.

I heard Oscar saying as the camera rolled, "Oscar Oranga reporting from the Star Light City mall. We were called here to cover an out of control Android. Not the phone, a real Android. Super Teen showed up and took the Android out. But she also took out the entire store and half the mall with a simple whiff of her feet! This begs the question, is Super Teen a Hero or a Zero?"

The cameraman scanned to show all the people lying out cold on the floor. The medics had arrived and were starting to bring people around.

I ignored the press and headed over to Krista. I gave her a little nudge. "Krista, wake up."

Her eyes popped open. She smiled. "Wow, you missed the most amazing thing!"

I shrugged. "Sorry, my stomach gets nervous during scary stuff like that."

She shrugged. "That's okay. We all can't be a Super Teen."

Oscar Oranga plunged a microphone into Krista's face. "Young lady, you were one of Super Teen's victims," he prodded. "How do you feel?"

Krista sat up. She smiled. "I feel great. Super Teen saved us all from that crazy HAR robotic-dude thing. It was awesome!"

Oscar waved the mic in front of her. "You don't mind that she knocked you silly? Reviewing footage from the store's security camera shows a simple whiff of her foot downed the entire store!"

Krista's eyes popped open. "Nah, it was the most relaxing thing I've ever experienced."

I stood there in amazement as almost everybody that Oscar Organa interviewed agreed with Krista. They were scared of the Android and grateful that Super Teen had saved them. They didn't mind being put to sleep because a little nap now and then was a good thing in today's hectic world. Even Chief Michaels noted that while he doesn't fully approve of super vigilantes, he appreciated the effort Super Teen made, and that was the best rest he'd had in years.

I couldn't be sure if Oscar liked what he was hearing. When the camera stopped rolling, I approached him.

"So, Super Teen is a hero?" I asked.

He looked at me with open eyes and a fake smile. "I guess she is."

I figured I should leave that comment well enough alone. Krista bought her shoes, and we headed home.

Dear Diary: Sometimes, I forget how powerful I truly am. It's both super cool and super frightening at the same time. To be able to beat a robot up with one hand and then drop an entire store and most of the mall with a whiff of my foot is crazy! I need to be careful, though. I love my new converse shoes, but I'm so glad nobody died.

Still not sure what to make of this reporter, dude. I'm starting to think he might feel it's a better story if Super Teen is a menace. I hope I'm wrong. Cause Super Teen can do a lot of good.

I think I need to look out for him, or he might be the death of my reputation.

Not So Social Media...

I walked Krista home to make sure she got there safely. She seemed a little loopy after getting a whiff of my feet. A couple of times, I had to put a hand on her back to steady her.

She smiled at me, "You're such a good friend, Lia."

"You sure you're okay?" I asked when we got to her front porch.

She nodded. "I feel fine. I don't know what Super Teen did, but that was the most relaxing sleep I've had since I was a kid. I dreamt I was floating on a cloud."

"So, the smell of her feet didn't make you want to throw up?" I asked.

Krista laughed. "No. Her feet were very *overpowering*, but it was kind of in a good way. It made me understand that she is WAY powerful, but we have nothing to fear. She'll always protect us!" She pointed to her door. "It's been such a fun shopping adventure, but I think I'd better get to my homework."

"Yes, me too," I agreed as I glanced at my watch and realized the time. "See you at school tomorrow, Krista." I smiled at her and waved goodbye.

Part of me felt good that by knocking people out with my slightly stinky feet, made them feel safe. But another part of me found that very weird and a little creepy. That's a lot of power for a young teen to have.

On my way home, I pulled out my phone to check my social media. Sure enough, it had been blowing up, most of it about Super Teen. And the reviews were mixed. There was even a hashtag now...#SUPTEENHERO

I had channel 13 news and Oscar Oranga to thank for that. At least that hashtag gave me the chance to easily see everything that everyone said about Super Teen.

Some people defended me. Jason led the defenders, or as he was known on Instagram…@COMICLOVERJ

@COMICLOVERJ: #SUPTEENHERO is a hero. She saved the shoe store from a crazy mad Android!

@WENDI: Is #SUPTEENHERO a hero? She didn't have to knock out the entire store to stop the Android. She did it on purpose to show her power. That was dangerous.

@KRISTA: I was there. It wasn't bad at all. I'm glad #SUPTEENHERO saved us. When I came too, I felt better than ever!

@WENDI: Krista…that's because #SUPTEENHERO probably has some weird whammy power that warps your brain.

That conversation went back and forth. Just like any other argument on Instagram or Facebook that nobody ever won. Everybody thought the same at the end as they did in the beginning. I sighed. Most of the other remarks went from either…"She's so cool!" or "She's a threat!" It seemed people were 40 / 60 in support of Super Teen. I smiled when I saw that. Brandon questioned Wendi about her comment. I had to admit, it was crazy when I watched everybody drop. Most of them hit the floor before my shoe did. Of course, the excitement was instantly followed by terror and me thinking, *OMG, I can't believe I did that. I hope they're all ok!*

Dear Diary: I'm so glad Krista and everybody else in the store is okay. And I'm so glad I stopped that crazy HAR…kind of worried that the people my dad works for were behind all that. But I'm more worried about how people feel about Super Teen from now on. I only want to help others, use my powers for good, make the world a better place. I'm starting to figure out some people will support me no matter what. But some people hate change, and Super Teen represents change. Those people won't accept change no matter what. Words won't change them, but maybe, just maybe, my actions will.

Family Ties...

I got home and found Mom sitting in the living room with Grandma Betsy and Great-Grandma Ellen. Man, the three of them could pass as sisters. They had a computer open and were skyping with Great, Great-Grandma Ann. She'd moved to the Andes mountains in Peru, so people wouldn't get suspicious of how little the Strong women aged. Grandma and Great-Grandma now even said they were sisters.

"Looks like you've had a busy day!" Mom said as I entered the room.

I saw on the TV they were watching the Channel 13 news. It was showing the people in the store all falling over. Of course, they had the hashtag: #SUPTEENHERO Underneath the picture. The headline sticker had such interesting updates:

-BM Science regrets Android HAR's actions, will give the school new cleaning Androids

-Mayor TJ Bass undecided if Super Teen is a threat

-Police Chief Michaels Claims he welcomes the help but is cautious

-Store Manager thankful for the help and that nobody got hurt

Grandma and Great-Grandma walked over to me and kissed me on the head.

"We came to help you with your family history report," Great-Grandma said. "We even have my mom online so she can chip in her knowledge. The woman did fight in a world war, after all."

Grandma gave me a firm hug. "Of course, we are here to talk about your powers as well. That's if you want to."

I sat down on the couch so I could see into the computer screen and waved to Great, Great-Grandma. "Hi, GGG!" I said. That's what I'd always call her. Now, of course, it finally made sense why I had so many grandmas, and they all still looked great.

"Hi, kiddo!" GGG said.

I sighed and knocked over the computer on the table. "Oops, sorry!" I giggled.

The grandmas laughed. "Just growing pains." Grandma Betsy said.

"Can I take my shoes off?" I asked them. "These things are a little tight."

"Sure," Great-Grandma Ellen said.

I kicked my shoes off. Mom and Grandma Betsy were sitting beside me. They both coughed a little.

"That is pretty powerful," Grandma Betsy said.

Mom nodded. "Yeah, that nervous sweat. It can have quite a kick."

Great-Grandma Ellen sat directly across from my feet. Her eyes seemed to be spinning in her head. I wiggled my toes without thinking. She slumped back over on the couch.

"Wow!" Mom said.

"Super impressive!" Grandma Betsy said.

"I didn't expect that!" I said.

"She'll come around in a minute or two," Grandma Betsy assured me. "You just caught her off guard. She wasn't prepared for that kind of power."

"Am I that powerful?" I gulped.

Mom and Grandma shrugged. "Apparently, but you'll figure it out with time."

Great-Grandma Ellen started to stir. She sat up. "Impressive young lady!" she smiled. "Very relaxing nap!"

I shook my head. "Yeah, I don't get that. Why do people I knock out with my foot odor seem so happy afterward?"

"Sounds like your pheromone power is developing," Mom explained, sounding like a scientist.

"Pheromones are the scents people give out to make themselves more attractive to others," Grandma Betsy added.

"Right, I remember Mom telling me about them."

Grandma Betsy smiled. "Trust me, honey, it's a great ability to have. Once you get control of it, you'll be able to help control any situation. Plus, it's fun. One time I was presenting a demonstration about a product that the company I worked for was trying to sell. I was in front of about 100 people. But there was a very rude man in the audience, calling out and embarrassing me in front of everyone. So, I made him think he was a pussycat, and he started meowing. Then he fell asleep in his chair! Everyone started laughing at him. It was a crack up!"

"Oh my gosh! So, it's like hypnosis?" I asked.

Mom shook her head. "No, with hypnosis, you can't make people do things they wouldn't normally do. With pheromones, you can."

"Wow," I said. "Another scary power."

Great-Grandma Ellen grinned at me. "It's just another tool in our kit."

"You're so brave," GGG said, "being the first one of us to openly use your powers in public!"

I dropped my head. "Not sure if it's brave or silly!"

Grandma Betsy put her arm around me. "Definitely brave!" she said.

I gave them a weak smile. "Thanks!"

Mom looked me in the eyes. "What else is on your mind, honey?"

I hesitated. "Well, I hate the fact that I have to give an oral report on family history and what the 1960s, 1970s, 1980s, and 1990s were like."

Mom shook her head. "Yeah, public speaking can be scary. But I think there's something else on your mind."

"Spit it out, girl!" GGG said from the computer screen.

I tossed myself back on the couch. "I'm worried that other friends or enemies might figure out I'm Super Teen. I mean, my costume isn't that fancy. Or tricky. I don't even wear glasses like Clark Kent in Superman. Not only do I not need them, but they'd look so bad on me. I'd love to do something extra to add to my disguise."

My two grandma's looked at each other. Grandma Betsy slid behind me. She took my hair gently in her hands and pulled it into two bunches at the sides of my head. "Your hair will look so good like this. And because you never wear it this way, it'll help to disguise you. Plus, it's easy to put up like this!"

Grandma Ellen held a mirror up for me.

I had to admit I did look different. For some reason, I never wore my hair tied up, and it seemed to change my look completely.

"Any other questions about being super?" Great-Grandma asked.

I nodded. "Well, how come these powers just kick in when we turn 13?"

Grandma put a hand on my shoulder. "Easy dear, our bodies require at least 4745 days to absorb the energy they need to charge our cells."

"Wow!" I said. "That's a lot of days in just 13 years. I never thought of it like that."

We spent the next few hours chatting about the history of the Strong family and how life has changed over the decades, and how it has remained the same. I learned that before the Strong women came to the US, we were mostly found in Great Britain. Great-Grandma thought maybe the Scotland area. Grandma thought Ireland. GGG thought Wales. The point being, the records back then were very thin. All we could determine was that we had ancestors from all over that area. I wondered if any of them were related to King Arthur or maybe even Merlin. Not sure why my mind just goes off track like that sometimes. But it's fun.

Mom must have noticed my mind was wandering as she gave me a little nudge to bring me back to the moment. "I understand this report will be half your grade for this semester," she prompted.

"I didn't tell you that," I said. In fact, I hadn't known that.

"Jason did," Mom said. "He thought I should remind you," she smiled.

"I like that Jason boy," he has potential, Grandma Betsy said.

"He's nice," Great-Grandma Ellen said slowly. "But he's just so normal."

"Normal is good!" GGG Ann chimed in via the computer.

Great-Grandma Ellen smiled. "Now that Brandon fellow! He's a catch. He's strong, a leader, smart and hot!"

168

"Great-Grandma!" I shouted, feeling my face turn red. It sounded so weird to hear her talk like that!

Her smile grew. "Hey, I may be old, but I still know hot when I see it." She paused for a moment, took a breath, then added, "A Strong woman needs a strong man."

"Give the girl time, Mom!" Betsy said to Ellen. "She just turned 13!"

"When I was 13, I was dating a senior in college!" Great-Grandma Ellen grinned, "But of course, he thought I was 18."

"A couple of us back in the day were married at 14," GGG chimed from the computer. "Not that I would advise that…. Just saying…"

"Can we please change the topic back to history?" I begged. For once, I wanted to talk about history. Nothing more embarrassing than having my grandmothers talk about my "relationship" status, or lack of a "relationship" status.

Mom spoke up to help me out. "Great-Grandma, can you tell us about life in the 1950s?" she asked.

For the next couple of hours, my three grandmas and my mom told me about life since the 1950s. It was then up to me to figure out what was alike and what was different from life nowadays.

I began to get really hungry halfway through, so we ordered pizza and wings and got one pizza with garlic and onions. Let me tell you, after eating that, the four of us could have dropped an army with our breath. And wow, it wouldn't have even been a close fight. GGG Ann kidded she could smell our breath over the computer.

Before winding up our discussion, Grandma Betsy had one more suggestion to help with my oral presentation. "Just pop your heels out of your shoes before you talk! Your pheromone power will make sure they all love it!"

"Mom!" my mother said.

Grandma Betsy looked at Mom. "Now, Isabel, you can't tell me you've never used your pheromones…."

Mom crossed her arms. "Mom! This isn't about me." She looked sternly at me. "I know you'll do what's right!"

I nodded and gave her a weak smile.

She walked over to me and gave me a big hug. "You might have only just developed your superpowers, but as far as I'm concerned, you've always had the power! Lia, your presentation will be a smash hit. You have nothing to worry about!"

I gulped nervously. Something told me that it was not going to be quite that easy.

Dear Diary: Amazing! All my grandmas are so alike and yet so different! I love each one of them. I'm glad now I finally understand why I have them all in my life. They were a great help to me tonight. There are some things you rely on friends for but other things you need a family to help you with. I also have to admit that I liked Grandma Betsy's idea of giving the class a little blast of my foot power. Not enough to drop them all, but enough to make them listen to my every word in awe.

But then I shook off that idea. For one, it was wrong. I can't use my powers to make my friends do what I want. Yeah, it would be cool, but it's not what a hero does. Plus, with my luck and lack of control, I might knock out the entire school. That just wouldn't be good, and awful hard to explain anyway. Besides, I was given this power for a reason. I want to help leave my mark on the world. I have an opportunity to make the world a better place. I can help those who can't help themselves. Oh my gosh, I'm so strong I can even help those who can help themselves. What I'm trying to say (and not doing a great job of) is that I want to make the world better. By better, I mean better for everybody, not just for me. Mom always says, "Competition is fine, but people accomplish great things when they cooperate." Now that I have this power, I finally get what Mom means. I could change the world, but not just as Super Teen, also as Lia Strong. My personality is as strong as any of my powers.

Okay, now I'm rambling on and getting a bit carried away. I get like this from time to time. Maybe I should nab more of that pizza? OMG! Why am I writing this down?

Another New Kid in Town?

Jason played it pretty smart during our walk to school on Monday. He was very tactful and didn't even mention that I knocked out an entire store and part of the mall with super foot odor.

Instead, he focused on our assignment. "How's the report coming along?"

"I feel much better about it now that I've talked with my grandmas," I replied. "I'm still nervous as anything about talking in front of the class, but at least I now have some good things to talk about."

Giggling, I continued, "One of them even suggested that I pop my shoes off before I talk, just to put everybody to sleep and then get them to love what I'm saying."

"Okay, I'm not sure what to make of that," Jason answered slowly. Hesitating for a moment, he continued, "Do you want to talk about what happened at the mall?"

I nodded, slightly embarrassed.

We were in front of Ms. Jewel's house. Her mean and nasty Doberman, Cuddles, began to run towards us. The dog stopped and sniffed the air. Then he turned and ran back into the house, tail between his legs. Ms. Jewel just waved to us from her porch. "Have a good day at school, kids!"

Jason and I waved back and kept walking, as that had become our new normal way of dealing with big fierce Cuddles, who realized it was me and then becoming a scared little puppy. It felt both good and weird at the same time.

"Yes, yes, I do want to talk about what happened at the mall," I nodded. "I need to talk it out with a friend."

Jason smiled. "I think it's cool, as long as you can learn how to control it."

I nodded again. "Yes, I'm working on it."

"How do YOU feel about it?" Jason asked curiously.

"On one hand, it feels great knowing I have this power. I stopped that HAR easily. I loved it. On the other hand, I'm a little worried that part of me got a tiny bit excited about knocking the store out so easily. I could have had an awesome shopping spree and taken whatever I wanted. Nobody could have stopped me." I noticed my heart pounding, and I was forced to take a couple of breaths to calm myself.

Jason smiled at me. "Lia, you stopped yourself from doing that. And that's what's important. It's only natural that you would question your power and want to experiment to see what you can do with it. We all have thoughts that are less than good now and then. It's part of human nature, I guess. Apparently, superhuman nature is no different."

"How'd you get so smart?" I asked him.

"You have feet that can drop a team of ninjas. I have brains!" He smiled.

"I'm smart too!" I said, giving him a little shove.

"Yeah, I have to agree with that, I guess," he grinned back at me.

"Hi, Lia! Hi, Lia's friend!" Felipe shouted from across the street. He stood waiting for the school bus. A short older blond kid stood next to him. It was nice the kid seemed to be looking out for Felipe. But that kid gave me a weird chill.

"Hi, Felipe!" I shouted back with a wave. "Hi, Felipe's friend!" I added.

Jason just waved.

We kept walking. "Do you know who the older kid with Felipe is?" I asked.

Jason nodded. "He's Felipe's older cousin Tomas. For some reason, he's staying with them for a while."

"Why doesn't he go to school with us?" I asked.

Jason shrugged. "I think he's homeschooled."

"How do you know everything?" I asked.

Jason shrugged again. "When you have open ears and eyes and your dad is police chief, you learn stuff."

I grinned at Jason. I loved that our relationship hadn't changed. It remained nice and normal.

Just then, I heard in my mind, *"You're a different girl!"*

Okay, so much for normal. I didn't know where that thought had come from. Or if I'd really heard it at all.

Jason looked at me curiously. "What's wrong?" he asked, a worried expression suddenly appearing on his face.

I shook my head. "I think I heard something in my head….it said…" I whispered to him, "You're a different girl!"

Jason patted me on the shoulder. "That's probably just your subconscious talking to you. Letting you know you *are* different. Which you are… but different is good."

"You sure?" I asked, eyebrows raised.

"Of course, I am. I got an A on my psychology report last year!" He grinned.

"Oh yes, that makes me feel SO much better," I told him.

When we finally approached the school building, Tony spotted us and held the door open as he waited for us to enter. "Come on, you two, let's not be late for homeroom," he prompted. Since I'd put Tony in his place last week, he'd been so nice to us both.

"Thanks, Tony," I said.

"Wait, no tip?" he asked.

I turned to look at him. He took a step back and grinned. "Just kidding you. My friends get into the school for free!"

"Tony, everybody should be let into the school for free," I lectured.

He smiled and opened up his arms. "Of course, they should, because they're all my friends! Now come on. Let's get to homeroom. We don't want to be tardy."

I grinned. I got the school bully to hold the door open and use the word tardy. Yeah, being super might have its bad points but overall, being super was, well, super. Sure, I had a strange voice in my mind. But I decided to take Jason's advice and ignore it. After all, who better to give psychology advice than a 13-year old who got an A on his paper?

Dear Diary: Jason is a great friend. I often wonder if he might be more than that someday. I kind of hope so. But I also kind of worry about that too. What if we broke up? I'd lose his friendship. That would crush me.

Oh, that Tomas kid gives me the creeps. Hard to believe he's related to cute little Felipe.

Bot rot...

As we walked towards our lockers, we saw Janitor Jan being trailed by a hovering domed robot with big white brushes on its bottom. A woman in a white lab coat and holding an iPad followed them both. The woman's lab coat had a BM Science logo on it. Looking closely at the robot, I saw that it, too, had the BM Science logo. Well, I had to give BM Science credit for being persistent. The mayor, TJ Bass, a big tall, gawky guy with curly hair, had previously come to our school and given us all a little speech. "We welcome the addition of this cleaning robot and thank BMS for their contribution. They truly want to help make Starlight City a better place."

At the time, we had all clapped politely. Then the mayor headed out to what I could only guess would be another short, meaningless speech somewhere else.

And now it seemed, the new addition was in action at our school. I wondered what Janitor Jan thought of it. I guessed she was probably worried that a robot would end up taking over her job. I watched as it cleaned the floor around the lockers.

Marie and Lori had just arrived at the locker area as well. Their attention turned to the robot as it used a laser beam from its dome to clean a spot on the floor.

"Not sure if that's cool or overkill!" Lori said.

Marie shuddered. "I don't like it," she said

The BM Science lady overheard them and commented, annoyed at their reaction. "I assure you this cleaning robot is 100% effective."

"Like the home aide robot in the mall yesterday?" Tim asked. He and Krista had just arrived as well. Tim pointed at Krista. "It scared my poor friend here!"

Krista dropped her head. "It only scared me a little."

176

The BM Science person rolled her eyes. "I'm sure the robot would have deactivated if that annoying Super Teen hadn't stepped in and destroyed it! That cost us a ton of money."

"See! Super Teen is a menace!" Wendi exclaimed, leaning on her locker. "Plus, she doesn't wear cool outfits at all! I don't know what everyone is going on about!" she added with a smirk.

Brandon seemed about to say something, but Wendi cut him off with a look. I like to think that Brandon is on my side. Well, the side of Team Super Kid.

"Yeah, she is dangerous," Lori agreed. "But gotta love her power!"

"I think she tries to help!" Marie said.

Wendi zoomed in on Krista. "Krista, you were there at the mall when it happened. Didn't she knock you out with her super foot odor?"

Krista nodded. "Yeah, I was there, and yes, she put me to sleep, but it was by accident."

Wendi shook her head. "Well, that's even worse than doing it on purpose!"

A couple of kids nodded and grunted in agreement. I decided to stand back and see how this played out. Jason got ready to jump to my defense, but I squeezed his arm, preventing him. I didn't need him to seem too eager.

"The thing is," Krista said slowly, "I don't think it was the smell that hit me. I just felt overwhelmed by her raw power."

A couple of the kids, with Tony as one of them, seemed impressed by that.

Wendi, of course, was not. "That doesn't make it any better to me."

"You wouldn't understand," came a voice from the back of the crowd. Jessie came forward. "Face it, Wendi, you have a very limited understanding of the world."

"Who do you think you are?" Wendi asked, making a fist and heading towards Jessie. Jessie held her ground.

The always calm Brandon stopped Wendi by grabbing her arm and pulling her back. "Wendi, don't worry about it," he said. How could she not calm down with him at her side? "I don't think Jessie meant anything by it."

Jessie shrugged. "Well, you've been in Starlight City all your life, so you see life through a very narrow lens, which is fine. You just need to accept that you don't know everything. In fact, you don't know much at all. You'll be happier when you do." Jessie walked by Wendi and Brandon and into the classroom.

Wendi opened her mouth to say something, and all eyes locked on her. But instead of speaking, Wendi sneezed. "Achoo! Achoo!! Achoo!!!"

Everybody cracked up, even Brandon. Wendi glared at us all. "Sneezing is not funny!"

Brandon hugged her. "Yeah, that was kind of funny, especially with the timing!" he insisted.

Before any of us could say anything else, the bell rang, announcing the start of a new school day. I guess the bell literally saved both Wendi and Jessie. Jessie certainly had a different way about her. I liked that!

The rest of the school day went fairly normal, at least as normal as middle school can ever get. I found the morning science class pretty interesting. After spending the last couple of weeks on the planets, we started talking about space travel this week. Mr. Ohm's little round face lit up when he talked about the future of man in space. We started learning about rockets and how it was so important for them to be launched with enough energy to escape Earth's pull of gravity. This was necessary to break past Earth's atmosphere into space.

For a while, I even forgot that I was super. That was until lunch when I was forced to pass on the baked beans. Even before I was super, those weren't a favorite. Now, they were a definite 'No.' I wasn't even sure why the cafeteria offered those.

Jessie sat with us at lunch again. She mostly read a book called Watership Down. But if we asked her a question, she would answer it with either a polite yes, or no, or maybe. Tim thought that meant she was warming up to us. I noticed Wendi shooting Jess the evil eye all through lunch. That was until the entire cafeteria cracked up when Bobby Parker slipped on a banana peel and spilled his chocolate milk all over Wendi. Wendi screamed and threatened to have poor Bobby banished from the school. But Brandon told her being school President didn't give a person that power. Plus, Brandon pointed out that Bobby was a good guy who had just slipped, and slips do happen.

I caught Jessie smirking through the entire event. She might have seemed cool and aloof, but she paid attention to what went on around her. A weird part of me started to wonder if Jessie had anything to do with the run of bad luck that was happening to Wendi. Nah, that's impossible. Right?

Of course, until last week, I thought it would be impossible for me to lift a moving car off the ground like it was a toy car and to drop a room full of people by popping off my shoe. So, I guess anything could be possible. Like Great-Grandma always said, "The world is a random wonderful crazy place!"

In History, Mr. P reminded us that we had until midweek to finish the oral part of our projects. The entire class groaned and moaned. I did too. We thought we'd have until the end of the week at least. Mr. P explained that because we each need to speak for ten minutes, he could only make this work to bring the deadline forward a bit. Each day, starting on Wednesday, he would randomly draw five names from a hat, and those five people had to be ready to present their oral project. The paper to go with the project would still be due next Monday. He apologized to us but then pointed out that life often changes the rules as it goes along.

Wendi raised her hand and even offered to go first since she was already organized. She said that because she had such an awesome family, the report had been easy. Mr. P thanked her but told her he'd still use the hat, although it was good that she was ready. Wendi knew he'd say that; she just wanted to brag about her family and already being prepared.

The rest of the school day happily passed by without any problems. A big kid, Ryan Taylor, accidentally bumped into me, and I had the good sense to fall down. I wanted to make sure nobody ever got a hint that I was Super Teen. Yep, I was pretty proud of that.

All in all, the day went well. Of course, that couldn't last. As I stood at my locker after school preparing for LAX practice, I heard a scream.

"Hey, you crazy robot. Stop that! Stop that now!"

Then in a robot tone: "You have dirt on your buns. Therefore I must clean it!"

ZAPP!!!!

"Ouch!! You crazy robot!"

I rushed towards the commotion. I saw the cleaning robot hitting Janitor Jan in the buns with a red beam of energy. The BM Science person ran behind the robot saying stuff like:

"Stop!"

"Abort!"

"Humans aren't dirt!"

The crazy robot (a phrase I've been using a lot lately) didn't listen. It hit Jan with another blast. Jan swatted the robot with her mop.

"Ha! It will take more than a cleaning device to stop me!" the robot taunted.

"Yeah, but how about a LAX stick!" Lori yelled.

Lori and Marie launched themselves at the crazy robot. Marie hit it over the dome with her stick! Lori threw a shoulder block at the robot. She hit it hard. But the robot bounced off her.

"Better than a mop!" the robot admitted. "But still not enough to harm me!"

I had to stop this robot. But I had to do it in a subtle way. Lori and Marie had it distracted as they whacked it with their sticks, but that wouldn't hold it for long. I thought about using heat vision, but that might be noticed. The last thing I needed now was people seeing heat coming out of my eyes and then realizing what was going on. I didn't believe I was even considering this, but it may very well be a time for super spit. Yep, super spit. Not ladylike at all, but it could work.

I rolled my tongue around my mouth to collect some spit. I aimed. I blew out a little wad of spit! The spit hit the robot in the midsection, breaking through the robot's metal shielding. The robot crumbled to the ground.

Lori and Marie raised their sticks in victory. I felt good for them. I also felt great that I'd saved the day even though nobody else knew it. I had used my brains to use my powers in a secretive but effective way!

Dear Diary: So now this is normal in my life, defeating robots that have gone mad. Well, at least nobody can say I have a boring life. I take pride in knowing I took the crazy bot down very intelligently without anybody knowing I did it! Gotta admit I did miss a bit of the praise and awe from other people, but I didn't miss the haters on social media, pretty much saying Super Teen isn't all that great at all. BTW, social media loved that Marie and Lori took out the robot and saved Janitor Jan. Sigh (yes, I wrote sigh). I guess normal kids doing heroic things are easier for people to deal with than Super Teen doing something heroic. I need to remind myself that I am Lia Strong. Super Teen is just a small part of my personality and not a defining part. Super Teen is a tool for me to get things done while still leading a normal life as Lia.

I talked to mom about that weird message I had heard in my mind. She told me that it was either 1) I was overtired 2) it was absolutely nothing 3) it was another super-being trying to communicate with me.

Mom did hint that there may be other advanced or supernatural beings around. She had never met any, but that didn't mean they couldn't or wouldn't exist. She told me, and I quote, "It's impossible to prove a negative." When I asked her to explain, she said it meant you couldn't prove something doesn't exist. The universe is always expanding.

So, who knows?

A different kind of kid...

During the next couple of days, life was pretty boring. But boring can be good. Boring lets you recharge and energize for the not-so-boring times, the times when you need all your wits and strength. I was glad that Super Teen could take time off and let me deal with just being Lia.

I put the finishing touches on my paper and oral report about my family history. On Wednesday, my heart pounded when Mr. P pulled the lucky names from the hat and announced who would go first: Carol Lester, Vanesa LeBlan, Meghan MacKenzie, and Buddy Jason.

I gotta say they all did way better than I could. Sure, they were probably the four smartest kids in the class (kind of weird how that happened), but they seemed to hold back any nervousness they had. Later, Jason told me the secret of public speaking was to picture everybody in their underwear, as it would help you to relax. Not sure I wanted to do that.

Walking home, we noticed Felipe being met at the bus by his cousin, Tomas. Felipe gave us an enthusiastic wave. Tomas gave us a polite nod. We decided to go over and introduce ourselves to Tomas. After all, being a new kid in town, he probably wanted to meet people.

"Hey, Felipe, we thought we'd come over and chat with you and get to meet your cousin, Tomas, a bit!" I said.

Felipe smiled. He stood there with his legs crossed. "Ah, ah great," he said. "But I have to rush to the bathroom now! I'll leave you guys to talk!" He leaped into the house.

"Well, thank you for coming over," Tomas said, not looking either of us in the eye. "It's hard meeting people when you're homeschooled. Plus, I'm kind of shy. Even when I go to the public library, I sit in the basement. It's quiet there, just me and my books. Well, not *my* books, but a bunch of books for me to read. I love books."

"I do too!" I said.

"I think we all love books," Jason said. "But why don't you go to the public school?"

Tomas looked up at him. "My family insists I am special. Too special for public schools!"

Okay, I got the impression Tomas didn't want to talk about this. But Jason, for all his brains, wasn't always the best person at picking up on somebody else's vibes. He pushed the matter. "You know, Starlight City Public Schools have a great reputation."

Tomas laughed. "That sounds like something Mayor TJ Bass would brag."

"Perhaps, but it's still true!" Jason said. "We get an excellent education, and we get to hang out with our friends."

I love Jason, but he could be such a dense geek when dealing with new people.

"Really?" Tomas said.

"Really!" Jason said.

Tomas crossed his arms. He looked at Jason. "I bet you don't even know how many moons Mars has?"

"Sure, I do, one hundred!" Jason said. "Wait, that's not right."

"I know you don't know the Pythagorean Theorem!"

Jason stomped a foot down. "A something equals CAT!" he said.

"Ah, Jason, that's not right! Not even close," I told him. Something weird was going on here.

"Let's do an easy one. I know you can't spell cat!" Tomas taunted.

Jason gave him a confident wave. "Oh please, that's so easy! I'm not even going to tell you!" he said, with a bravado in his voice I hadn't ever heard from Jason.

"You can't do it!" Tomas laughed.

I turned to Jason. "Jason, you can spell…cat!"

Jason nodded. "I can, but I won't!" he said, taking a step away from me.

This was very unusual behavior from Jason.

"Show us how you spell CAT!" Tomas ordered.

Jason spoke slowly like he really didn't want to, "C – A – N!" He said.

"Jason, he means CAT like the animal!" I said.

"Right!" Jason said, standing up straight. "I got this."

"No, you don't!" Tomas grinned.

"K-A-T!" Jason said proudly.

Tomas laughed.

"Well, it was close," I said, patting Jason on the shoulder.

Tomas shooed Jason away. "Skip along home now so that the smart people can talk!"

"Right, boss!" Jason said. He turned and skipped across the street.

I curled my hands into fists. I showed Tomas my fists. "Listen, buddy. I don't like people playing with my friends like that!"

Tomas took a step back, eyebrows raised. "Calm down!" he said. "Just having a little fun. You like fun!"

I took a step closer to him. "I will not calm down!" I shouted. The force of my voice sent him reeling backward.

Tomas held up both hands for me to stop. "I knew you smelled different!" he said.

"What?" I said, storming towards him.

"Don't get me wrong, you smell fine. Just way more powerful than normal humans. I knew you were her. But when you didn't respond to my mental message, I thought maybe I was wrong."

"So, you're the one who tried talking in my mind?"

Tomas nodded. "I didn't try. I did talk to your mind. You just didn't respond. Not my fault."

I rolled my eyes. "It kind of was, since I had no idea what was going on!"

Now Tomas rolled his eyes. "I thought that because you're super, you'd figure it out!"

I put a finger to my mouth. "Sssh, don't say that out loud!"

Tomas smiled. "Don't worry! We can talk privately. Anybody within listening distance is asleep on their feet right now." He smiled. "It's amazing, but my powers don't work on you!"

I stopped and looked around. Mrs. Spring, who had been weeding her flower bed, had her eyes closed. A couple of kids playing tag stood there asleep. Mr. Pool slept as he held a hose and watered his grass. You could hear the snoring from here.

"What are you?" I asked.

Tomas held out his hand. "Tomas Richards, half-vampire at your service, ma'am!"

"Half-vampire?" I asked.

"On my mom's side," Tomas answered, as though this was a perfectly normal thing.

"What does being a half-vampire mean?"

Tomas got excited. "It means I can go out in the sun, and I don't care about blood. I can make simple minds do what I want them to do. And I'm way strong!" He smiled. "Once on a camping trip, I ran into a grizzly bear. He growled at me. I farted at him. I used him as a footrest for the rest of the trip."

"Ah, cool, I guess."

Tomas looked me in the eyes. "Don't worry. I didn't do any real damage. I just showed him who's boss. Like you did to that herd of cattle."

I put a hand over my chest. "What? Me?"

Tomas laughed. "Oh, come on! I know victims of a super fart when I see them on the news. Not that I've ever seen them before. That's why I asked my mom if my aunt could homeschool me for a bit. I wanted to meet you. It's hard being super and not having somebody to share being super with, who is your age."

"I know the feeling," I sighed. My sigh pushed him back some.

"Wow! You *are* powerful!" he said, eyes popping open.

"Just be glad I didn't have any garlic today," I added.

He looked at me. "So, you want to hang out sometime?"

"I have an idea. Tomorrow, why don't you meet the gang and me at Mr. T's after school? You do eat, right?"

"I do!" Tomas said. "But not sure I should go. I don't do well with normal people."

"I find it's nice to be around regular people," I told him. "I try not to stand out."

"I'm not a big fan of regular people, as you call them," Tomas told me.

I looked him in the eyes. "Trust me, give them a chance!"

Tomas hesitated, then said, "Fair enough. I will meet you there."

"My friend will be okay, right?" I asked.

Tomas grinned. "Yeah, he will. He won't even remember I turned him into a dunce."

"Okay, I have to go now... but I'll see you tomorrow!" I told him.

"Great, I look forward to it!"

"Do you mind if I tell my mom about you? She's super too."

"Go for it!" Tomas said.

I turned towards home, thinking, "OMG! I just met a vampire, well half-vampire." I stopped and turned back to Tomas. "Wait! Does this mean Felipe is a half-vampire too?"

Tomas shrugged. "He is my blood. So, you do the math!"

Dear Diary: Never think life can't get any stranger. Now, not only was I super, but I was neighbors with a half-vampire teen. A kid who can make people do whatever he wanted and could drop a grizzly with a fart. I could relate.

Mom wasn't shocked at all. She told me she figured if we could be super, there had to be other "non-normal-beings" around. She wouldn't be surprised if more started to show up now that I had kind of presented myself to the public. People were figuring out that supers and normals could live together. I hoped. I wanted to make people understand that being super didn't mean a person wasn't normal.

Robots not in disguise...

      Thursday started as my most normal day in a long time. No strange things happened in the morning. At lunch, Jessie even answered our questions when we talked to her.

      I felt relief again in History class when my name wasn't one of the four picked from the hat. Instead, the cheerleaders, Michelle Noah and Cindy Kay, were picked, along with the debate team captain, Jackson Jacobs. Jessie was also chosen. They all seemed far less nervous than me. Jackson spoke for twice as long as required. Michelle and Cindy both spoke with a lot of passion. Jessie's speech was quite deep. She talked about persecution in the past. I guess it's true what Grandma Betsy says, lots of stuff goes on for people that we don't even know about.

      The good news was that there were no robot attacks in school. BM Science insisted they had taken all the bugs and defects out, and Jan the Janitor seemed happy to have the help. As well, I made it to LAX practice without anything abnormal, funky, or weird happening.

      But of course, that didn't last.

      I had a pretty good practice. First, we ran drills. I like drills because I enjoy repetition. There is something comforting about doing something over and over and watching yourself improve.

      After that, we scrimmaged a bit. I scored a nice goal where I tucked the ball into the corner of the net above the goalie, Kelly Richard's shoulder. "Great shot!" Krista said, giving me a high five. Marie followed with a fist bump. Even Kelly acknowledged me with a nod of her head.

      That's when I heard inside my head:

      "Lia, this is your dad. I'm broadcasting on a frequency only you (and probably your mom and grandmas) can hear. We have a

problem at BM Science, and we need your help! Over and out, Dad."

My first thought was to ignore it. After all, I haven't heard from my father in over ten years, and now suddenly he reaches out to me just because I'm super. And only because he needs me! But he was my dad. And he did need me.

I smiled, knowing Mr. Coach Blue was our coach today. I guess I should clear that up some. We have two coach Blues for LAX. They are a husband and wife coaching team. She usually coaches us, and he coaches the guys, but now and then, they switch. And Mr. Blue always took it easier on us than Mrs. Blue.

I walked up to Coach Blue, holding my stomach and bending over. "Coach, something I ate at lunch didn't agree with me at all" I leaned in close to him and whispered, "I think I'm going to vomit…."

Coach put an arm on my shoulder. "Take the rest of the practice off, go home and get some rest."

I dragged myself off the field, holding my stomach. I heard Wendi mumble under her breath, "Wimp." Couldn't let her bother me now.

I got to the locker room and collected my stuff. Good thing I kept my Super Teen outfit in a bag in my book bag. I also kept a pair of old socks in that bag to stop anybody from looking into it. The smell was even better than a padlock.

A text appeared on my phone.

JASON>My dad has been called 2 BMS…something weird is going on.

I texted back> OMW there

I moved into the bathroom, changed at super speed, and leaped out the window. I leaped and bounded my way to BM Science, keeping my book bag by my side. After a few minutes of super hopping, the BM Science lab complex came into view. The place was surrounded by a big fence. Police cars lined the gates, but the guards at BM wouldn't let them pass.

Using super hearing, I heard Captain Michaels arguing with the guards about how the police had a call regarding an out-of-control robot. The guards insisted the call was a mistake and shouldn't have been made. My extra super hearing zoned in on people running and screaming in a courtyard beyond the main building. I knew something bad was going down. I stored my book bag in the highest branch of a nearby tree then leaped over the BM Science fence. Another bound and I was on the flat roof of the main building. For a high-tech lab or whatever, the building itself looked like a boring white warehouse.

Peering down from the roof to the court and lunch yard below, I could see a big blue robot that looked like a 10-foot-tall robot boxer. People were running in fear as the robot smashed lunch table after lunch table. A couple of security people tried to stop it, but the robot pushed them aside like they were flies.

I saw my dad and a couple of people in lab coats watching from inside the main building. I could see them shaking their heads.

The big blue robot lumbered towards a small blond woman who stood there trembling with fear.

The robot raised an arm and shouted, "I will prove I am the best. I can't be beaten!"

I leaped down between the robot and the woman and caught the robot's arm on the way down before it could smash the lady.

"Not happening on my watch!" I told the robot as I ripped off its arm.

I felt good about that. The robot reacted fast, way faster than I expected. It swatted me across the face with its remaining arm. That blow sent me staggering back a little.

"Ha! Human! Your fighting is almost as bad as your banter!" It taunted. It swung at me again. This time though, I blocked it. Then I moved forward and hit it with an open palm to its robot stomach. My blow sent it reeling back. The big squared head bot looked at me and smiled. "Not bad, tiny human!" it said.

The bot took a boxing stance. "I have been programmed to fight!"

I dropped back into a karate stance, "Good, I'd hate to beat up a non-fighting robot!"

"I must warn you, silly human. I have been programmed with every style of fisticuffs and martial arts known to man!"

Okay, I didn't like the sound of that. I had to hope the robot was bluffing. I leaped up, sending a flying kick to the robot's chin. It swatted me to the ground before I got to it. I rolled away as it tried to stomp on me. I bounced to my feet.

The robot laughed, "Ha, I saw that pitiful move coming before you knew you were going to do it!" it shouted.

I pointed at the bot very dramatically, "Your maker must be so proud!"

The robot's stiff face showed a slight smile. "I am not programmed for emotion or to recognize emotion, but yes, I do believe they are."

"Then why are you attacking them?" I asked. I didn't care. I just needed time to catch my breath and maybe figure out a plan of attack on this big blue bot.

"They wanted me to show them what I can do. So, I did. I figured you would show up. I wanted to beat the strongest human in the world!"

I kind of liked being called the strongest human in the world. But now I needed to show this bot what that meant. I just didn't know how. After all, yeah, I may have been strong and know karate, but I still didn't have much fighting experience. In karate, they never prepare you for facing off against a 10-foot-tall metal robot.

"I see you are using delaying tactics in order to catch your breath," the robot laughed. "I gave you a sporting chance, but enough is enough." It started running towards me faster than I thought a bot that size should be able to move.

The bot was on top of me before I knew it. It grabbed me with its good arm and lifted me off the ground, then threw me down heavily. I rolled up again and noticed a "me" sized dent in the ground.

"Is that the best you've got?" I taunted.

The big blue bot stalked towards me again. "You can take a beating; I'll give you that! I would be impressed, except..."

"You're not programmed for emotions," I said.

I leaped up into the air, bounced off a lunch table, and sprang up over the bot. I forced myself down, jamming my legs on top of the bot's head. "Like Mario squishing a goomba!" I told the bot.

The bot crinkled but didn't break. Now it was maybe nine feet tall instead of ten. It still had fight in it, though. "Figures you'd make a geek reference!"

"Look, if you're trying to taunt me again by calling me a geek, it won't work!" I told the bot. "I'm proud of being a geek!"

The bot let out a chuckle. "Yeah, only a geek would think a pink shirt with green jeans covered in stars, topped off with a black mask, would look good!"

"Nope, that won't work either!" I pointed to the outfit. "I know this is cool, plus you have no taste."

"Hmm, then once I take you down, I will head to town and knock the town to the ground!" the robot said.

Now that made me mad! One, I hated the rhyme. And two, no robot was going to threaten my friends and my town. I felt the anger building up inside of me. My eyes began to glow. Beams of red-hot heat flew from my eyes into the robot.

The robot exploded with a wondrous BOOM! Robot parts rained down around me. I thought of cold things like eating ice cubes, then blew on the robot parts with icy breath. The robot parts shattered into dust.

I leaped up in the air. I was due at Mr. T's 20 minutes ago!

193

Vamp Out...

I felt so powerful! Not only had I taken out a crazy robot, but my leaps were also growing by leaps and bounds. I made it all the way from BM Science to the tree where I'd stashed my book bag in a millisecond. I grabbed the book bag and made another leap. Within a minute, the city had come into clear view. I bounded home, got changed, and then headed to Mr. T's.

When I walked into Mr. T's, my mouth fell open. A kid named Jimmy Wall sat there sucking his thumb. Tony, the bully, danced like a ballerina. Mr. T and Mrs. T were asleep on the counter. Jason clucked like a chicken. Marie and Lori played clapping games with each other. Brandon ran around on all fours barking like a dog. He chased Wendi, who hissed like a cat. Krista sat at our table, but she was sitting on her head. Tim walked back and forth, arms stiff like he was a zombie.

Everybody in Mr. T's was either sound asleep or acting crazily. Well, everybody but Tomas, who sat in a chair. The cheerleaders, Michelle and Cindy, massaged his feet. Oh, and for some reason, Jessie sat there at a corner table reading War and Peace.

"Hey, Lia," Jessie said as I walked by.

I stopped. "You're still you!"

Jessie nodded. "Yeah, the little half-vamp is too smart to try and mess with me," she said.

"Ah, why is that?" I asked.

Jessie pointed to Tomas and the two poor cheerleaders massaging his feet. "Don't you have more important things to do right now?"

"Good point." I turned and headed to Tomas.

"Tomas, what are you doing?" I shouted.

Tomas looked at me. "You're late."

194

"Yeah, something came up!"

Tomas pointed over his shoulder to the TV that was showing my fight with the bot. "You look cool!"

"Ssh," I told him.

Tomas grinned. "None of these people can hear anything besides my commands. Well, besides the witch, and she already knows!"

I looked over my shoulder at Jessie. She gave me a wave. "You're a witch??"

Jessie nodded. "Don't fret. I'm a mostly good witch." She pointed at Tomas. "Deal with the issue at hand."

Shaking my head in disbelief, I looked directly at Tomas, "Why are you doing this?"

"You told me these people were nice and that I could fit in. But when I told them I was a half-vamp, they laughed!" He pointed to the cheerleaders massaging his feet. "Ha! I'm the one laughing now!"

I thought about how to approach this. For one thing, Tomas' feet certainly did smell. I have no idea how Michelle and Cindy were handling it. I pointed to the two poor cheerleaders. "How come they can do that without fainting?" I asked.

Tomas took a sip from a milkshake. "I won't let them faint. This is too much fun!"

I sighed, and my breath knocked Tomas off the chair. The two cheerleaders smiled.

"We're free!" they said.

Then they both passed out on the floor.

"Man, you are strong!" Tomas groaned, standing up.

"Listen, Tomas, these people are nice, or mostly nice, or kind of nice, but they don't take different that easily. You can't just tell them you are a vampire!"

"Half-vampire."

"You can't tell them you are a half-vampire and expect them to believe you and not think it's a joke or that you're crazy! That doesn't mean they are bad or unaccepting. They are just used to their world being a certain way."

"But the world changes," Tomas argued.

"Agreed, but we need to ease people into the changes," I told him sincerely.

He pointed to all the people now acting as animals or babies or statues. "Ya gotta admit this is fun!"

"You do have a certain, ah, flare, I'll give you that… but can you make them all normal again?"

Tomas looked at me and frowned.

"Please!" I asked, putting my hands together.

"Fine!" he sighed.

I pointed to his shoes. "Oh, put your shoes on first, so they don't all faint after you bring them back to being themselves!"

"Man, you are no fun!" Tomas complained as he slipped his feet into his shoes.

He snapped his fingers. "Everybody, back to how you were. You don't remember anything about the last ten minutes!"

Everybody snapped back to normal. They all acted as if nothing had happened.

"Oh, hi!" Krista said to me. "I hope you're feeling better."

"Hey girl, when did you get here?" Tim asked.

Jason came over to our table. "Nice to see you're feeling better!" he told me. He took a bite of a fry. "Why are these cold?"

I sat down. "I invited Tomas to join us today. Since he's homeschooled, I thought it would be nice if he got to meet you all!"

Brandon walked by our table, with Wendi close by his side, of course. I smiled. Brandon stopped. "You are feeling better, Lia?" he asked. I swear his white teeth sparkled almost as much as his eyes.

My face became a giant grin. Brandon had noticed me. "Yes, thanks," I replied, my cheeks flushing with happiness.

Wendi dragged Brandon away. "She's fine. She probably just got a whiff of her own breath. That would make anybody want to throw up!"

"Now, Wendi, that's not nice. Lia smells just fine!"

"Stop smelling other girls!" Wendi ordered.

My group all stared at me as I dropped down in my chair. Trying to take their attention from me, I directed the conversation towards Tomas. "So, Tomas, tell us what you like to do?"

"Do you play any sports?" Tim asked.

"Do you have a girlfriend?" Krista asked?

Jason simply rolled his eyes at me. Was Jason jealous of the way I acted around Brandon?

"I like chess and ping pong," Tomas said.

"That's cool!" Tim said with a nod. "We should play sometime."

"Which one?" Tomas asked him.

Tim took a sip of his milkshake. "Either." He frowned. "Weird, this milkshake has turned warm."

Tomas pointed to the TV. My fight was shown on half the screen while Oscar Oranga interviewed people on the other half, asking them what they thought. As always, a lot of the people liked me. Some of the people thought I could be dangerous.

"I think she's great!" Jason said.

"I think she's amazing!" Krista agreed.

"I think she's cute!" Tim said.

"She does have a cool look about her!" Krista added.

Tomas took a bite out of a burger. "So, you guys aren't scared of her? But she can drop you all with a whiff of her feet."

Krista waved at him dismissively. "Nah, I've experienced that. It's not bad!"

Jason nodded. "That's what I heard too!" He smiled at me.

"Man, I wished she'd knock me out!" Tim said. "Then she could give me mouth to mouth!"

"Oh gross!" we all said.

Tim grinned cheekily. Then we all laughed. Even Tomas almost grinned. We sat there for the next hour or so, just munching and talking. Talking about everything, talking about nothing. I believe Tomas even cracked a smile or two.

Around dinner time, Tomas, Jason, and I started walking home. Jason asked if I was glad about not having to give my speech yet. I nodded and told him yes, but I also wanted to get it over with. Tomas said how he loved being homeschooled as it was less drama. Jason told him that the drama makes life interesting. Tomas just laughed and said he finds life interesting enough without the drama of school.

I said goodbye to the guys and headed to my house.

"That was fun!" I heard Tomas say in my brain.

"*Okay, this is weird!*" I thought back.

"*Not weird, we're just advanced… Would you go out with me sometime?*"

Now that was something I hadn't expected.

"*Tomas, I like you, but I just want to be friends,*" I thought back.

"*I get it. I'll see you later.*" He cut his reply short, and I didn't hear anything further.

I walked into the house. I hoped he was okay and wasn't upset with me. I guessed it could have gone better. These things always could. Before I could overthink it, though, my phone vibrated. Two messages. One from Jason.

JASON> Great job 2day! U were awesome! (muscle)

I texted back: Tnks!

The second message was from my dad.

DR DAD>Thanks for your help, my dear. Love Dad!

Wow! My dad really was back in my life!

Dear Diary: Okay, I'm not sure what the coolest and weirdest moments were with these recent events. Certainly, beating up the big blue robot felt great. Once that big blue jerk threatened my town and friends, I knew I had to put him down and hard. I certainly do have a lot of punch! The excitement from that made me tingle all over. But that also showed me how I have to keep my calm. I can't go firing off heat ray vision by accident. Man! That would be bad. Using the freezing breath was, pardon the bad joke, cool.

On the weirder side, Tomas has an interesting way about him. Not sure what freaked me out more, the fact that he could mind control the entire room or how calm he acted. You know it's been a strange day when you find out that one of your new friends is a witch, and that isn't even the oddest part of the day.

Still, the highlight had to be my dad reaching out to me. It's great to have him in my life again. Sure, he summoned me with a mental broadcast, but I even found that neat. Sure, he wanted me to defeat a crazy robot. Sure, mom thinks Dad may have been testing my limits. But then he texted me afterward! He told me, good job. I bet he was proud of me. I knew he was. He didn't have to text me. But he did. Yep, my dad was now a part of my life, and I liked it.

Oh, getting back to the males in my life…it was kind of odd that Tomas would ask me out after only knowing me for a few days. After all, Jason and I have been friends forever, and he's never asked me out. Of course, maybe that's why Jason never asked me out. We were such good friends. Whatever! I just hoped I handled it okay. I do want Tomas to be a friend or buddy. You can't have too many friends, and man, he would be a tough enemy. I had to hope for the best. Sometimes even superheroes have to hope for the best. Hmmm…the new normal!

Vamps and Witches, Oh my!...

That evening, I had dinner with Mom and Grandma Betsy. It was a phones off, let's talk and chat dinner, of grilled chicken breast with Mom's gourmet sauce and her special salad. Yum!

"Proud of you for taking out the crazy blue droid!" Grandma Betsy told me. (She was a big Star Wars fan...)

Mom put a hand on my shoulder, "I am too." She hesitated a moment. "Just be careful with your dad... That man always has something up his lab coat sleeve."

I nodded.

"Ah, Isabelle, you just don't like that he always called you Isa," Grandma said with a smirk.

Changing the subject, I asked. "Have either of you dealt with vampires and witches?"

They both shook their heads. "Like I've said before," explained Grandma Betsy, "I've always surmised they existed...but they've stayed hidden away."

"As have we," she added, grinning at me with her eyes as much as her mouth. "You, my dear, have opened up the world to a lot of new things!"

Mom nodded in agreement, and I gave them both a weak smile in return. I just hoped opening up the world would be a good thing.

After dinner, I went to my room to do some homework and practice my speech. I worked for about twenty minutes then realized my phone was still off. I turned it back on and texted Jason. I thought for sure that he'd want to chat about my battle with the crazy blue robot.

LIA>How's the night going?

Nothing. I waited a few moments before sending another text.

201

LIA>Knock!

Still nothing.

A quick check of my social (or unsocial) media showed people once again debating the pros and cons of Super Teen. Surprisingly though, Wendi wasn't complaining about me. She was worried that she hadn't been able to contact Brandon all evening. She'd asked his parents, but they didn't seem concerned, and that was strange.

Now was that just a coincidence?

I heard a knock. Not on my door, but on my window, which was extra weird considering I'm on the second floor. Turning to the window, I saw Jessie floating there. I jumped up, opened the window, and helped her in.

"Jessie, what's going on?"

Jessie looked around my room. "Hmm, I thought there'd be pictures of pink ponies or unicorns or something. Not LAX posters."

"I took the unicorns down when I hit 12, but still, a girl can like unicorns, ponies, and LAX as well," I admitted. "But that's not why you are here!"

Jessie shook her head. "No, I figured you might be worried about your buddy, Jason, and the boring perfect looking kid."

"Brandon?"

Jessie nodded. "Yeah, that one, he's so blah with his straight teeth and dimples," she stuck out her tongue.

"Jessie, to the point!"

"The half-vamp nabbed them!"

"Why?" I asked.

Jessie shrugged. "Don't know...vamps are weird." She looked me in the eyes. "My guess is he's jealous!"

"What? You're kidding me!" I stared at her. "Do you know where he took them?"

"Kind of," Jessie told me. "I did a locator spell, and it showed me Main Street... vamps can be hard to get a lock on!"

As soon as she said Main Street, I knew where Tomas was keeping them. "The library!" I said. "Tomas said he loves to hang out in the dark basement of the library!"

Jessie smiled. "Vamps can be so cool!"

I headed towards my window. "You coming?" I asked.

Jessie smiled again. "Wouldn't miss it!"

We arrived at the library quickly. Since it was dark, I figured I'd handle this as Lia Strong, not Super Teen. After all, this was personal, not heroic. We found one of the library's main windows had been forced open. We climbed in the window. It felt kind of freaky being in a dark library. The good thing was that my super sight seemed to see perfectly well in the dark.

The shelves of books made a maze for us to navigate through.

"I'm pretty sure they are in the basement," I said.

Jessie seemed giddy. "This is so cool," she said.

After working our way up an aisle of books and then down a row of books, we found the door to the basement. The door had been smashed open. Pointing at the broken lock, I stated the obvious, "They're down there for sure."

Jessie rolled her eyes. "Wow, brilliant, Sherlock!"

I shot her a look. She took a step back. "Sorry, I can get cynical when I'm excited!"

We made our way down the dark staircase. There, sitting in the middle of the basement, was Tomas. He was reading a book by flashlight. Tomas sat on top of Brandon and used Jason as a footrest.

"Oh, so not cool, Tomas!" I said.

Tomas turned to me. I noticed he was reading The Art of War.

He stood up quickly. He staggered. He put his hands behind his back, "Oh, hi. Funny finding you here! This isn't what it looks like!"

"It looks like you've got it in for Brandon and Jason!" I said, thrusting a finger at him.

Tomas dropped his head. "Okay, it is what it looks like then."

I walked over and lifted Tomas off the ground with one finger. "What's your problem?"

"You like them better than me!" he replied.

"Like duh!" Jessie said.

I shot Jessie a look. She backed up a step and said, "Come on now, that was obvious as well!"

I let Tomas fall to the ground. I took a deep calming breath. Then another and another. "Look, Tomas, I've known Jason all my life. Well, at least for all of my life that I can remember. He's always been there for me. I've always been there for him. We're great friends. Will we ever be more than that?" I shrugged. "I don't know. Maybe we know each other too well. But whatever there is between Jason and me has nothing to do with you." I poked him with my finger. "Get it?"

He rubbed the spot where I had poked him. "Yeah, I get it." He motioned with his head towards Brandon, who was kneeling on the floor on all fours. "What about pretty boy?"

"Oh, please, he's Wendi's boyfriend. He's not even interested in me!" I said, my face turning red.

Tomas laughed. "Oh, come on! You're smart, you're pretty, and you're super powered! Of course, he's interested in you!"

"Duh, again," Jessie said.

A part of me liked hearing that. Wow!

Another part of me told that part to calm down. I had a lot of flaws...not the least being that one of my farts could drop a town. "Look, Tomas, I appreciate the comments and your feelings... I do...but when I said I'm not ready for a relationship, it has nothing to do with these two guys or with you. You're great in your own strange way."

"Thanks. I think," Tomas said.

"Tomas, my life is bizarre right now. I have a lot to take in and a lot to learn about myself. I don't want to be more than friends with anybody, not yet. Not until I have a better idea of who I am and my place in this world. This world that gets crazier for me by the day."

Tomas looked at the two guys and ordered. "Get up, walk up the stairs, out the window, and go home. If anybody asks, you've been studying late!"

The two boys obediently stood up and walked away.

"Thanks, Tomas," I said.

He shrugged. "Felipe says I have to learn to read human clues better."

"He's a smart kid!" I said.

Jessie came up and put her arm around Tomas. "You know, being a mostly good witch, I'm already aware of my place in this world."

The two of them smiled at each other.

"I'll just leave you two alone!" I said, heading out of there as fast as possible. "Thanks for your help, Jessie!"

"No, thank you!" Jessie told me with a wink.

I smiled and caught up with Jason on the walk home. He was confused. So, I thought it best that I made sure he got home safely.

"You know, I have a weird feeling that something strange just happened," Jason told me as we reached his house.

I shrugged. "Well, the world is a weird and wonderful place, Jason."

He nodded. "True, but that still doesn't explain why I smell feet?"

Dear Diary: First off, vampires and witches are strange, but in a kind of interesting way. I also have to admit that Tomas made me begin to come to terms with my feelings about Jason and Brandon, kind of.

The big day...

On Friday morning, I had a feeling of dread. That could only mean one thing. Today would be the day I got chosen to give my oral report. I stayed longer than usual in bed. Shep, our loyal dog, walked into the room. He nudged me with his nose. Shep hated it when I slept late, especially on school days.

I turned to him. "Oh, Shep..." I said. But I couldn't finish, as the second my breath hit him, he whimpered, went stiff, and fell over. I shot my hand over my mouth. It seemed like my morning breath of death was back. Yeah, that's not ever a good sign of things to come. This showed how unique my life had become. I thought nothing of a whiff of my breath knocking out a 100-pound dog.

After good teeth brushing and breakfast, Jason and I headed to school. Jason seemed no worse for the events of the night before. He told me he'd had the wildest dreams.

All through the school day, I hoped something would happen that would call for Super Teen to save the day, anything that would give me an excuse to have to leave the school grounds. But of course, they never do when you want a super villain or something to show up.

Before I knew it, I was sitting in history class. Mr. P probably was the neatest man in the world. He never had a hair out of place. It seemed like his clothing never wrinkled. Not sure why I noticed all of that right then. It's funny the things you pick up on when you're trying not to freak out.

Mr. P pulled out a name from the hat, "Lia."

"Lia, who?" I asked, grasping at straws.

The class laughed.

Jason bent over and patted me on the back. "You can do this!"

I stood up. I walked to the front of the class.

"*You can do this, honey!*" I heard Grandma Betsy say in my brain. Not sure how she did that, but it made me feel better. "*Just breathe!*" she mentally coached. "*And don't fart, LOL!*" she added. Yeah, she said LOL.

I stood in front of the class. Stay calm, I told myself. My knees started to shake. I felt my palms sweat. I took a breath. I closed my eyes, and then I decided to imagine the entire class in their PJs. Somehow mentally picturing Wendi wearing bright orange Sponge Bob PJs put me more at ease. I smiled.

Then I started out talking about how my first ancestors came here in the 1600s. Before that, most of my family lived in England, Scotland, and Ireland.

"In other words, Great Britain," Mr. P lectured.

I went on to talk about how things have changed. How man has walked on the moon. How today, we all walk around with little computers in our pockets that are more powerful than the most powerful computer on Earth at the time man walked on the moon. How the internet has given us all access to unbelievable amounts of information. How these days, the trick is to work out what information is true and what isn't. I talked about how Netflix and Chill were unheard of, not even ten years earlier. I also joked about how my grandma can't wait for her car to be able to drive her to the shopping center of its own accord.

I closed with what I considered the strong point of my talk. "Probably though, the biggest thing I learned doing this project is, the more things change, the more people stay the same. In fact, despite all the technology today and the fast-paced life we have, a pace so fast we have to text by leaving out letters or using cool emoticons or LOLs, we are all still much like our ancestors and each other. We all want to be safe and happy. We all want to be part of something larger than ourselves. Rather, we call it a community, a clan, a tribe, a team, or a club. We all want to belong, and that's because we know things are better when we work together. We all have a role to play! The trick, of course, is finding that role!"

Mr. P gave me a little applause. "Very good, Lia!" I especially loved the conclusion.

When I looked at the class, they all were smiling, even Wendi. Then they all began to applaud as well. I took that as a sign of success.

Before I could soak in the glory for too long, though, an announcement came over the PA system. "This is Vice-Principle MacaDoo! The rest of the school day and all after-school practices have been canceled. All students and teachers, please go to the basement! THERE IS A GIANT ROBOT HEADING TOWARDS OUR CITY!"

Of course, there was!

Mr. P quickly turned on the TV in the classroom. There, stomping towards town, was a giant robot that looked like a huge three-story tall square box with long coil legs and five metal arms with claws attached. The police shot at it, but their bullets just bounced off. From the TV, we heard Oscar Oranga broadcasting from the street, "This demolition bot has escaped from BM Science's facility. BM says they regret any inconvenience this may cause, and they will reimburse people for any damages."

"Quick, everybody, to the basement!" Mr. P yelled.

People shot up from their chairs. I rushed over to Jason. "Cover for me!" I said.

"I have your back," Jason told me.

Dear Diary: Speaking in public may be even scarier than fighting giant robots. But I did it!

Bot Battle...

I rushed at super speed through the hallway to grab my outfit out of my book bag.

I heard a mental broadcast from my dad, *"Honey, this robot is nasty. It's meant to bring down skyscrapers, so be careful!"*

Then I heard my mom in my head, *"Since I know I can't talk you out of this, your grandma and I are on the way to lend a hand!"*

"Thanks, Mom and Grandma!" I thought back.

"If you need witch help, give me a shout!" Jessie thought to me.

"Thanks all," I thought back at them as I opened my locker. I grabbed my bag and headed to the bathroom for a quick change.

With everybody moving in the other direction, I had a clear path to the bathroom. Until I saw Vice Principle Macadoo standing in front of the door, that was. I stopped in my tracks. "Ah, sir, I need to use the facilities," I crossed my legs. "I'm so nervous."

VP Macadoo was a mountain of a man. He crossed his log-sized arms and stood in front of the door. "Sorry, Lia, but you have to use the one in the basement. It's safer."

"No, *I'm* sorry!" I said. Okay, I needed to use my pheromone sweat power to convince VP Mac to let me pass. I just had to be careful. I wanted to influence him, not knock him. I knew my feet had to be really sweaty from both the talk and now the nerves of knowing I'd be facing a giant robot. I popped my heel gently out of my shoe, just enough until I got a slight whiff of my foot. Then I quickly popped my heel back into the shoe. VP Mac now had a silly smile on his face.

"You will let me pass!" I said softly but firmly.

He smiled at me and stepped to the side. "Of course, master!" he answered.

I shook my head. Okay, that was mega odd. "Go down and join the others, and please don't call me master!"

He bowed and headed off.

I super speeded into the bathroom, changed, and leaped off to fight a giant robot.

In less than a minute, I had the robot in sight. Following the loud clangs of its feet smashing into the streets made it easy to track. I landed on the ground, maybe a quarter of a mile in front of the giant crazy machine.

The police had the robot surrounded, but their shots, even from heavy weapons, bounced harmlessly off the bot. Mom and Grandma stood behind the police.

"Captain Michaels, have your men stop firing, their shots aren't doing any good against the robot, but they might harm Super Teen!" I heard Grandma command the captain.

"Stop firing, men!" Captain Michaels ordered.

The robot stopped in its tracks. "Ah, Super Teen. I am so filled with joy that you would show up. After all, you are the reason I am here! I want to prove to my makers that I am the most powerful machine or person or animal or vegetable on Earth!"

I bent my knees then sprang forward at the big bad bot. I extended my fist and rammed the bot in the midsection.

I made a little dent.

The bot swatted me to the ground with an open claw hand the size of my body.

I hit the street.

"Oh, that's going to leave a mark!" the bot laughed.

"She can't stop it! Fire men! Fire!!!" Captain Michaels ordered.

The police started raining bullets at the giant bot. The bullets bounced off the bot's hard metal surface, not even scratching it.

"Police, hold your fire! It's useless!" I heard Grandma Betsy order.

212

"Only Super Teen can stop this thing!" Mom scolded the police.

The hail of bullets stopped.

I rose to my feet. I saw the big "me" sized dent in the road.

"Told you!" the bot said, thrusting a finger the size of my face in my face.

I swung at the finger with my fist. The bot pulled away. I missed and fell again, face first into the pavement.

"I've been watching you!" the giant white robot gloated. "I know all your moves before you do!" He pointed to his square robot head. "I have a lot of processing power!"

I pushed myself up off the ground and rammed the robot between its legs. The force of my blow lifted it up off the ground. But it thrust itself back down without losing any balance.

The bot reached down with a hand. "If I had been a human male, that attack would have made me at least talk funny," it told me in a high-pitched voice. "But I am not!" the bot continued in a trembling roar. Then, it began to squeeze.

I felt pain for the first time since I've been super. A part of me didn't like it at all. But another part of me realized that the pain made me angry. I could use that anger. I pushed out on the robot's hand with my hands and slowly forced the big cold metal hand open.

I shot up! I blasted the bot's head with my heat ray vision. Two intense red beams of sheer power blazed from my eyes into the bot's head. The head turned from white to pink, lost shape, and then melted into the body! The bot stood there motionless. The crowd of onlookers cheered!

The top of the bot started to rumble and churn. A new head popped up. "I'm built with the newest and coolest Nano Technology. You break something, and it repairs itself," the robot laughed.

Oh, this was bad, so so bad. The bot extended a fist over its head. It pounded the fist down at me. I jumped to the

213

side. The fist shattered the road. I leaped backward. The bot struck at me again and again with multiple arms. I retreated, dodging blow after blow. I didn't have time to think.

"Dad, how could you crazy scientists make such a monster robot?" I asked in my thoughts.

"It's because you've been holding back, honey!" Dad said in my mind.

"What?" I screamed in my head.

"Yeah, what!?" Mom screamed too. It seemed that suddenly I had a conference call going on in my brain.

"Lia, honey, you haven't been pushing your powers because you've either been afraid of hurting somebody, or you haven't been pushed. My team and I have been developing this robot to help you be the best you can be. Exceed the limits you put on yourself!"

The big robot lumbered towards me slowly. He shook his new head. "Oh, Super Teen, I had hoped you'd be more of a challenge." Lumbering towards me, it lifted up two of its arms and sniffed. "I haven't even worked up a sweat!" The arms dropped, and the robot laughed. "Ha! Ha! Robot humor."

Well, I certainly didn't love the fact that my dad had invented a giant robot just to help push me to be my best. A little part of me thought that was kind of sweet. A bigger part thought, my gosh, this is crazy! But I couldn't let this robot hurt my town or my friends. Nope! It was not going to happen! I had to stop this huge humongous thing. I just had no idea if I could. I needed a moment to think and collect my thoughts. The problem was, I didn't have a moment. The bot moved towards me. It's fresh head taunting. "Takes more than you to stop me!"

From behind the robot, I saw Tomas holding up Felipe with one arm. Tomas tossed Felipe like he was a football. Felipe flew towards the giant bot, yelling, "Yahoo!"

Felipe hit the robot in the back of the head. The giant robot spun his head around 360 degrees to see what had smacked him. Felipe dropped to the ground next to me.

"Felipe, thanks for the help! But people will recognize you now!" I told him.

Felipe smiled. "Nah, I have a vampire blur on. Regular people just see a weird streak. They have no idea what it is. Silly regular people."

"Okay, thanks for the little break," I told him.

Felipe streaked back to Tomas.

The robot shook its head and turned back to me. "Now that was hard to compute. What isn't hard to compute is that I am going to clobber you."

"*Hey, Lia, this is Jessie broadcasting to you in your brain now. I'm linking you to the thoughts of your friends.*"
I heard a variety of remarks...

Please, Super Teen, do this.

I know she won't let us down.

Give him a belting– (that was from Brandon...)

Come on, Lia, launch that big ugly bot! (That had to be from Jason!)

I smiled. I had this. Not sure how though, but I'd figure that out as I went along.

I leaped up at the big bot, then spun and hit him with a fart, right in the face. The bot stopped for a second. "How rude!" it told me. "My air sensors tell me that I am lucky I don't need to breathe air."

Yes, I figured that fart wouldn't stop it, but it gave me time to think. I thought of eating ice cream in an igloo. Inhaling, I blasted the top of the bot with super cold breath.

The robot froze solid. I dropped to the ground.

The robot started to glow red. "Nice try, but I will just turn my internal heat controls up to melt this ice."

Now I had my chance. I leaped behind the robot. I grabbed one of its arms, then jumped into the air and started spinning. The higher I went, the faster I spun. After ten or more rotations, I had created quite a lot of force. And the bot and I were way off the ground.

"Crashing from this height won't harm me that much at all!" the robot laughed.

"I figured as much!"

Keeping my head straight as we spun, I saw the ground, then space, the ground, then space, the ground, then space. I needed to time this just right. After about ten more rotations facing ground, then space, I had the timing sorted out. I faced the ground. I rotated towards the sky. I forced myself to stop. I released my hold on the big bot, flinging it forward with all my might and sending it flying even higher into the sky. I hovered there. (Not sure how…) I watched as the robot soared higher and higher. With super vision, I saw the robot heating up. It kept flying higher and higher. I heard a little boom when the robot broke the sound barrier. I saw it drift off into space. Yep, it'd be no problem now!

I let myself glide back down to the ground.

"*Yahoo! You tossed the robot out of the Earth's atmosphere! Yes, that cost my company millions of dollars, but money well spent!*" I heard Dad say in my head.

I landed softly on the ground. "That was amazing!" Oscar Oranga said, rushing up to me. He stuck a microphone in my face. "Super Teen, any words for our viewers!"

I smiled and shrugged. "I just want to do my best!" I said.

Mom rushed over to me, holding her doctor's bag. "Super Teen, I'm a doctor. Do you need any assistance?" she asked in her most official voice. She started looking me over from head to toe.

"I'm fine, doctor," I replied in my most official voice.

Mom looked at my midsection, stopping at a large bullet hole in my shirt. She knelt down and examined the hole, and looked for a wound.

"*Oh my,*" she said in my head, which was even weirder with her being next to me. "*A ricocheting bullet must have hit you….but there's not even a burn mark on your skin.*"

I shrugged. "*Didn't feel it….*"

216

"Wow," Mom said out loud. "You are fine!"

I leaped up in the air and headed back towards my home. Yeah, I know my book bag and stuff were at school, but after a day that featured an oral exam and a giant robot that I had to throw off Earth to defeat, I needed to get home.

That night after a long shower, I had a celebration pizza dinner with Mom, Grandma, Great-Grandma, Jason, and strangely enough, Jessie and Tomas, and Felipe. It turns out that Felipe being half-vampire, really did know I was Super Teen all along. Man, that kid is sharp. So, we had pretty much everybody who knew I was Super Teen at our house, except for my dad. Mom wouldn't let him in the door. I guess I couldn't blame her.

"To Lia!" Grandma Betsy said, raising a glass of milk to me!

"To Lia!" everybody else at the table joined in.

"Thanks, everyone! I couldn't have done it without you!" I grinned happily back at them.

We talked and ate into the night.

Dear Diary: OMG! What can I say or write? Unbelievable! I can hover in the air now to the point that it's like I'm flying. I am so strong I can throw a huge robot into outer space, at least when I'm angry. I feel I'm getting good at using my powers. I am developing some control. Plus, best of all, I gave an oral report and didn't do anything to embarrass myself. In fact, the report went really well. That actually felt as good as being super.

On the weird side (with me, there's always a weird side), it's nice to have my father back in my life. Of course, it would be nicer if he didn't work for the company that created robots just to test me.

But, oh well, I guess no parent is perfect. ☺

Epilogue...

I laid awake in bed, checking my social media. Sure enough, some people complained about the damage Super Teen caused. I figured out that no matter what, you're never going to make everybody happy. On the bright side, many more people were happy that I saved the day and were impressed by what I did. Even Chief Michaels and Wendi commented on how that robot would have done major damage to the town if it weren't for Super Teen. Of course, Wendi did bring up the point that maybe BM Science would leave us alone if Super Teen wasn't around. More people blamed BM Science. BM Science joined the conversation, saying they were building the city a new park and recreation center.

My head hit the pillow, knowing I had done well.

"*Honey, are you awake?*" I heard Dad in my mind.

I replied, "*Yes, Dad, I am!*"

"*Sorry, we had to do that to you, honey....*"

"*Yeah, it's kind of strange knowing my father helped design a gigantic robot to test my limits!*" I mentally sighed.

"*Believe me, honey, it's for the world's good!*" Dad said in my head. (Yeah, I'm still not used to that.)

"*Ah, why?*"

"*Honey, aliens are coming! Earth will need you to be as strong as possible!*"

The end for now...

***

Book 3

The Power of Teamwork!

Ape in the Morning...

I leaped through the air. I spotted the huge ape bounding down the street carrying a big bag of jewels in one arm and a bunch of bananas in the other. Yeppers, this was not the way I envisioned starting my first morning of summer break. I wanted to be sleeping in a bit, at least until 10, not chasing down a crazy gorilla that the police couldn't stop. But this was my life now that I was super. I really shouldn't complain; after all, I probably am the strongest person on Earth. Like Mom tells me, with power comes responsibility. I just wish I could be responsible, especially after a nice breakfast.

"Stop, Ape!" I shouted. I was not really expecting him (or her) to listen. After all, he (or she) was an ape.

The ape stopped and turned to me. "Actually, I'm a gorilla," she said in a female voice.

I landed near the ape, ah gorilla. "Okay, fine," I said. I had to admit to being surprised the big gorilla had responded.

The gorilla pointed to me. "You know, being a superhero, I think you should know these things!"

I shrugged. "Sorry, it's summer break. My mind is on vacation. Plus, it's not even 8 am!"

The gorilla looked at a watch on her arm. "So it isn't," she laughed. "Like they say, the early gorilla robs the jewelry store and the grocery store and gets away!"

I shook my head. "Ah, nobody says that…."

The gorilla grinned and hopped up and down, itching her armpits. "Well, they will now!"

Looking over this strange gorilla, I noticed she had a bandage around her head that seemed to be anchored to her temples by metallic disks. I guessed that these were what made this big gorilla, not your average gorilla."

I dropped my hands to my hips, trying to look relaxed. By now, the police had caught up with us and had positioned themselves all around. "Look, you can't win this," I said to her as I pointed to the police.

Channel 13's Oscar Oranga was also there filming with his crew. I was still not used to seeing myself in the news.

"They can't shoot me because I'm an endangered species," the gorilla laughed. "And I'm way too strong to be stopped by tranquilizer guns!" The gorilla laughed louder. She pounded her chest. "I feel so powerful; I don't even think bullets could stop me!" she bragged. She put the jewels and bananas down. Something told me this wasn't because she wanted to surrender. She took a Kung Fu stance. Oh, there are times when it's a pain to be right. She motioned to me with her lead paw. "Come, little human, let's see what you got…."

"Fine, two can play that game," I told her. I also took a Kung Fu stance, one arm high, one arm low, legs bent, ready to pounce. Yep, this is what my life had become, Kung Fu fighting with a 600-pound bionic gorilla. I took a deep breath. I exhaled. "HIYA!"

My breath shot across the road and hit the big gorilla. Her nostrils flared. "Oh my...." She whimpered. Her eyes rolled to the back of her head. Her arms locked to her side. Her legs buckled. She fell to the ground stiff as a board. My super hearing could still hear her heart beating. Lucky for the big gorilla, my breath hit from six feet away.

I pointed at her. "See, this is what happens when you make me fight crime first thing in the morning before I get a chance to brush my teeth!"

I covered my mouth, turned to the police, and said. "Take her away!"

Leaping up into the air, I headed home. I didn't want to accidentally knock out the entire police force with my breath. That never goes over well.

Dear Diary: Yeah, I just clobbered a big strong gorilla with a whiff of my breath. It's a feeling of empowerment and embarrassment at the same time. I suppose I should worry a bit about who is turning gorillas into super strong, intelligent thieves. But something tells me I'm going to find out soon enough!

Breakfast of Champions...

A couple of leaps and bounds brought me home. After a quick shower and a good tooth brushing, I met Mom downstairs at the breakfast table. She had the TV on and was watching my battle. The headline read: 'Super Teen drops 700-pound Super Gorilla with Super Morning Breath.' I still didn't know if I should be proud or ashamed or both.

"Busy morning," Mom said, sipping on a cup of great smelling coffee.

I sat down and gulped some orange juice. "You know, same old, same old." I smiled. "I don't think that gorilla was much more than 600 pounds," I added. "Plus, they all kind of got excited by the fact that my breath knocked the thing out, rather than the fact that it was an extremely intelligent gorilla robbing banks and stores!"

Mom pointed to my pancakes. "Eat! You know as well as anybody we can't control what the press says," She shrugged. "Some people will love you, and some people will be jealous; others might be scared of you. Your job is to do your best to make the world a better place. The more you do that, the more people you will have on your side. No matter how many of them you KO with morning breath."

"Or BO or foot odor or farts," I added, chomping down on a blueberry pancake.

"Yeah, just more of who you are," Mom laughed. "And don't talk with your mouth full!"

I nodded, "You're right."

I knew I wasn't supposed to have my phone at the table, but I couldn't resist a quick glance at my social media. Of course, Wendi and some of her crew think I'm a menace and should never leave the house, especially in such an outfit. Do you believe they still don't like my outfit?"

"Honey, you could wear the exact same clothes that Wendi wears, and she wouldn't think they looked good on you at all."

"Yeah, you're probably right!"

"Jason texted me earlier. Of course, he's worried about an intelligent gorilla popping up. Thinks this might be the start of a trend."

Mom bit on a piece of bacon. "You should ask your dad if he knows anything about this. This is the type of stuff BM Science loves to tinker and toy with."

I took a big bite of bacon. Man, I love bacon. "Yeah, Dad said he wanted to do lunch with me today."

Mom rolled her eyes. "That may not be a coincidence."

"Plus, he wants me to meet him in his lab," I added.

Mom steadied her gaze on me. "Yeah, definitely not a coincidence."

"Should I cancel?" I asked her.

She smiled and shook her head. "No, the man is your father. Sure, he has flaws, lots and lots and lots and lots."

"I get it, Mom."

"...of flaws. But he would never do anything to intentionally harm you." Mom finished.

"He built robots to test me!" I said.

She grinned. "Yeah, but he knew you could handle those." She paused and took a sip of coffee. "Besides, your dad knows if you went missing, your grandmas and I would rip that BM Science building to the ground!"

I grinned. "Yeah, Grandma Betsy says she'd love to knock the place down with one of her farts."

Mom nodded. "She would, and she could. Your dad knows that."

I took a sip of hot cocoa. Sure, it was a hot day, but any day is a good day for hot cocoa.

"Yep, this is what my life has become, fighting super robots and super cyborg gorillas. Plus, having a grandma who can fart down a building. Not to mention having a couple of half-vampires living in my street and a witch in town. All the while juggling the same problems other kids do: school, social media, and boy-girl crushes."

Mom got up and hugged me. "Poor baby, the strongest person on Earth."

I hugged her back, and although I knew she was a bit cynical, it was still a lot to accept. "Don't get me wrong. I love my life and most parts of being super. But ya gotta admit, vampires and witches, are weird!"

Mom shook her head. "Not weird, just different. I'm sure they simply have family mutations that allow them to do things most people can't do."

I liked Mom's way of looking at it. I had to admit that Jess, Felipe, and Tomas did seem mostly normal. I still preferred them way more to 'Miss Perfect Wendi.' That girl had been driving me crazy since third grade, always putting me down, and it seemed that would never change.

Mom started gathering the dishes. "I have a busy day at the hospital today. I'm scrubbing in with one of our newer doctors, Donna Dangerfield. She's brilliant, and her research is cutting edge. We've been recruiting her for years, trying to get her to come on board. She finally said yes a month ago. She's now working for us, the university, and BM Science as well."

"Wait, I've heard that name...before...." I said.

Mom nodded as she headed to the sink. "Yep, back in the day, she was an MMA fighter. The woman is strong and smart."

"Impressive!" I said. "Can you get her autograph?"

"Nah, that wouldn't be professional, but you can ask her when you start volunteering at the hospital. You haven't forgotten have you?"

I finished off my cocoa. "Nope, it will be fun. That and my LAX coaching are my normal kid activities for the summer. They keep me grounded!"

Dear Diary: I am so glad my mom is so grounded. She's been through what I am going through and came through it just great. Man, I wrote "through" a lot. Back on topic, I love that my mom may be super, but she is still so normal and sane!

Sweet Dreams?...

After Mom left for work, I had a few hours of free time before meeting my dad for lunch. Being the first day of my break after a long year of school, I figured the best course of action would be to head upstairs and get some much-needed sleep. So, I did.

I fought back the urge to check my Instagram and Facebook accounts just to see what people were saying. I've been Super Teen long enough now to know I had some fans and some haters and some people in between. No matter what I did, some people were going to like me. Other people just weren't going to like me.

Whatever, I couldn't bend them to my will and make them like me. Well, I could maybe do that, but then I wouldn't like me. I knew that was the important thing, and I needed to like myself. And I did. Yeah, sure, I wasn't perfect. In fact, far from it. But I was making my part of the world a better place by being Super Teen and Lia Strong. Sure, Super Teen could do amazing things. But Super Teen was only a small part of me. Lia Strong was who I was. And Lia Strong did a lot of good. I worked with kids. I was going to start working at the hospital. I'm true to my friends. And I don't turn people I dislike into dust with my heat vision. That last one made me giggle.

I set the timer on my phone for two hours and laid down on my bed for a much-deserved nap.

My head hit the pillow. The next thing I knew, I found myself standing on a pavilion in a park. The sun shined brightly above in a clear blue sky. The birds sang sweetly. I noticed I was wearing a long white dress. It felt like silk. Oh wow, this was a wedding gown, a long flowing beautiful wedding gown. I felt something pull on my hair. Christa and Marie stood behind me, adding the final touches. The strange thing was, Marie had an electronic device on her temple, much like the gorilla I fought today.

Christa walked in front of me. "Oh, you make such a beautiful bride!" she gushed. She had a makeup brush in her hand. She shook her head. "Girl, woman, your complexion is perfect as always!"

The wedding march started to play. "They're playing your song!" Marie told me with a smile.

Dad walked up to me. He had a white tuxedo on. By the way, he walked, he looked like a robot that needed oiling. I knew he felt awkward, so dressed up. He held out an arm for me. "You ready, honey?"

I took his arm. We began walking down the aisle. Man, it looked like the entire town was there. Wait! Was that the president? What! Is that Liam Hemsworth here too! Ah, he looks sad I'm getting married. Then I noticed the band had Taylor Swift singing for them.

I walked past my mom and all my grandmas. They smiled and blew me kisses. Wendi sat in the second row. But it looked like she was alone. No Brandon! Hey, wow, maybe I was marrying Brandon? Or could it possibly be Jason? Jason has been my BFF for as long as I can remember. I always thought it could turn into more… Maybe somebody else? Whoever my groom was, they had their back turned to me. Not very traditional, but part of me realized this was a wonderful, strange dream.

Suddenly my stomach began to rumble. I put my hand on top of the rumble to ease it. No, no, I thought. This is not the time to fart! Okay, I guess there's never a good time to fart, but certainly not when you're at your own wedding. 'Hold it in, hold it in,' I thought to myself. But you know, sometimes these things have a mind of their own. A tiny silent fart snuck out. I smiled when it didn't make a noise. Phew, that was a close one. But I heard a bunch of gasps behind me. Looking over my shoulder, I saw the entire crowd had fallen over holding their throats. A flock of birds dropped from the sky. I think I saw a plane crashing off in the distance. Woe, talk about silent but deadly...

OMG, I just wiped out my wedding! I just dropped my entire family, all my friends, Liam Hemsworth, the President, Taylor Swift, and my husband.

I woke up in a cold sweat and looked around me. "I hoped that dream wasn't prophetic!"

Trying to calm my racing pulse, I sat up in bed and stretched, the dream still racing through my head.

Whoa, it smelled like I needed another quick shower before I went to lunch with Jason and Dad. I believed this was a record; two showers before midday! Part of the price I paid for being super.

Dear Diary: It's amazing how fast a dream can turn into a nightmare. Does it work the other way around? Can you turn a nightmare into a dream? Truthfully, I'm not sure. I think about silly things. Well, at least my wedding gown was way awesome!

Lunch with Dad...

I was glad Dad invited Jason to our lunch at BM Science. Dad likes Jason because he says Jason reminds him of a young him. Not sure if that's good or bad. I am sure that Jason is my BFF and helps to keep me grounded. I love hanging out with him. I always feel more secure when he's around. I know without any doubt, Jason has my back and my best interests in mind.

"I'm glad your Dad invited me!" Jason said as we biked towards the BM Science complex.

One of the great things about Star Light City is the city has everything a kid or adult would want, and it's all very well laid out. Everything is easy to get to. They have a great public transportation system, and the Uber service is the best! On days like this, though, nothing beats getting around on our bikes. (Well, besides leaping and running at super speed.)

"Me too," I told Jason.

"Not only does BMS have the best and latest high-tech gadgets, but they do have a great cafeteria!" Jason smiled.

"Plus, you get to hang out with me!" I told him.

He beamed at me. "That's a given, Lia!"

There are times when Jason knew the right thing to say.

He rubbed his stomach. "Plus, I swear their cafeteria has the best French fries in the world!"

Of course, other times, he thought more with his stomach.

"Plus, the servers are robots!" he added.

Then there was the geek side of Jason. I did like the way that no matter what the situation, Jason was always Jason. I found that refreshing and comforting. When your life is changing fast, some constants are needed.

Jason, my family, and my friends were those constants. Yeah, sure, they would grow and change just like me, but they were always there to support me. Even superheroes need the support of others.

We biked up to the security gate of BM Science. Three guards in green uniforms were there to greet us. The guards

233

smiled when they noticed who we were. The lead guard, a tall man with a big jaw, gave me a salute, "Ms. Strong, it's an honor to see you and your friend again."

He pointed to a bike rack (with two spaces) on the other side of the fence. "You and Mr. Michaels may park your transportation there. A shuttle is on the way to accompany you to your father's office area."

"Thank you," I said, though it felt weird being saluted.

As we parked our bikes, Jason whispered to me, "Do these guys know that you're Super Teen?"

I shrugged my shoulders. "I have no idea."

A driverless red golf cart rolled up to us, and a computerized voice said, "Greetings, Lia and Jason. I am the Machine Automatic Communication System, MACS for short."

"Hi, MACS," I said.

"Nice to meet you," Jason said.

"Your father is quite anxious to see you both!" MACS continued. He beeped happily. "Now, please enjoy the ride."

We sat down in the back seat. MACS pulled out. Both of the back seats had a little information screen in front of them.

"We are ten minutes away from your father's office space. Do you wish to watch anything? Would you like me to play some music? I am also capable of telling jokes...."

Two glasses of water popped out from under the back seat. "I have estimated you must be thirsty after your bike ride."

Jason and I both took our waters. "Thanks!" Jason grinned.

He sat back in his seat. "I could get used to this!"

"I have a massage setting for both the seats if you wish," MACS said.

"Sure," Jason laughed. "And tell us a joke, please."

"My pleasure, Jason. Why is seven the scariest number?"

"No idea," Jason replied.

"Ms. Strong?" MACS prompted me.

"I don't know either," I grinned.

"Because seven eight nine," MACS responded in his robotic voice. He added a ba bump, bump drum sound.

"Funny!" I said with a smile towards Jason.

"Now, what type of music choices do you have?" Jason asked, clearly getting into this.

"I have all the music from Bach, as that music has been known to stimulate the brain," MACS answered.

"Fine, hit us," Jason said.

"Mr. Jason, when you are in control of a car, hitting things is not an option," MACS replied.

"Just play the music."

Music started to play. It sounded better than I thought. I couldn't help but be impressed, not only by MACS but by how the BM Science facility had grown in just a few months. There were even taller, shinier buildings than before, and each building had more floors than I remembered. The grounds were perfectly manicured. Of course, the most interesting part was that robots of all sizes wandered around interacting with the human workers. The humans acted like this was perfectly normal. I guess for them, it was. Could this be the future?

We drove through the large compound until we reached a tall round shiny glass building. MACS pulled up to the double doors of the building. "Your father is on the 20th floor...."

Looking up at the shimmering tower, Jason gulped, "Wow!"

What MACS didn't tell us was that my dad's office took up the ENTIRE 20th floor of the building. The room was large enough for us to have a LAX game and maybe even two, side by side. As I exited the high-speed elevator, I could barely see my dad's desk across the room.

"Wow," Jason gulped again as we walked in. "I want to be a scientist when I get older!"

Another red cart zoomed up. "Hello again," MACS voice said from the cart. "Would you like a ride to your father's thinking area?"

I shook my head. "No thanks, we'll walk."

"Yes, soak it all in!" MACS said.

After a bit of walking, we got close enough to dad's desk to see him clearly without using super-vision. He had been sitting there talking to a person I can only describe as the best-looking woman or person I had ever seen. The woman had long blond hair that danced down her shoulders, big blue eyes, and a perfect porcelain complexion. She had the tall slim build of a master ballerina.

"Wow, your dad's assistant is beautiful!" Jason said, far louder than he should have.

The sound of Jason's voice was heard by Dad and his stunning assistant, and they both looked at us.

"Thank you, Jason," the beautiful woman said.

Dad smiled. He pointed to the woman, "Lia, Jason, I'd like you to meet Hana."

We reached Dad's large desk. Hana held out a hand to each of us. "Lia, Jason, I've heard and read so much about you two."

We each shook her hand. Her grip felt much more powerful than I would have guessed. Yeah, she had to be some kind of athlete.

"The pleasure is mine," Jason said, unable to take his eyes off Hana.

"Nice to meet you, Hana," I said. I raised an eyebrow. "I've heard nothing about you."

Hana smiled and released our hands. "Your father is a man of many secrets. He doesn't believe in revealing them until the right moment. And then he likes to be dramatic!"

"You seem to know him well. How long have you been working with my dad?" I prompted.

Hana smiled. "Oh, for as long as I can remember."

I shot Dad a look. Not sure why. He and Mom hadn't been together for a LONG time, but I still felt weird that he hadn't told us his assistant happened to be the most beautiful woman in the world.

Hana noticed my look. Dad either didn't notice or didn't care.

"I'll go prepare the meal!" Hana said, walking away.

Dad pointed to a couple of chairs across from his desk. "Come and sit!" he smiled. "I'm so glad you are here!"

"The place is amazing!" Jason said. "And so is Hana!"

"Thanks!" Dad smiled. "Now that I am mega senior VP of science and research, I have some perks!"

"So, I noticed," I said, a bit of contempt in my voice.

Dad looked at me, his eyes wide open. "Honey, why the attitude?"

If he didn't know, I wasn't going to tell him. "Nothing," I sighed.

The force of my breath knocked him over in his chair.

I shot up from my seat. "Dad, sorry," I said, leaning over his desk. "Sometimes, I still forget how strong I am!"

He laughed as he stood back up. "No problem, honey! I know it can't be easy being super. That's why I want to help."

"Help?" I looked over my shoulder. "Oh no, you're not going to attack me with another robot. Are you?" I looked back at him. "Really, dad, that gets old fast!"

Dad laughed again. "No, you've passed all those tests with flying colors."

"Is this about aliens?" I asked. "You mentioned aliens before."

Dad's face became serious. "Yes, honey, I believe we are not alone in this wide universe. There may be many universes. The odds of us being the only intelligent beings

237

is...." Dad raised his eyes to the ceiling as he did some calculations in his head.

"Very small," Jason said.

"Exactly!" Dad smiled. "I think I can safely say we are not alone. In fact, aliens may be watching us. I'd be shocked if they weren't interested in Super Teen. You and other super beings may be the next evolution of man."

"Wow!" Jason said.

Now, that was a lot to take in.

Dad shrugged. "Then again, you might not be. You just might be genetic freak accidents that mean nothing to the course of human evolution."

"Gee, thanks, Dad!"

Dad grinned. "Just stating a possibility. The thing is, no matter what, you are important to the here and now. That's why I am here to help."

"How so?"

Dad stood up. "Honey, I've built you a new uniform!"

Dear Diary: My dad may be a bit crazy, but he's still my dad, and I love him. Could I be the next step in evolution? Nah! He just said that to toss me off guard so I wouldn't question him having such a beautiful assistant.

Uniform 2.0...

"Dad, you don't build a uniform!" I told him.

"I do!" he said proudly, probably more proudly than he should have. Especially coming from a guy who seemed only comfortable in a lab coat or sweatpants.

Dad pushed a button on his desk. A table popped up next to the desk. I saw a white bodysuit, a pair of plain looking shoes, two clip-on earrings, and a watch on that table. The watch looked cool. But definitely nothing else.

"Tada!" Dad said, once again sounding much more proud than I thought he should.

"So mega cool!" Jason was clearly impressed.

I got up and walked towards the table. I picked up the plain white bodysuit. It seemed to be made of many little balls. The shoes also appeared to be made of the same substance. I showed them to Dad. "You gotta be kidding! I can't wear this in public!"

Dad's eyes popped open again. One of them began to twitch. "You don't understand. This is the latest in NACT: Nano Adaptive Clothing Technology."

I looked at it again. "It looks weird and high-tech. I'll give you that. But I can't wear this under my clothing or out in public!"

Dad shook his head. "Yes, this can be worn under your outfit if you wish, but it's also perfectly capable of being the only outfit you need. It has self-cleaning nano-bots, so you can wear it continuously for at least 24 hours without having to worry about pit stains or odor."

"Oh, gross, Dad!"

Dad nodded. "A normal human could wear it for weeks without the nano-bots needing to recharge. But in your case, thanks to your powerful sweat…24 hours should be the max. Then take it off so it can recharge."

"Gee, thanks, Dad!"

"Honey, I'm just stating facts."

I showed him the suit. "But this thing is ugly as anything!"

Dad turned to Jason. "Do you want to tell her? After all, this was your idea."

"What?" I asked, turning to Jason.

"Jase has been emailing me his ideas. They're great!" Dad smiled.

Nice to know my dad talked more with my BFF than he did with me. But I let that go for now. If Jason had thought of this, there had to be more to it. I showed the outfit to Jason. "What am I missing here?"

Dad pushed another button on his desk. A screen started lowering itself from the ceiling.

"What the?"

"Just put it on!" Dad said.

The screen landed between myself and dad and Jason, giving me some privacy. I looked at the white outfit made of balls. I stuck out my tongue. Since Dad and Jason couldn't see me, I made a loud "Blah" sound.

"Just put it on!" Jason shouted.

I kicked my shoes off. I kind of hoped my feet stank just to teach them a lesson. Sadly, for once, they didn't. I sighed and put on the suit and the shoes.

"Don't forget the watch and the earrings!" Dad shouted over the screen.

"Watches are so 1990s!" I called back.

"Retro is cool!" Jason yelled.

I slipped the watch on over my wrist. It sealed itself automatically. A smile appeared on the watch's face. "Hello again!" MACS voice said from the watch.

"MACS?"

"Yes, Ms. Lia, I am the interface for this suit and earrings. Please put on the earrings. Accessories are so important!"

I popped on the earrings. They were little studs that sat on my earlobes. I finally had an idea where this was going.

"Okay, raise the screen!" I called to Dad.

The screen started back up towards the ceiling. Did Dad have the screen installed on his ceiling just for this? Okay, Lia, think big picture here, I thought to myself. I turned my attention to Dad and Jason, who were smiling at me like I was the coolest Christmas present in the world. "You guys going to tell me how this works?" I asked.

"This will allow you to switch instantly from your regular clothes to your choice of uniform and back to your normal clothes again," Dad said.

"No need to carry your disguise around!" Jason added.

"I can't go around in public in this, and with no mask!"

Dad and Jason just smiled at each other. "MACS uniform style one."

My suit of white balls instantly turned into a pretty pink top that buttoned down the front and a fitted black skirt. The earrings projected a black mask over my eyes. "Okay, wow!" I said, jumping up and down in excitement. "What else can it do?"

"Touch the screen or ask MACS?" Dad replied. "He'll tell you anything you want to know. He makes Siri look sad." Dad smiled.

"Good one, Doc!" Jason told Dad.

I groaned. Dad jokes are the worst, especially when they come from your own dad.

"MACS show Lia her options...."

"Please look at my screen," MACS instructed me. "I can scroll through outfits on a timer, or you can flick left or right. To select an outfit, just tap it."

A cool red outfit appeared on the screen. "I can also modify any colors choices you want," MACS explained.

I flipped through one, then another, then another. A super adorable yellow dress with little shoulder straps popped up on the screen. I smiled. I tapped the screen. The next thing I knew, I had that outfit on.

"This would be perfect in light blue," I said.

The outfit instantly changed to a light blue color. "I'd like the shoes to be dark blue," I said.

My shoes became the exact shade I wanted. "How about some heels?" I asked.

"Sorry, don't do heels," MACS said.

Dad laughed. "Yeah, your mom would clobber me!"

I looked at dad and Jason. "You guys did good!"

"Oh great! She likes the NACT!" Hana said, walking back into the room, pushing a cart. The cart had BBQ chicken, hamburgers, and hot dogs on it. Plus, there was fresh corn on the cob, a huge bowl of French fries, and a platter of salad. To drink, we had lemonade.

"I have prepared the lunch!" Hana said proudly.

A picnic table popped up from the floor. Jason raced over to the table. "I'm famished!" Jason said.

"What a surprise!" I laughed.

Dad walked over and joined us as Hana began to prepare plates. Hana handed me a plate loaded with chicken, corn, and salad.

"Thanks!" I said.

"My pleasure!" Hana told me.

Suddenly it hit me. I sniffed Hana. "You don't have a scent!" I told her.

Hana smiled. "I will take that as a compliment!"

"Here's the thing. Every person I know has a scent!" I exclaimed.

Hana shrugged. "Perhaps they need to shower more?"

"I'm not saying they smell. Well, some of them do. But my super smelling power can smell the differences from person to person."

"Good for you!" Hana said, patting me on the shoulder.

I sniffed her. "You're a robot!" I said.

Hana grinned. "Actually, the proper term is android."

Dear Diary: So...instead of hiring the most beautiful woman in the world to be his assistant, dad built her. I'm not sure that's better! But at least she isn't beautiful and human. Wow, my dad is so smart...and weird...

A Bit of Business...

I shot Dad a look. "You built an android that looks like the perfect woman!"

Dad munched on a chicken leg. He looked at me. "Yes, yes I did," he smirked.

Jason stood up and walked towards Hana. "You look so amazingly lifelike."

Hana nodded. "I am alive. Just in a different way than you are."

Dad popped a French fry into his mouth. "We at BM Science are very proud of Hana. After all, she was a team project. She helped us build her."

"Ah, come again?" I asked.

"They built my brain and interface system first. That enabled me to consult on the rest of my specs!" Hana said proudly.

"Best billion dollars this company has ever spent!" Dad said, drinking some lemonade. He spilled some on his lab coat but didn't seem to mind. Yes, even in Dad's big fancy office, he still wore his lab coat. I could see why now.

Hana looked at my dad. "You were right about Lia. It's amazing how quickly she deduced I was not human."

"That's my daughter!" Dad said, trying to clean the spill off his lab coat. Of course, he just made it worse.

Hana looked me in the eyes. Her eyes seemed incredibly human at first glance, but when I peered deeper, something was missing. I just couldn't be sure what. Maybe it was my brain playing tricks with me now.

"I'd love to spar with you sometime," Hana told me.

"Ah, sure," I said slowly, not quite sure how to respond.

"Man, I'd pay to see that!" Jason said.

I shot Jason an unimpressed look. He turned back to his seat, sat down, and started to eat. "Great chicken!" he told my dad, a little awkwardly.

I turned my focus back to Hana. "Sure, some other time. Today I have LAX coaching with my team."

Hana nodded, "Yes, I know. I put it on your father's calendar." She paused. "I look forward to a stimulating sparring session with you."

I looked at Dad. "Any other surprises for me today?"

Dad popped some lettuce into his mouth. "Actually, there is one more."

Of course, there was. It wouldn't be Dad if he didn't keep popping out surprises.

He took another bite of lettuce. "Yum, I love this dressing!"

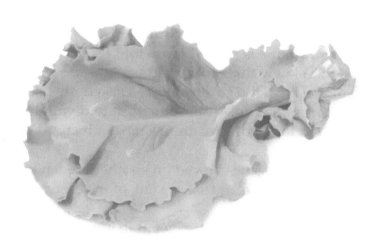

"Dad, what's the other surprise?" I shouted.

The force of my voice knocked both dad and Jason backward. A few strands of Hana's hair flew out of place. She shook her head, and the hairs dropped back into place.

"Remember that gorilla you fought?" Dad asked.

"You mean the one I fought a few hours ago?" I asked.

Dad nodded. "Yep."

"Hard to forget a super strong, intelligent bionic gorilla," I noted. "Especially when the fight was this morning!"

"Actually, it's not bionic. It's cybernetic," Dad corrected.

"I knew that," I said. "Bionic just seemed more dramatic."

Dad laughed. "Do you need more drama in your life?"

"Good point," I sighed. "Dad, where are you going with this?"

He sat back in his chair and put his hands behind his head. The chair started to tip. He sat forward. "We have the gorilla now."

"What?" I asked.

"Josh's dad knew the gorilla was too much for the Star Light City Police to handle. I mean, come on, they just aren't equipped for a cybernetic super gorilla."

"Ah, my name is Jason," Jason told Dad.

"Right, I knew that!" Dad said.

"So, you have the gorilla now?" I asked my dad.

"Of course, we do! Your father just told you that!" Hana answered for Dad. "We are the most advanced facility on Earth."

Dad nodded as he chewed on another French fry. "We have her locked up nice and safe in one of the basement facilities."

I got quickly to my feet. "I want to see her!"

Dad smiled. "I knew you would. Let's just finish eating, and Hana and I will escort you down to the subbasement!"

"Subbasement? So cool!" Jason said.

I looked at Dad. His smile didn't waver. "Trust me, honey, the gorilla is fine. Better than fine!"

I decided to trust him. After all, he was my dad.

Dear Diary: Seems like the more I get to know my dad, the more I realize there's a lot I don't know about him. The man is brilliant. He built me a great uniform that will save time and help keep my identity safe. (And it keeps me smell-free for a day!) But he also built a perfect android that wants to spar with me. Plus, he's holding the gorilla I fought with this morning. Man, parents are complicated!

Going Ape...

We finished lunch and then ate a dessert of fried ice cream made by Hanna. After that, Hanna and Dad escorted Jason and me down to the subbasement. I wasn't sure how far underground the subbasement was buried, but it seemed to take forever for the secure elevator to make its way down there.

The elevator opened up into a brightly lit hallway that spanned as far as the eye could see. Hana walked out and pointed down the hall.

"This way, please," she instructed us.

"Is the gorilla alright?" I asked nervously. "She got a good whiff of my morning breath. That could drop a herd of elephants from a hundred yards away."

Dad smiled. "She was a little out of it when our team picked her up. Your breath does pack quite the punch. But my team tells me she is fine now."

We continued to walk for what seemed like forever. I don't know what I found to be weirder, me knocking out gorillas with my breath or Dad having a team. I never really thought of dad as an in-charge kind of guy.

"How's she doing now?" I asked.

Dad hesitated.

"Dad, tell me!" I ordered. Not sure if I fired off some of my pheromones or not. I still had no control of that power.

"We removed her cybernetic attachments," he said slowly.

"And?" I prompted.

We came to a door. Hana put her hand on the door. It popped open. "See for yourself!"

I walked into a room that had a big cage in it. Still, as far as cages go, this was a nice one. There was a lot of green grass in the cage, a tree, and a little stream of water. A couple of keepers in orange suits were feeding the gorilla some greens.

"She seems happy," Jason said.

"She does," I agreed.

Hana looked at me. "Before we removed her attachments she told us her name was Jodi with an i…." She motioned towards Jodi. "You can go visit with her. She's fine."

I walked forwards slowly. "Hiya, Jodi," I said with a smile.

Jodi tilted her head. She farted. Then she started laughing and clapping!

Dad laughed too. "Since we removed the attachments, she's become a normal gorilla, a normal gorilla with a sense of humor."

I stuck my hand into the cage.

One of the attendants warned me. "I wouldn't do that ma'am. Even in this state, she's very strong!"

I ignored the attendant. I didn't like being called 'ma'am, but I knew they were trying to be polite and helpful. "I'll be fine," I said. "She'll be gentle with me."

Jodi took my hand. Her hand engulfed mine. I wasn't sure if she recognized me without my costume and without her super intelligence, but the look in her eyes seemed to suggest that she did. She shook my hand lightly. She smiled at me. I returned the smile.

"Good girl, Jodi!" I said.

"Hoo, Hoo!" She responded.

"See, she's fine," Dad said. "Sadly, the enhancement cybernetics disintegrated the moment they were separated from her. But Jodi shows no ill effects. We do know the implants must have been put on her recently since she had that wrap around her head."

"What's going to happen to her?" I asked, still keeping my eyes on her.

"She will go to a nice gorilla sanctuary down south," Hana told me. "There are five others of her kind there. She will be comfortable."

"Do you know where she came from?" Jason asked, always looking for clues.

Dad shook his head. "Nope. There have been no reports of missing gorillas, and I'll tell you a missing gorilla is hard to miss."

"Do you know who did this to her?" I asked.

Dad hesitated again.

"Dad tell me, please!"

He took a step back. He looked at the ground. I knew he didn't want to say anything. "We have no proof yet," he said.

"Dad."

Hana spoke up. "The work has a resemblance to the groundbreaking work of Doctor Donna Dangerfield. She has done a lot of study on enhancing people through cybernetics."

"She just moved here like a month ago! That can't be a coincidence!" I said.

Dad shook his head. "Actually, it can be. A lot of people now are working on cybernetics, including us. It's a hot field. The number of older people in the world is growing rapidly. It would be great if we found ways to make growing old easier. Cybernetics offers a lot of promise."

"But why pick on a harmless gorilla?" I asked.

"Cause gorillas are a lot like people," Jason said.

"Exactly," Dad said. He pointed to Jason. "I like this Joey guy!"

"Jason!" Jason, Hana, and I all told dad.

"Right, Jackson," Dad said. He smiled. "I know it's Jason." Dad's smile straightened out. He put his arms on my shoulder. "Listen, honey, don't go accusing Doctor Dangerfield yet because..."

I lowered my head. "She may be innocent?"

Dad shrugged. "Yeah, she may be, but if she isn't, we don't want to scare her off by thinking we are on to her. So, if you meet her, just act normally!"

"I'll try, dad. I'll try."

Jason pulled out his phone. "Speaking of normal, we've got to coach a LAX game in less than an hour."

Dear Diary: I was so happy to see Jodi safe and content. I'm not thrilled that somebody would experiment on her like that. When I find out who did, they are in trouble. PS: Dad really has to get Jason's name right!

LAX...

Peddling as fast as we could (without me using my superpowers), we got to the LAX field five minutes before the "game" was scheduled to start. Luckily, our other coaches, Marie and Christa, had the kids lined up and doing drills. Well, as much as you can with kids their age. When they are seven and eight years old, it's pretty much like herding cats.

Today, our green team was playing the red team. Normally, who they played was no big deal. After all, these games were supposed to be about having fun and learning the basics of LAX, so the score didn't matter. Today's but since we were playing the red team coached by Wendi (and Brandon and Lori and an older girl named Tanya Cone).

Yeah, I know it probably shouldn't have. After all, Brandon is always nice and certainly has a great smile. Lori, for all her roughness, is a nice person too. She is a faithful teammate. During our season, she made a great pass to me as I made the winning goal of the last game of the year. That felt good. Oh, and Tanya is a very cool kid. She must be fifteen or sixteen and only coaches this level because her little sister, Kayla, plays on the team. Kayla's a cute kid too, with dark hair and dimples. Like a miniature version of Tanya. The entire red team and their coaches are fine. They are all lovely normal kids. Sure, they can be high-strung and annoying, and at times, it's tempting to pop my shoes off and put them all to sleep with super foot odor. But I know they're just kids being kids. They aren't the problem.

The problem is Ms. Perfect Wendi. I knew if her kids beat my kids, I would never hear the end of it. Sure, we weren't supposed to keep score, but the kids do, and so do the coaches. I guess it's human nature. Being superhuman doesn't change that with me. I wanted to make sure her kids didn't beat my kids. I had a secret weapon, and his name was Felipe.

When Felipe saw me, he came running over and hugged me. "Yeah, Lia, you're here!"

Felipe's cousins Tomas and Jess were also there to cheer on Felipe.

"Hey, Lia," Tomas said.

"Beautiful day for a game," I told them.

Jess smiled. "I wouldn't have it any other way."

Tomas used to have a crush on me, but I didn't return his feelings. He's nice and all, but I don't think I'd want to date a half-vampire. (Even though vampires aren't really vampires like in the movies, just humans with slightly different genes...) Still, I didn't like him that way. And I was happy that he and Jess, the witch, had hooked up.

Felipe motioned to me to bend down to him. I did. He whispered in my ear, "Now I'm not supposed to use my powers of speed and strength here. Right?"

"Felipe, today we'll make an exception. Do you know what that means?"

His face lit up. "That I can have lots of fun!"

I nodded. "Yes, but we want to keep the game close."

"Got it!" Felipe said, running towards the other players on the field.

The referee, who happened to be Janitor Jan from school, blew her whistle for the two teams to meet in the middle of the field.

My coaches and I walked out to meet Wendi and the other coaches. Wendi shot me a look. I shot her a look. I had to concentrate to NOT use heat vision on her.

"Remember, coaches, these games are for fun and learning," Ref Jan warned us all.

"Of course," Brandon said with a beautiful smile. "It's all about sportsmanship and a good game!"

"And having fun!" Jason added.

"And learning the rules," Lori added.

"And staying safe," Marie added.

"And sportsmanship," Christa said, looking at Wendi and me.

I held a hand out to Wendi. "To a good game!"

Wendi took my hand without looking at me. "Good game."

We returned to the sidelines. Jan blew the whistle, and the game began. Both teams just pretty much ran up and down the field, chasing each other and occasionally making a pass. Most of the kids simply enjoyed the running.

The coaches would yell things like:

"Pass pass!"

"Fall back on defense!"

"Watch your man!!!"

"Keep those sticks high!"

"Stop chasing butterflies!"

"Guys, you're running off the field."

"Guys, stop having a burping contest in the middle of the field!"

You know that kind of stuff. Like I said, it would mostly be easier to herd cats. The one exception on our team was Felipe. He darted up the field, dodged other kids, and tossed the ball into the net. Wendi's team also had their own star player, Kayla Cane. For every goal, Felipe scored, Kayla would fly up the field and score right back. I thought, wow, this kid's amazing, as Kayla ran up the field with the ball in her stick.

She approached the goal.   Suddenly everything froze in place—everything except Kayla, her sister Tanya, and me. But I still stood motionless, just to see what was going on. Tanya walked out to Kayla on the field.

"Kayla, you know this is a no, no!" Tanya scolded, her finger wagging.

Kayla sighed. "I know you told me not to slow time this much, but I was tired from all this running, and I needed a little break. This time control stuff is hard!"

Tanya crossed her arms and glared at her little sister. "Yes, yes it is. That's why we're not supposed to do it. Only in extreme emergencies. Playing a lacrosse game isn't an emergency."

"But I need juice now!" Kayla pouted. She pointed to our side. "We can take some of the other team's juice!"

Tanya shook her head. "No, that would be wrong."

Kayla pointed at me. "Hey, that girl is moving."

"What do you mean, Kayla?"

"Tanya, I saw her blink. When we time slow, people can't blink!"

Tanya and Kayla locked their eyes on me. I stood there trying not to blink. The thing is…when you try not to blink, it makes you want to blink. I blinked. I sighed. I walked towards them.

"Yeah, I'm not frozen," I admitted. "Everything seems heavier than normal, but I can move through it all. It's weird."

Tanya nodded. "Yep, that's the time displacement you're feeling."

"How can she move?" Kayla asked. "Only you, mommy, and I are supposed to be able to move." She looked at her sister questioningly.

Tanya held out a hand to me. "Lia Strong, nice to formally meet. Oh, should I call you Super Teen?"

I grinned and shook her hand. "Let's stick with Lia, please. So how did you guys get your powers?"

Tanya looked at me. "Wow, not big on small talk, are you?"

I dropped my head. "Sorry, but your powers are just so cool."

Tanya smiled. "Our grandma was pregnant during the Chernobyl accident in Russia. Our mom, Meesha, was born with the ability to slow time. And now, so can we." She shrugged. "No idea why or how. What about you?"

"I come from a long line of superwomen. When we turn 12, we've absorbed enough energy to activate our powers." I explained.

It felt good to talk to another who had powers and seemed normal. I mean, I like Jess and Tomas, but he's a little creepy, and she's a little aloof.

"So, we're going to keep each other's secrets?" Tanya asked.

"Of course!" I said.

"Good! Now let's get back to the sidelines and get this game over with, I mean going again." She looked Kayla in the eyes. "And no more stopping time!"

Kayla groaned. "OK!"

Dear Diary: Well, Mom and Dad have always thought that there would be other super people out there. And now that I was super, I would most likely notice them. This is something I don't often say, but wow, my parents were so right. I'm hoping I can be friends with Tanya as it would be so cool to have another super kid I can chat with about being super. Somebody who can relate to the ups and downs. Plus,
having a friend who can slow time could come in handy!

Post-Game Meet and Greet…

The game ended in a 10-10 tie. We gathered up our kids and our gear. The kids lined up in the middle of the field and shook hands, giving each other high fives. I liked teaching the kids the importance of being good sports, even against Wendi's team.

Speaking of Wendi, I saw her heading towards me. A tall red-headed woman accompanied Wendi.

"Good game, Strong," Wendi said, a little begrudgingly.

"Thanks, Wendi," I said with as much sincerity as I could fake.

Wendi pointed to the somehow familiar woman. "My aunt wanted to meet you. She's kind of new in town, but also famous and a great doctor. Your mom works for her."

The woman stepped forward and offered her hand to me. Her arm was ripped with muscles. "Lia, I'm Doctor Donna Dangerfield. And I work *alongside* your wonderful mother." Doctor Dangerfield said with a smile.

I shook her hand. "Nice to meet you, Doctor."

She released my hand. "Please call me Donna."

By now, Jason, Christa, and Marie had noticed Donna. Jason and Marie rushed over.

"Doctor Dangerfield, I've been a fan of yours for a long time!" Jason gushed. "I've followed your research in cybernetics and your fighting career!" he babbled on, turning a slight shade of red.

Donna turned to him and smiled. "Wow, I don't find many people who follow both my careers."

Jason turned even redder. He took a step back. He tried to talk but failed.

Marie stepped forward and grinned. "Doctor Donna, so nice to meet you. It's an honor to be volunteering in your lab!"

Donna smiled. "Ah, so you're one of my student lab rats, as Doctor Stone calls them."

Everybody else laughed, thinking it to be a joke. But after the events of today, I wasn't so sure.

Marie grinned. "Yes, my friend Lori and I are hoping for careers in medicine and science!"

Lori joined the conversation. "I just loved your MMA work...how you systematically destroyed your opponents. I respect that!"

Donna nodded. "Thank you, I guess," Donna turned her attention back to me. "Well, I just wanted to introduce myself and to say you are always welcome in my lab at the hospital."

"Ah, thanks," I said.

Donna put her arms around Wendi and Lori. "Come on, and I'll take you both out for ice cream, doctor's orders!" Donna turned to us. "Would you guys like to join us?"

"Sorry, we're taking our team to Mr. T's for food," I answered.

Wendi pulled on her aunt. "Come on, Aunt Donna, you'll see them at the hospital."

"Another time then," Donna said.

The three of them walked away.

"Wow, she's amazing!" Jason said, his mouth gaping open.

"Close your mouth," I told him.

Marie pointed to our equipment. "I'll go help Christa pick up our gear." Maybe Marie sensed I needed to talk to Jason.

I nudged Jason. "Remember, Doctor Donna may be an evil mad scientist!" I said softly.

"She doesn't seem evil to me!" Jason replied.

The thing was, she didn't seem evil to me either.

Dear Diary: I don't know what's more annoying, the fact that Doctor Donna Dangerfield is Wendi's aunt or that she appears to be so lovely. I mean, I really should like this woman. She's smart and strong and everything I strive for. Yet I can't help thinking about what somebody did to that poor sweet gorilla, Jodi. If that was done by Doctor Donna, then she truly isn't a good person. I mean, can you do something like that and still be good?

Senior Heist...

Not sure why but I always loved going to Mr. T's after the game with our kids and their parents. Sure, chaos reigned when we were there. Instead of herding cats, it became herding cats on sugar. But I loved it. Christa says it's because I love punishment. I enjoyed the bonding of team and family and food. Jason says it's because I'm a leader but also a team player. Not sure if he's right about the leader part.

Today as an extra treat, Tanya and Kayla joined us. Sure, Kayla wasn't on our team, but she knew every kid from school. That's one of the smallish town advantages, and everybody knows everybody. Of course, that could also be a disadvantage at times. But like Grandma Betsy says, you take the good with not so good and the bad and the terrible. It all evens out.

We pretty much took over Mr. T's. But Mr. T and Mrs. T didn't seem to mind. They enjoyed this mixed crowd even more than I did. Of course, they were making money out of us, so obviously, that helped.

We sat at a coach's table. The parents sat at a couple of parent's tables next to us. And the kids pretty much just ran around stopping by their parents' tables to snack now and then.

I sat and munched. I soaked in the atmosphere. Jason must have seen me smiling. He nudged me. "Wow, you seem happy."

I nodded. "I am. It's been a good day. "

Just as those words left my mouth, we heard police sirens. Lots and lots of police sirens. Darn, I shouldn't have mentioned the words, 'good day.'

Jason looked at his phone. He turned to me and whispered, "This might be a good time to test your new uniform."

I stood up. "I'm going to go check out those sirens."

Of course, the entire restaurant had already headed out the door to see what was going on. There's something about sirens and possible danger that gets people so excited.

Jason walked out with me. He showed me his phone. It read: Bank robbery in progress Star City National Bank.

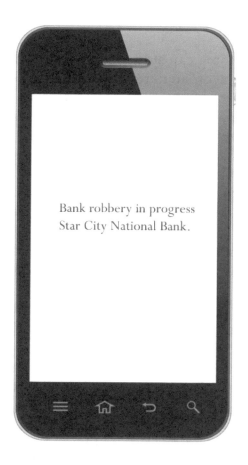

Since the bank was located right across from Mr. T's, we had a birds-eye view. Four police cars had pulled up in front of the bank. Four policemen took position behind their cars. Four other officers carefully approached the bank. Their guns were drawn. The four officers, three men, and a woman entered the bank.

"Looks like the police have this under control!" I said.

The three policemen came flying out of the bank. They crashed to the ground – out cold.

"Okay, maybe not." I groaned.

An old-looking bald man in shorts and a white t-shirt walked out of the bank holding two big bags of money. His white shirt had an orange ink stain on it, but he didn't seem to care.

"Ha! Nothing can stop me!" the man shouted.

The policewoman darted out of the bank. She aimed her gun. "Halt!"

The old man bent down and wiggled his butt in her general direction. The police lady dropped her gun, grabbed her throat, and fell over, blue. The old man laughed. "Ha! Silent but deadly!"

The police all looked at Captain Michaels for direction. Captain Michaels aimed his weapon. "Last chance! Hands up, or we shoot!"

The old man grinned. "You got me. Nobody ever says that Grandpa John is a dummy." He lifted his arms up. His smile grew.

The police in front of Grandpa John grabbed their throats and mumbled, "Oh the stench…" and fell over.

The cloud of old man underarm odor crept across the street. Everybody on the street dropped at once. I felt a little dizzy, but okay. I fell over, pretending to be affected. I wanted to catch the old guy off guard.

Grandpa John sniffed his armpits, "You wimps! They don't smell THAT bad!" He started laughing and walking down the street.

I pushed the button on my watch to activate my new uniform and got to my feet. I had to admit that it was handy to have this uniform. "Excuse me, it's wrong to fart and use super BO without saying excuse me!" I shouted. Okay, not the best and wittiest comeback, but I was still new to this.

I raced down the street at super speed. I moved in front of Grandpa John. I held out my hand. "You're lucky you didn't kill anybody. Give up the money now, and I'm sure the courts will go easy on you." I noticed he had two electronic disks attached to the side of his forehead near his temples. The disks were pulsating.

Grandpa John looked at the bags of money. He looked at me. He shook his head. "I need this money. I might want to go to an old folk's home someday, and those things are expensive. They are a rip-off! I don't need an old folk's home. I need this money for a nice tropical vacation. Maybe I'll go with some beautiful swimsuit models. That Christy Brinkley is still very beautiful and only about 20 years younger than me. She'll come!"

I shook my head. "I doubt you'll get her or any other model to go with you!"

"But I'm rich now!" he shrugged.

"It's not your money," I told him.

He shook his head. "Possession is 99 percent of the law."

Now I shook my head. "Nope, that's not how it works."

He dropped his bags of money and made a fist at me. "What do you know? You're just a kid!" He shouted like I had been standing on his lawn.

"His name is John Johnson," MACS said to me from my watch.

That caught me off guard.

"I am constantly monitoring your situation," MACS told me.

I put my watch close to my face. "How can you see him?"

"I got his image from the bank's security camera," MACS informed me.

Grandpa John moved towards me. "You young kids, ya can't go three minutes without looking at your fancy-dancy

263

technology." He showed me his muscles. "Back in my day, our muscles were our technology."

"Okay, you know that makes no sense. Right, Grandpa?"

"It makes sense in its own way!" he insisted.

I shook my head. "Nope, it doesn't!"

He curled his hands into fists. "Young lady, I boxed in the army!"

He threw a punch at me. I caught his hand. I hit him with an open palm to his chest. He went flying backward and fell over.

"Okay, I never claimed I was a good boxer," he groaned from the ground.

He jumped back up to his feet. He turned and aimed his butt at me. "I hate to do this to such a pretty young thing, but you asked for it!" He let out what had to be the loudest fart I've ever heard: PPRRRTTTTP!!!!!!!!!

"Oops, that may have been a wet one!" he laughed.

I staggered back a step or two. "Is that all you got?"

He dropped his head. "It is…those big ones take the wind out of me."

"Now, are you going to give up nice and quietly?" I asked, moving towards him.

He pulled out a pair of glasses from his shorts. He popped his glasses on his nose. "Look, you can't hit a man with glasses!" he told me.

"Fine, have it your way!" I told him.

"You're letting me go?" He asked.

"Oh no, giving you a taste of your own bad medicine," I told him.

"Say what?" he said.

I turned and hit him with one of my own farts. A quiet, ladylike pft…

I heard him drop to the ground before I even turned around. Yep, I had out-farted a pumped-up old man. But I still wasn't sure if I should be proud or ashamed.

"Your father would like pictures of the cybernetic disks he's wearing," MACS told me.

I bent down next to the out-cold Grandpa John. The disks on his forehead melted away. "I so hope my fart didn't do that!" I said.

Dear Diary: First super gorillas, now super senior citizens. I need to get to the bottom of this and fast. The good news was, my new uniform worked great. Plus, having MACS as my contact "machine" would probably be useful. Maybe even get me closer to my dad! I'm glad that Dad's back in my life.

Evening with Mom

Luckily, the people on the street all recovered quickly. Since they were all out cold I didn't have to explain why Super Teen showed up while I was missing.

That night, Jason and I talked about the situation with my mom and grandma Betsy. It turns out Grandma knew this John Johnson guy.

"John Johnson is a good man," Grandma told us as we sat around the dining room table. "A bit on the crazy side, but I like that in a man."

On the TV we saw Oscar Oranga doing an exposé on whether super people were dangerous and what we could do to protect ourselves. Checking my social media, people seemed split as they pretty much always were. Some of the people pointed out that Super Teen showed up to save the day. Others, like Wendi, claimed that no super people popped up until Super Teen showed up. Others blamed BM Science. BM Science's online rep assured people they had nothing to do with this or with Super Teen, who was a treasure. I smiled at that.

"Lia, put your phone down and pay attention," Mom told me.

"Sorry," I groaned. "It's just good to know what people are saying. Lots of them are on my side, which is good. I still think this is that Doctor Donna's fault. And I'm not just saying that because she's related to Wendi."

Grandma nodded. "Your dad did say the tech used on the gorilla, and John seemed to resemble the tech that Dangerfield has experimented with!"

Mom shook her head. "The woman is brilliant, she has an M.D. and Ph.D. in physics, and she's a Vet, and I believe she's a lawyer as well. She and her junior associate, Doctor Gem Stone, even makes house calls!"

"Doesn't mean she can't be evil," I said.

"She's also a world-class athlete and pretty good looking," Jason added.

I shot him a look.

Jason held his ground. "She is!"

"The boy's right honey, she is a hotty," Grandma told me.

I heard a knock at the door. "Who could that be?" I asked.

Mom pointed to the door. "I suggest you check!"

I opened the door to see Janitor Jan standing on my porch. "Ah, hi…" I said.

Jan walked past me. "I think you ladies need to hear what's going on."

I staggered. "Wait? What?"

I grabbed Jan by the arm. "What are you talking about?"

Jan looked at me like I was a child, a very dim child. "Oh, so your mom hasn't told you yet?"

"Told me what?" I said with a tap of my foot.

Jan reached into her purse and pulled out a card. She showed it to me.

"Ah, Jan, that's a coupon for odor eaters," I said.

Jan put a finger up. "Right, very important item." She put the coupon back and pulled out another card.

I read the card. "This is a gift certificate to MacDonalds," I sighed.

"So, it seems!" Jan said, holding up the card with far more pride than I thought she should have. She shook the card and shouted, "WAMMO: card be true!" The letters on the card started moving around and reforming until they read: Sorceress Supreme.

I looked at the card and wiggled my head. I blinked my eyes.

"You see it right! I'm Sorceress Supreme!" she said proudly.

"But you clean our school!" I exclaimed.

Jan started towards the dining room table to join the group. "Who says a lady can't have two jobs? The school gives me health insurance and dental. Plus, I keep an eye on you!"

Jan looked at my mom. "I thought you told her Isabelle?"

"I was waiting for the proper time," Mom said.

Jason stood up, "Do you want me to get you a seat?"

Jan grinned. "Sorry, kiddo, I like you, but this conversation is just for us ladies," She pointed at Jason, "WAMMO! You're a stool!"

In a flash of bright energy, Jason glowed, shrank, and became a stool. Jan walked over and sat on him.

"Ah, I'd like to point out you just did that to my BFF!" I told Jan.

Jan laughed. "Don't worry, it's not permanent, and I probably won't fart."

Mom leaned on the table. "Jan, what do you have to tell us?"

Jan crossed her arms and adjusted her butt on Jason. Now that was another phrase I never thought I'd say. "Yesterday, when I was cleaning the hospital, I saw that John Johnson guy visit Doctor Dangerfield's office."

"Wait, you work at the hospital now?"

"Big picture, honey," Mom told me.

"Right," I looked at Mom. "So, Jan's at my school to keep watch on me?"

"And to clean," Jan said. "I love cleaning things!"

"It was her idea," Mom told me. "And when Jan gets an idea in her head, you don't get in her way, unless you want to spend a few days as her shoe insoles," Mom said as if she had been talking from experience.

"Darn straight!" Jan said. "Can we get back to the business of who the bad guy or gal is before I turn you all into shoe insoles!"

"Right," I said. I set my gaze on Jan. "What did you learn at the hospital?"

Jan rolled her eyes. "I just told you! I saw that John Johnson talking to Doctor Dangerfield and her people. That can't be a coincidence."

"See, Mom!" I said.

Mom put her head in her hand and leaned on the table. "I admit it looks bad. Let's just not focus on her, though. It could be a setup."

"Well, at least there will be three of us in the hospital, starting tomorrow," Jan stood up. "I gotta be at work early tomorrow, so I'd better get rolling."

Jan stood up and looked at the Jason stool. "He'll turn back in a bit."

"Hey, why'd you zap him? You didn't tell us anything he couldn't have heard?"

Jan walked by me and smiled. "I know. He just dropped some paper on the floor. He didn't mean to, but littering makes me mad."

Jason popped back into himself. "Wait? What did I miss? Why does my back hurt? Why do I smell a butt smell?"

I patted him on the shoulder. "From now on, be sure to keep the school as clean as possible!"

That night, getting ready for bed, I put on a pair of clean pink PJs. MACS sent me a text (which was weird, BTW) saying that it would be good if I removed the suit after the day I'd had, so the nanobots had an easier time keeping it fresh. I would have taken it off anyhow. There are times when you want to wear your usual comfortable clothing, and tonight I wanted a bit of comfort sameness.

Out of curiosity, I sniffed the armpit area of the nano suit. It smelled a little but not THAT bad. I picked up one of my nano shoes and sniffed it. It had a little kick to it, but I was pretty sure they weren't lethal. I guessed the suit and even the shoes could keep up with me as long as I wasn't overstressed. The good news was...I could lift my arms up without having to worry about knocking everybody out. The not-so-good news was that I'd lost a potential weapon. But I figured if I got nervous or angry enough, I could sweat through those nanobots. ☺

Shep popped into my room. He loved sleeping by my side, and I loved having him with me. Shep, as always, just couldn't resist sniffing my shoes. I'm not sure why. I guess he wasn't as smart as he seemed. Shep walked over to the shoes beside my bed and took a whiff of them. He didn't drop over stiff. Instead, he laid down and went to sleep. He started dog snoring and sounded so cute. So yeah, my shoes still had some punch, just not an instantly drop everything in their tracks punch.

MACS sent me another text from the nightstand I had put him on.

MACS: Okay, even the latest tech can't quite keep up with your feet.

For some strange reason that made me feel good.

Dear Diary: Wow, busy day today. I got a new uniform. I met an android. I met some siblings who can slow time, and I learned our school janitor is also a sorceress. Who would have thought that out-farting a super senior citizen wouldn't be the strangest thing that happened in my day?

Doctor Stone...

On the drive to the hospital, Jason and I went over our plan with Mom the next day. "Now remember," Mom said from the driver's seat. "You have no actual proof Doctor Dangerfield is behind this!"

"True," Jason chimed in from the back. "My dad interviewed her, and she seemed very honest. She admits that the technology used on the gorilla and the old guy, John, was very similar to hers, but not hers."

"She talked to John at the hospital!" I insisted. Yeah, I know I was a bit stubborn and pigheaded here, but this woman was related to Wendi.

"She showed my dad the video," Jason said. "They talked about John's poor health problems and his frequent farting and burping. Doctor Dangerfield told him her work wouldn't help him with any of those! At least not yet."

I looked across the seat at Jason. "I'm just glad you'll be working in her lab so you can keep an eye on her!"

Jason nodded. "Oh, I plan to... she's so smart and strong and pretty," he sighed, a dreamy look on his face.

"Lia, just make sure you're not biased just because she's related to Wendi!" Mom warned me. "Our hospital administrator, Mr. Thom, spent a lot of time and money recruiting Doctor Dangerfield. Plus, she's working with the University and with your dad's company."

"I'll try," I said, shaking my head in frustration.

We pulled into the hospital parking lot. The hospital was an impressive brick building with large windows that looked out onto the well-groomed patio that led into the main building. The original building had to be one of the oldest structures in Star Light City, but it had been updated many times. According to Mom, we now offered all the latest services and some cutting-edge technology that wasn't available anywhere else. Mom insisted we were lucky to add

Donna Dangerfield to the list of talented staff who worked there. I still wasn't sure.

Walking into the reception area of the hospital, I was reminded of how big the place was. Mom had signed me up for volunteer work because she thought it would be good for me. I guess she didn't like my initial summer plan of sitting around all day just chilling and relaxing. I told her I needed my downtime to recharge and fight crime and stuff. She insisted that donating three hours of time each morning to the hospital would allow me plenty of time to recharge. Plus, she said it would make me feel better about myself. It would show me I can contribute to society as Lia. I knew she had a point. That's why I didn't put up too much of a fight. Of course, now that Doctor Dangerfield worked here, I figured I could keep an eye on her as well.

We found Marie and Lori standing in the lobby. They were talking to a short, pale-skinned, red-haired woman in a pink lab coat. Marie and Lori pointed at Jason. The pink lab coat lady nodded and started walking over to us.

"Who's the lady in pink?" I asked Mom.

"She's Doctor Gem Stone, junior associate to Doctor Dangerfield."

Doctor Stone nodded to my mother. "Doctor Strong, nice to see you as always."

Doctor Stone looked at Jason. "Jason, I'm here to introduce you to the Dangerfield lab. I'm sure you will find this to be a rewarding experience. Doctor Dangerfield may be fairly new to our town, but she is a leader in many fields."

"Yes, I'm very excited!" Jason said.

Doctor Stone pointed to Marie and Lori. "Go join the girls. There is an introductory welcome speech being given by Mr. Thomas in the conference center. Doctor Dangerfield would like her interns, as she calls you, to sit together. Then I will escort you to the lab."

"Excellent!" Jason said. I could feel his excitement. I even heard his heart rate speed up.

Doctor Stone turned her attention to me. "You must be Lia Strong," she said, extending a hand to me.

I shook her hand. Her grip was surprisingly strong.

"Nice to meet you, Doctor Stone," I said.

"Your mother is part of our hospital family. Call me Doctor Gem."

"Nice to meet you, Doctor Gem," I said.

Doctor Gem grinned. "We wanted you to be part of our group too, but your mother told us she'd prefer you to have more general duties. Of course, we honored your mother's wishes. After all, she is one of the finest doctors in the hospital." Doctor Gem paused. "Well, I'd better get back to my charges. I hope you have a great time here! I look forward to seeing you around!"

Once Doctor Gem was out of earshot, I turned to Mom. "Wait, I could have been in Doctor Dangerfield's lab? I could have been watching her all the time?"

Mom sighed. "It's good you're not there. I don't want you obsessing."

"I don't obsess!" I insisted.

Mom put her hands on her hips. "You're obsessing now!" she insisted.

"I'm persistent," I admitted.

Mom pointed to a blue hallway. "Follow the blue hallway. You'll find the conference center."

I knew enough not to push my luck any further with Mom. I hugged her then started towards the conference center.

Dear Diary: I know I shouldn't jump to the conclusion that Doctor Dangerfield is guilty. But my gut says...don't trust her. I trust my gut.

The Talk...

Christa had saved a seat for me next to her in the conference room, which to me was actually more of a small auditorium. There were about 30 of us kids there. My friends and I were certainly the youngest. I recognized some of the older kids, Tanya and Michelle Lee. Tanya gave me a cool nod. Surprisingly, Jess also sat there on the other side of Christa.

"Jess, nice to see you here," I told her.

Jess nodded. "Thanks, it looks good on the resume."

"Never thought of you as the type of person who would worry about resumes," I said.

She smiled. "Hey, Witch College can be very competitive!"

On the stage on a podium stood a big bearded man in a suit that seemed too tight. The man cleared his throat. We all turned our attention to him. "Greetings and salutations to our Lab Learners and Helping Hands, student volunteers," the man said. "I am Mr. Thomas, the lead administrator at this hospital. This program was my idea, along with Doctor Strong and Doctor Dora. You won't meet Doctor Dora because she is exploring the Amazon. But our newest doctor, Doctor Donna Dangerfield, has agreed to take her place in this program and accept Lab Learners. We are pleased to have you all here. I am sure you will help us as much as we will help you prepare for the future. I now pass you over to Nurse Payne."

Mr. Thomas sat down. A tall skinny woman in a white nurse's uniform took the podium. She adjusted her hair, and it seemed to make her bun even tighter. "You will all be given uniforms to wear over your regular outfits. The Lab Learners will be given green lab coats. The helping hands will be given light blue smocks. Please note, these are only on loan to you all. We expect you to keep them clean."

Nurse Payne took a deep breath then continued. "The rules for you all are very simple. Lab Learners, you are to watch and learn from your doctors. You may do anything they ask you to do. You may not do anything they don't ask you to do. It's very easy. Any questions?"

By the look that Nurse Payne gave the group of Lab Learners, she obviously didn't want any questions. "Good." She turned her attention to us helping hands. "Now for you helping hands, your rules are a little more complicated. Your role here is to aid the patients. You must give them an extra human touch. So, here is what you must always do: offer them something to read, talk with them, hold their hands, change the channel on the TV, help them with their computers and phones."

She paused to let that sink in, even though it wasn't that tricky.

"Now, here are the things you can do IF, and ONLY IF, a nurse or doctor says you may: Give them a snack or water, raise their bed, take them for a walk." She paused again. "I know these things sound simple and harmless, but for some patients, they could be disastrous. So do not perform any of those tasks without checking with a nurse or doctor."

We all nodded.

"Finally, if a nurse or doctor or technician asks you to do something, you do it. If they want coffee, you get it for them. If they need something taken from floor 1 to floor 10, you do that. Even if it's pee. If they have a spill that needs to be cleaned, you do that. By making the nurses happy, you also help make the patients happy. Any questions?"

Christa raised her hand.

"Yes, young lady?" Nurse Payne said.

"Will anybody vomit on us?" Christa asked.

Nurse Payne smiled. "Good question. And most likely, yes. If that happens, though, we will issue you with a new gown."

Dear Diary: Oh yeah, I am volunteering to get vomited on! Man, being a superhero in real life isn't nearly as glamorous as in the comics and on TV. I'm not at all happy with my mom for signing me up for this, but at least I can keep an eye on Doctor Dangerfield.

Anthony...

First, I read a story to a cute little girl named Tiz. She needed to have her tonsils removed, and my mom was her doctor. I assured Tiz the operation would be over in a snap, and she would be fine. Tiz seemed happy knowing that her doctor was a mom.

Next, I met with a young woman named Tess and her husband, Juan. Juan paced up and down the room nervously, as they were expecting their first child. He showed me his hand. It was red from Tess squeezing it so hard. I let Tess squeeze on my hand for a bit. All the while, I patted her head with a wet towel the nurse had given me. Both the nurse and Juan seemed grateful for my help.

After that, I checked in on an older man. The man sat up in his bed and smiled when I walked in. He put down the American Science magazine he'd been reading.

"Well, hello there, young lady!" he told me.

"Hi, my name is Lia, and I'm a helpful hands volunteer," I smiled.

The man put his hands behind his head. "I'm Anthony," he said with a slight grimace. "Sorry, sometimes my arthritis gets to me a bit."

"Anything I can do for you?" I asked.

"Can you make me 50 years younger?" he asked.

"Sorry, no," I said with a little shake of my head.

He patted a chair next to his bed. "Then come sit, talk for a bit."

I did as he asked. After all, I liked talking and sitting.

"You don't mind talking to an old man?" he asked.

"Nah," I said with a little wave of my hand. "I know that older men know stuff!"

He laughed. "Only thing I know is, I wish I knew what I know now when I was younger. I could have done something about it then!"

"What are you in here for, Anthony?"

He pointed to his hip. "Getting a new hip. Went eighty years with the original. They tell me this one will last just as long."

"I hope it doesn't hurt too much," I said.

"Lia, I fought in two wars. This is nothing," He laughed. "Got shot in the buns in Korea!"

"Say what?" I said, trying not to snicker.

"You can laugh, honey. It was pretty dang funny if you weren't me! Oh, I wasn't running away. A sniper hit me from behind in the behind."

"Good to know," I giggled.

"I got a purple heart for my butt!" he said proudly. "If I can handle being shot in the butt, I can handle a new hip. I was hoping for one of those fancy new cybernetic implants."

"Really?" I said.

He bobbed his head. "Yes, ma'am. I'm an engineer by trade, so I love all the new technology. Sure, I can't figure out how to lock my phone and keep it from pocket dialing, but I still love it."

"So, you met with Doctor Dangerfield?" I asked.

"Yeah, nice lady. She didn't think I qualified. She told the other guy and me there she would like to help, but her techniques are still too new to try on older patients."

"Oh..." I said. "Do you remember the other guy?"

"Nice guy, John something. He farted a lot, but pretty much everybody does at our age." He looked at the ceiling, then back at me. "Funny thing is, her assistant doctor came to us afterward. She gave us her card and told us she might be able to help us."

"But you didn't take her up on that offer?" I asked.

"Nah, I'm too old to want to be a lab rat!" Anthony said with a grin.

An announcement came over the hospital intercom. "Doctor Sparks, please report to the basement level."

I knew there was no Doctor Sparks in this hospital. In fact, that happened to be the emergency code for security to show up. Something weird was going on in the basement. I needed to check it out. First of all, as Lia, then if needed, as Super Teen.

I looked Anthony in the eyes and took his hand. "I'll be back to see you! I promise!"

He grinned at me. "I'll be counting on it!"

Dear Diary: I've found working in the hospital to be very rewarding. I don't say this often, but maybe Mom was right! Anthony was such a nice old man. Not only that. But I learned something interesting...

Doctor Dangerfield discouraged patients from working with her.
And more interesting, Doctor Stone didn't agree with that.

Lab Rats?...

I slipped down to the basement at super speed so I wouldn't be spotted. When I arrived, my mouth dropped open. There, standing in the hallway, stood the biggest gray rat I had ever seen. The rat stood so large he took up the entire width of the hall. Two security men stood in front of it. Their guns were drawn.

A man in a lab coat stood between the rat and the security people. "Don't shoot Algernon!" the man pleaded. "He's just scared...."

"Okay, now this is different," I mumbled.

The big lab rat started forward, pushing the doctor down. The security men opened fire.

"No!" I shouted.

Everything froze in place. "Did I do that?" I said out loud.

"Ah, no!" I heard from behind me. I turned to see Jess and Tanya standing there. "I did," Tanya said.

"We thought you might need some help!" Jess told me.

"Thanks," I said. "We're like a teen or almost teen girl justice league!"

Tanya walked up to me. "You can pick team names and costumes afterward. First things first." She pointed at the bullets frozen in flight. "You grab the bullets. They're too hot for me. I'll disarm the guards."

"Nah, I got the guards' weapons," Jess said. She waved her hands, and the guns vanished from the guard's hands. "I love vanishing things!" Jess said.

Meanwhile, I walked forward and grabbed both the bullets out of the air. I crushed them to dust in my fist. I pointed to the cameras. "What about those?"

Jess grinned. "I've been jamming them with magic."

I walked forward and picked up the giant rat. Its breath reeked of cheese. "I'll put it back in its cage," I carried the rat down the hall. I found a room that was a giant maze. I dropped the rat into the middle of the maze. I worked my way back out. "Now that was weird," I said. "I wonder why the hospital has a giant rat and maze?"

"I'll un-slow time, and then Jess can interview the scientist," Tanya said.

"Want me to turn the guards into lab rats?" Jess suggested. "I don't like that they were going to shoot a poor defenseless giant rat!" She pondered what she had said. "I stand by my words."

"Just make the guards go away," I said.

Jess raised her arms. "You mean make them vanish?"

"No, just make them forget and go back to work."

"Right, I knew that," Jess said, flicking her red hair behind her shoulder.

Tanya snapped her fingers, and time started moving at regular intervals again.

The guards and the scientist seemed confused. "What the..." they all said.

Jess waved her hands in front of the guard's eyes. "Return to work. Nothing to see here! Nothing happened here," she ordered.

"Yes, master," they said as they walked away.

The scientist stood up and straightened out his lab coat. "My gosh, what are you girls?"

"We're the cool teen girl league of super people!" I said. I turned to the other two. "Okay, yeah, I'll work on that name."

Jess walked up to the scientist. "You won't remember any of this."

The scientist shrugged. "Of course not. I'm a brilliant but absent-minded kind of guy. Now, what do you wish to know?"

I had to admit that I was a bit envious of Jess's control of her mind control power. I wished I could control mine as well.

"Why the giant rat?" Jess asked the doctor.

"Well, funding is always tight, so we're using the same rat to do a growth study while working on treating memory loss. We made an extra smart giant lab rat. He's a nice rat. We just accidentally left the door to his maze unlocked, and he got out. Rats are curious creatures. He got scared when the guards showed up. He'd never hurt another creature. Except for a cat, he hates cats."

"So, you'll make sure this never happens again?" I told the doctor.

"I thought you'd erase my memory like the security people?" The doctor answered.

Jess grinned. "Oh, I will, but I'll let you remember that."

"Sure," the doctor said.

Jess locked her eyes on the doctor's eyes. "Look into my eyes, and you will do whatever I wish. You will forget about all this, except leaving the door unlocked."

"As you wish, master, your wish is my command," he said with a bow. He turned and walked back into the maze room.

I looked at Jess. Jess shrugged. "I might have hit him with too much power."

I put my arms around Jess and Tanya and walked them back towards the elevator.

"A girl could get used to this teamwork!" I told them.

"I'm only available in emergencies," Tanya said, "playing with time is not something that should be taken lightly!"

"I'm only available for things I find fun!" Jess said.

Dear Diary: Okay, I gotta say it was great having other super kids on my side. Not only does that give me people who are also different, but there are some things, probably most things, that are easy to solve with teamwork.

The talk...

I waited for Jason outside of Doctor Dangerfield's office and labs. As I sat there checking out social media on my phone, Doctor Gem Stone walked by. She stopped when she saw me.

"You're Lia Strong, correct?" she said.

I looked her in the eyes. "Yes, Doctor, I am." I didn't point out that she had just met me a few hours ago.

Doctor Stone smiled. "Lia, no need to be so formal. After all, your mother is senior staff here. She's part of the reason Doctor Dangerfield wanted to come here. Please call me Doctor Gem."

"Thanks, Doctor Gem," I said. I paused for a moment, then asked. "How goes your research?"

Doctor Gem smiled, and her face lit up. "You've heard of cutting edge? Well, our technology is laser cutting edge! It's the latest and greatest. We are helping the old and weak feel young and strong, very strong."

"Wow, that's great!" I told her.

Doctor Gem patted me on the shoulder. "My dear girl, we are helping to make the entire human race better. Soon we could have an entire planet of people who are as strong, if not stronger, than Super Teen!"

"So that's good, right?"

Doctor Gem's eyes shot open wide, almost taking up the top half of her head. "My gosh, yes! So so good! They will have the power, yet they'll also have control. They can remove their shoes without knocking out a mall!"

"Ah, I think Super Teen just knocked out a part of the mall," I said defensively, probably more so than I should have.

Doctor Gem looked at me with a tilted head. "Yes, knocking out part of a mall with super stink foot is SO much better!"

"Many of the people that Super Teen put to sleep claimed it was a pleasant experience," I pointed out, unable to stop myself.

"Yes, well, their heads were most likely spinning from whatever pheromones Super Teen zapped them with!" Doctor Gem retorted.

Before I could respond, Jason came popping out of the lab. He had an extra kick in his step. Jason must have heard our conversation as he seemed anxious to break it up.

"Ah, hi, Lia and Doctor Gem! It's been a great morning, and now I'm ready to walk home." Jason grabbed me by the arm. "Come on, Lia, let's get moving."

I didn't budge. Jason pulled back. He knew if I didn't want to move, he couldn't move me. Still, he knew he had to make me move. Jason gave me a friendly nudge. "Come on. Ice cream is on me! I'm so anxious to tell you about all I saw in this amazing lab!"

Somehow that brought me back to my senses. I took a deep breath. I took another deep breath. I looked Doctor Gem in her green eyes. "I look forward to learning more about your amazing technology!"

"I'd love to demo it for you any time!" Doctor Gem told me. She pulled an old pocket watch out of her lab coat pocket. "Look at the time. I have an appointment with a potential patient!"

Doctor Gem walked into her lab. Jason and I started walking home. Jason pretty much rushed me out of the hospital, just in case I was tempted to start up my conversation with Doctor Gem again.

"So, how was your morning?" Jason asked, giving me a little nudge.

"You know, same old, same old," I told him. "Met a few nice people, including this older gentleman named Anthony, who wanted to be a patient of Doctor Dangerfield's. Oh, and of course, I had to carry a GIANT HUMONGOUS lab rat back into his maze!"

"Oh man, you got to meet Algernon!" Jason sighed in a weird mix of sadness and jealousy and awe.

I stopped walking. "Wait, you know about this?"

He nodded. "Yes, of course. Doctor Dangerfield is very open about all her research with us. She says she wants to encourage great young minds like ours to go to college and do amazing things."

"So, the good doctor does cyber implants and grows giant rats?" I asked.

"Well, yes, she's more interested in the intelligence aspect of it, though. She's all about helping people to improve. She's also into robotics," Jason spat his words with excitement. He was talking a million words a minute.

I wiped a bit of spit from my face.

"Oops, sorry," Jason said. "I do get excited sometimes." He paused. "Wait, you met one of our potential patients?"

"Yeah, a nice man named Anthony. He was cool. But Doctor Dangerfield didn't think he was a good fit."

"She said the same thing to the lady we met today," Jason told me.

"Okay, can you get her name and address?" I asked Jason.

"Sure, I think so, but why?" he asked.

"I want to talk to her, to see if Doctor Gem offered her anything," I said. "My gut tells me something is rotten. Now I'm not sure if it's Doctor Gem or Doctor Dangerfield!"

Jason looked at me. "So, you've opened up your mind?"

"I'm willing to consider other options."

Jason smiled. "I'll see what I can find." He tapped me on the shoulder. "You know you can use google too!"

I nodded. "Yes, I am aware of that. I just don't have your flair for it. I believe your superpower is being a wiz with computers," I smiled.

"You're flattering me, Lia."

"With the truth, Jason."

He sighed. "I'll see what I can do."

We arrived at our home. "Okay, Jason, thanks. When you find out that info, please let me know as soon as possible."

Jason nodded. "I think her last name was Gold... but I'll check."

As I headed into my house, I thought Gold? I wonder if she's related to Brandon.

Strange Visit...

I walked into my house and kicked off my shoes. Funny thing, Shep didn't rush up to meet me. I picked up my shoes and sniffed them. Could they have knocked Shep out from a distance? "No, they weren't THAT bad...."

I moved into the living room. I dropped down on the couch. Sure, I had only spent a half-day at the hospital, but it had been an eventful half a day. I saw Shep sleeping in the kitchen. Now that struck me as strange. Shep usually got up as soon as he saw me enter the house.

"Man, I didn't think my shoes smelled that bad?" I said out loud.

"I don't believe they are near-lethal to mammals," I heard a familiar voice say. "Your father's and my nano-technology is working just great."

I turned to see Hana coming in from the kitchen. I jumped up. "What the heck are you doing here?"

Hana looked at me. "Your father wanted me to check in on you," Hana said innocently.

I pointed at Shep. "If you hurt my dog!"

Hana shook her head. She turned her head around at an abnormal angle, to look at Shep. That creeped me out. She looked at me. "No, he seemed nervous about me being in your home, so I used a sonic beam to put him to sleep."

"Why?" I asked.

Hana grinned. "I don't want him to interfere with our testing."

I tilted my head. "Wait, are you checking in or testing me?" I asked, sounding far more confused than I wanted to.

Hana walked towards me. "For me, checking in and testing is the same." Her arms expanded outwards. She grabbed me and lifted me up. "Remember, yesterday you said we could spar!"

"Put me down!" I ordered.

"If you insist!" Hana said. She flung me across the room. I crashed into a wall, leaving a big dent. I rolled down the wall and landed on my feet. Before I could say, 'what's going on?' I saw two fists racing towards me. I ducked. The fists each left more dents in the wall.

I looked over my shoulder at the dents. "If I don't rip you to shreds, my mom will."

Hana walked towards me slowly. "Don't worry. Our construction people will make all repairs."

I rolled my sleeves up. "Let's hope they can put you back together again!" I said. I leaped at her, "Actually, let's hope they can't!"

I hit Hana so hard that her head popped off. The head flew up, crashed off the ceiling, then hit the floor. Her eyes looked up. Her hands, on her now separated body, pointed to the new cracks in the ceiling. "Now that is your fault!" she said. Her body walked over, reached down, and picked up her head. The head molded itself back to the body.

Hana took a fighting position. "I hope you can do better!"

My initial reaction was to flatten her with a fart, but Shep was behind her, and I didn't want to risk hurting (or killing) him. I dropped back into a fighting stance. I waved her forward with my front hand. "Come on, machine, let's see what you have!"

I felt kind of excited about the chance to be able to test out my powers. Normally, I have to be extra cautious when dealing with people or animals. But here and now, I could let it rip. And boy, did I!

I flashed forward at Hana. I pummeled her with at least a hundred punches in less than ten seconds. Each punch, I felt her body bending and contorting a bit. I pulled back. Hana looked like a beat-up trashcan. But I had to give her credit. She stayed on her feet.

I blew on her. She fell to the ground. Just to make sure she stayed there, I thought cold thoughts: ice, ice cream, icebergs. I covered her with a blast of frozen super breath.

My watch beeped. I put it up to my face. Dad's face appeared on the watch face. He smiled. "Wow, that was amazing!"

"Dad, why did you send your Android assistant after me?"

Dad didn't stop grinning. "I wanted to test you and help you let your power out! I knew she couldn't hurt you."

I showed him the house. "Yeah, well, our house isn't nearly as indestructible as I am!"

Dad still had that grin on his face. "Repair crew will be there in five. They will also return Hana to me."

"Yeah, I don't think all the king's horses and all the king's men will be able to put Hana together again...," I said. "She won't be rebooting!"

"Don't fret!" Dad said. "I've got Hana 2.0 here!" Behind Dad, I saw another Hana stick her head over his shoulder. She gave me a thumbs up. Gee, whenever I think my life can't get any weirder, it does.

Dear Diary: My dad sent a super Android out to test me, and by testing me, I mean attempting to rip me apart. Luckily for both of us, I'm pretty strong and tough. Extra lucky for Dad that his crew was able to put our house back together before mom got home. They worked fast. I give them that. I must admit, I did enjoy cutting loose. I guess Dad knew I would. After all, this wasn't the first time I'd battled a super machine made by Dad's company. I wonder if I should worry about that?

TXT U...

That night after dinner, I sat on the couch. Mom rested next to me, pretending to be reading a medical journal, but I knew she would sneak peeks at what I was watching. I planned to veg out and just watch some of my favorite TV shows. I wanted to turn my mind off and relax. That's when I got a text from Jason.

JASON>Got her name. It's Greta Gold

LIA>Great! Thks! Address?

JASON>She's unlisted

LIA>Think she's related to Brandon????

JASON>Want me to ask him?

I had to think about this reply for all of one second.

LIA>I'll txt him

JASON>U sure? U'll risk the wrath of Wendi!

LIA>I'll take my chances

JASON>Good luck.

Mom looked at me. "What's going on?" she asked.

I shrugged. "Just a text from Jason."

I could tell Mom wanted to pry more. So, I gave her just enough information to keep her happy. "Just work stuff!" I smiled.

"I hope you're not asking Jason to be your spy on Doctor Dangerfield!" Mom said. Yeah, Mom read me well.

"No, no," I assured her. "This isn't about Doctor Dangerfield!" I didn't lie.

Okay, I had to be careful with this text to Brandon. I mean, after all, Brandon was the best-looking boy in the school. Yeah, he went out with Wendi, proving he wasn't perfect. But outside of that, he seemed pretty darn close. I found him to be smart, handsome and really nice. Plus, he seemed to enjoy being school president. And I know Jason says Brandon makes a great teammate in LAX. But still, he does go out with Wendi. Well, like Grandma Betsy says, "no accounting for taste."

I wanted to word my text carefully. My phone gave me an alert.

JASON> Don't overthink this. Just ask him about his grandma. Tell him it's 4 work

Man, Jason knew me well too.

LIA>I am not overthinking!

JASON> Have you sent it yet?

LIA>Been talking to my mom...

JASON>Sure...sure

Oh man, he really did know me

LIA>Sending it now

LIA>Just want to make sure it's perfect!

JASON> You know I like the guy, but he's not perfect. He farts like everybody else!

JASON>Okay, actually I've never heard him fart

JASON>Oh NM

JASON>C U 2morrow

My my, did I detect a bit of jealousy from Jason? Jason is so nice. Even when he's jealous, he still can't put a guy down. I smiled. But I got off track.

I sent this text: LIA STRONG>Hey Brandon, this is Lia, just wondering if your grandma's name is Greta?

But I didn't expect an immediate reply. My eyes popped open when I received a sudden alert from my phone. From the sound, I knew it wasn't Jason. Looking down, I saw...

BRANDON GOLD>Hey Lia, yes, as a matter of fact, Grams is named Greta. Why?

Oh, how cute! He called his grandma, Grams. Could that Brandon get any more adorable?

LIA STRONG> She left her reading glasses at the hospital. I'd like to return them to her. After all, she is such a sweet woman.

BRANDON GOLD>Yeah, Grams is the best! But yes, she's forgetful. I can pick up the glasses from u and bring them to her!

OMG, Brandon offered to come to my house! That would be great. I took a breath. Except, of course, for the fact that I didn't have any glasses to return, and I needed to talk to Grandma Gold. I pressed back the urge to say, sure.

LIA STRONG> That's so nice of u, but I better do this myself. It's my job

BRANDON GOLD>Ok, that's great!

LIA STRONG>Can I have her address?

BRANDON GOLD>Doesn't the hospital have it?

Oh, that was a good point. Brandon wasn't just a handsome face. Think, Lia, think. Come on, brain.

LIA STRONG>Yes, of course they do. But silly me, I was so excited about my first day, I misplaced it. I don't want to look bad. Sorry…. ☹

BRANDON GOLD>No, I get it. She lives at 72 Creek Street

LIA STRONG>Thanks Brandon, ur great. Please don't tell anybody

BRANDON GOLD>I think most people know I'm great

What the?

BRANDON GOLD>LOL ☺

So, I had it.

I texted Jason.

LIA> I got it. 72 Creek Street

JASON> Great

LIA> We can visit her before work tomorrow…Creek Street is on the way 2 the hospital.

JASON>Sure

LIA>Oh, by any chance, do you have an extra pair of reading glasses?

JASON>I will c what I cn do!

Dear Diary: How did kids talk before texting? I mean, yeah, they probably used the phone and talked in person, but texting is so fast and fun.

Morning has broken...

I got up, grabbed a quick breakfast, and left mom a note saying because it was such a nice day, Jason and I had decided to walk to the hospital. I knew she'd suspect something was up, but she wouldn't be able to ask me about it until after she got off her shift. By then, the deed would have been done. Nothing to be done about it after that. I don't think even Tanya can reverse time.

Heading out my door, I noticed none other than Wendi pacing up and down in front of my house. I swear I could see steam coming out of her ears. My first instinct was to super speed by her. But no, I couldn't do that. This was a real-world problem, and I needed to deal with it in a real way. My second instinct was to just knock her out. One fart in her general direction, and she'd be toast for the day. But nope, as good as that might have felt and as tempting as it may have been, I needed to face Wendi. I had done nothing wrong.

I took a deep breath as I opened the door. Wendi shot across the yard towards me. Her face was growing redder, and her eyes were growing smaller with each step. "Strong, what are you doing texting Brandon?" she shouted.

I walked towards her slowly, like I'd approach a very dangerous cobra.

"Ah, Wendi…" I said.

Wendi got in my face, so close that I could smell her breath. Of course, it smelled pleasant. "Don't oh hi me! I invented the innocent, oh hi!"

I put up a hand. "Wendi, I just texted Brandon about his Grandma Greta."

"Wait. What? Who? Why?"

I took a step back. "Wendi, we had some contact with Grandma Greta at the hospital. She left her reading glasses there. Jason and I were going to return them to her in person. She seemed like such a sweet lady."

Wendi put a finger in my face. She wanted me to get upset and lose my calm. "Of course, she's sweet! She's related to Brandon. The guy is as sweet as they come."

I fought back the urge to say, "yeah, what the heck does he see in you?" Wendi dropped back, slouched, and sighed. "Sometimes, I think he's even too sweet for me." She

300

took a breath. She looked up at me. "I mean, I've never even seen him in a bad mood or complain. He got a 90 on a test once and told me how it was his fault for not working harder."

"Yeah, I can see where that could be annoying," I said, stopping myself from rolling my eyes.

Wendi put a hand on my shoulder. She looked me in the eyes. "Good, I'm glad. Most people think it must be great having a perfect boyfriend. But I tell you, it's a lot of pressure. I guess that's why I get so defensive. I'm always afraid he'll see I'm not good enough for him and leave me."

I'd never seen this vulnerable side to Wendi before. I kind of liked it. I put my hand on her shoulder. "I assure you, Wendi, the texts were purely business. His grandma seems like a nice lady who Jason and I want to help out. That's it. I'm sure Brandon won't break up with you." I took a step back and pointed at her. "Look at you. You're pretty, you're smart, you're a great LAX player! You're pretty perfect yourself." Okay, my stomach churned with nausea just a little, saying those last words.

Wendi looked at me. "I've got nothing to worry about?"

I shook my head. "Nope," I told her. Then added, "Well, except maybe global warming. I think we should all be worried about that."

Wendi laughed. "That's what I like about you, Lia. You're funny in your own simple way!"

"Gee, thanks..." I said.

She patted me on the shoulder. "I don't know WHAT I was thinking! No way Brandon would ever leave me for anybody. And certainly not you! Woah, sorry to bother you, girl. Thanks for returning Grandma's glasses."

Wendi turned and walked away. I fought back the huge urge I had to burn her in the butt with my heat ray vision. I gave myself a pat on the back. Not only for not burning Wendi's butt, but also for solving a real-world problem without using any superpowers.

I saw Jason walking towards me. He had a pair of glasses in his hands. Yep, Jason always comes through. "What was that all about?"

"Ah, Wendi was jealous that I was texting Brandon. She thought he might leave her for me."

Jason laughed. "Yeah, like that would happen!"

Okay, now I had to fight the temptation to burn Jason in the butt.

He straightened himself up. "Sorry, I didn't mean to laugh. I mean, you are way nice, but Wendi is just..." he sighed.

I gave him a nudge. "Come on, let's go see Grandma Greta!"

Dear Diary: I did see another side of Wendi. I guess even she has fears about not being good enough. Who would have thought that!. It still doesn't give her permission to brag about herself over the rest of us. But at least, now I sort of see where she's coming from.

Man, I still would have loved burning her in the butt with heat vision.

GGG...

We found Grandma Greta outside, pulling weeds from a garden in front of her home. The house even had a lovely white picket fence surrounding the yard. Jason and I unlatched the gate and walked up to Grandma Greta. She was focused so intently on her weeding; she didn't even notice us.

I gave a polite cough.

Grandma Greta looked up at us. "Oh, hello kids, are you selling cookies?"

"No ma'am, I'm Lia Strong, and this is Jason Michaels! We volunteer at the hospital."

Greta smiled. "Oh right. Your mom is the doctor, and your dad is the sheriff, and your mom is a judge!"

"Actually, my dad is police captain," Jason said.

Greta grinned. "Yes, sorry, my memory is not what it was. That's why I went to see that nice Doctor Strange."

"It's Doctor Dangerfield," Jason corrected.

Greta popped herself in the forehead. "Like I said, my mind isn't as sharp as it used to be...too bad Doctor Strange Dangerfield told me her treatment wasn't ready yet." She pointed to her brain and spun her finger around. "Oh well, at least I am happy. So why you kids here?"

I nudged Jason. He took the glasses out of his back pocket. "I believe you left your reading glasses at the hospital," He showed the glasses to her.

Greta leaned forward and squinted. She stood up. She walked towards us. Shaking her head, she said, "Silly me, I didn't even remember I used reading glasses!" She took the glasses from Jason and put them on her head. They fell off. "Silly me again!" she said.

I bent down and picked up the glasses. "You know, I bet silly Jason made a mistake, and these weren't your glasses after all!" I said.

I handed the glasses to Jason. "Yes, silly me!" Jason said.

Greta chuckled. "Well, it was nice of you sweet kids anyhow!" She scratched her head. "Hey, do you young ones know my grandson, Brandon?"

"Yes, ma'am, he and I play LAX together," Jason said.

"I'm on the girl's LAX team, so I know him too!" I said quickly.

"Oh, I didn't know Brandon played LAX. I thought he only played Lacrosse, basketball, and football."

"LAX is what we call lacrosse, ma'am," Jason said.

"You kids today with LAX and LOL and hashtag and inyourfacebook! I can't keep up!" She paused. "My grandson, Brandon, is quite the handsome young man. Isn't he?" she beamed.

"I guess..." Jason shrugged.

"Oh, I hadn't noticed," I said shyly.

Her eyes popped open. "Oh really?"

"Yeah, oh really?" Jason said cynically.

Greta nodded. "Probably for the better. Brandon seems taken with that lovely Wendi girl!"

"Not to change the subject, ma'am, but I was wondering if Doctor Stone talked to you after Doctor Dangerfield did?"

"You mean the lady with the pretty green eyes?" Greta asked.

"Yes ma'am...."

Greta's eyes lit up. "Yes, she did. She said she would like to talk to me about another project she was working on. She thought I'd be perfect for it. She wants to meet with me tomorrow."

"At the hospital?" Jason asked.

"Nope," Greta said. "She told me by doing it outside of the hospital, she can do it much cheaper. I will get the details tomorrow."

"Ah, by any chance, do you have the address she wanted to meet you at?" I asked.

"Of course!" Greta said. "She wrote it down for me."

"Can I have it?" I asked, probably with more excitement than I needed to.

"Ah, why is that?" Grandma Greta asked.

"We just need it for official purposes," Jason said, using his most adult voice.

"I have her card inside on my stand by the door. I'll be right back!" Grandma turned and headed towards her door.

"Nice save there!" I told Jason.

"Hey, I may not be as good-looking as that Brandon guy you 'never' notice, but I still have my uses," he grinned. "So, what's the plan once we have the address?" he asked curiously.

"We go check out the place after work and see what we can find," I replied.

"I pretty much thought you were going to say that," He laughed.

"You know me well."

"Maybe too well," Jason added.

We waited a few minutes. Then finally, Grandma Greta came out of the door, smiling and holding a card. She walked over and handed it to me. I read the card: 1 LOLIPOP LANE.

"Why does that name sound so familiar?" I thought out loud.

"It's the old animal hospital," Jason told me. Man, Jason did know everything.

"I also called that nice Doctor Gem and told her how great it was for her to send some students over to check up on me," Greta said with a smile.

I took a step back. "And what did she say?"

Greta shrugged. "I don't know. I just got her machine. You know doctors are always too busy to talk to actual people."

All right, now this changed our schedule a bit. "Thanks, Grandma Greta," I said. "We'd better get to the hospital now!"

Once we got down the street, Jason turned to me. "We're not going to the hospital. Are we?"

"Nope..." I said. "I need to get to the bottom of this ASAP. Now that Doctor Stone has been warned, we have to act fast."

"We could lose our jobs at the hospital," Jason pointed out.

I increased my pace. "We're volunteers; we make our own hours."

"Good point!"

Dear Diary: I felt a little bad tricking Grandma Greta like that, but it had to be done to help get to the bottom of this. Plus, I did lie when I said I've never noticed Brandon. I notice him the minute he walks into a room. Sometimes I have to force myself to take my eyes off him. But I can't help the way I feel. He's so good-looking!

Angry Birds...

"What are we going to do when we get to Lollipop Lane?" Jason asked me.

I hadn't considered that very carefully. I pretty much just wanted to see what we could find to help prove that Doctor Stone or maybe even Doctor Dangerfield was behind these recent crazy cybernetic people (and animals). Once I got there, I'd figure out a way to stop it.

"We're going to see what we can see!" I said, making a fist.

"Oh, in other words, you don't really have a plan." He sighed.

I couldn't argue with that statement.

We made it to Lollipop lane in record time. The lane was just a long road that led to one building, the old animal hospital. The place had to be 100 years old, so they shut it down last year and opened a sparkling new facility on the other side of town. The new place has a lot of windows and a green area. Even Shep likes to go there. This old building, not so much. It was grey and dingy. It looked like the roof was made of tin foil.

"Okay, Jason, be on the lookout for anything strange!"

Jason pointed up at a flock of birds coming towards us. "Like those pigeons."

I looked up at them. "They look like normal birds."

Jason shook his head. "Nope, they aren't flying like normal pigeons!"

I have no idea how Jason knew this. But I knew enough to trust him. Using super-vision, I zoomed in on the birds carefully. They each had a small cybernetic disk on their heads. "Yep, you are right. This is strange."

The birds flew past us. They pooped over us.

"Incoming poop!" I shouted.

Jason and I dodged the gross poop. It splattered on the ground and burned holes wherever it landed.

"Acid poop!" Jason gasped.

"Man, that is so wrong and so nasty!" I said.

I realized this was just too dangerous for Jason. I may be super and able to take a lot of damage, but Jason is just a regular guy. He's smart and great and all that, but he's not built to take on poop acid. I wasn't sure I was either. But I didn't have much choice.

I pointed in the opposite direction. "Jason, run! Get to the hospital and tell Mom what I'm doing and what's going on!"

"You could text her…or dare I say it, call her…." Jason suggested.

"No, I don't want to give her a chance to tell me not to do this," I said.

"Yes, of course. Why bring common sense into this when we are facing ACID POOPING PIGEONS!!" He pointed up at the birds. "They're turning around and getting ready for another run at us."

"So, get out of here!" I yelled at him. "Go! I'll rush the building. They'll have to follow me!"

Jason stood there, his eyes locked eyes with mine.

"Please do what I ask…." I said.

Jason frowned, clearly worried about the situation, and for a moment, he didn't budge.

Then he nodded and took off. "I'm bringing back help!"

Acid poop started raining down on me. Most of it missed, leaving sizzling holes in the ground. "Who thinks of this stuff!" I said. "MACS, activate my uniform!" I shouted.

"No need to shout, Ms. Lia," MACS told me. "Do you wish me to alert your father to this situation? I am sure he would want to help."

"No, not yet," I answered.

"Very well, ma'am."

"Don't call me ma'am!"

"Yes, Lia, ma'am!"

309

I leaped up into the air towards the ugly old animal hospital. As I jumped, a couple of pieces of acid poop (man, I never thought I'd say that) hit my shoulder. It sizzled my suit and then burned through to my skin. It hurt, but not nearly as much as I thought acid on me should hurt. Still, it bothered me enough to upset my leap.

I landed on my face about halfway to the building.

"I am repairing your suit now!" MACS told me. 'The acid is extremely powerful, but I believe I can counteract it. After all, acid and pigeons are old school, and I am very new school!"

I pushed myself up off the ground. I turned and looked up to see another barrage of white poop acid falling towards me. Out of pure reflex, I inhaled quickly, then exhaled -- hard. My breath shot the acid back up at the pigeons who were pooping on me. Half of them began to caw and flap their wings wildly after being splattered by their own acid. A few dropped to the ground. I felt bad doing that to the birds, but I had no choice. The remaining birds regrouped. They dive-bombed towards me.

"Okay, I've made the angry birds even angrier."

"Lia, this may be a good time to tell you that your dad designed your suit with a secret airtight pocket."

I looked at the birds closing in on me. "Thanks, MACS! Nice to know I have a pocket and all, but it's not that helpful just now!"

"Your dad put a piece of condensed garlic in that pocket," MACS continued.

"Now that's something worth knowing about!" I told MACS. A pocket on my suit popped open. I reached in and grabbed a small piece of something that felt like a nut. I tossed it into my mouth. It tasted like garlic. Luckily for me, I like garlic. I looked up at the birds. I opened my mouth. The flock of birds dropped from the sky.

"My, that packs a punch!" I said. "If I talk to anybody, I'll drop them in their tracks!"

"Your father calculated the garlic dose so it would wear off in three minutes," MACS told me.

"Well, let's hope that if I need extra super bad breath, it will be in the next three minutes!" I leaped towards the building.

Dear Diary: Jason really is a good friend. He always has the best ideas and my best interests at heart. That's why I couldn't risk him getting hurt in this fight. It was my battle. And as great as Jason is, he is just a regular guy. A super smart and loyal normal guy, but still just a guy. As for my dad, I love the way his strange brain works!

Not Monkeying Around...

I peered into one of the windows of the old animal hospital. I saw a bunch of big and small cages along the wall. A couple of large freezers sat in each corner. The middle of the room had a long lab table with all sorts of specialized-looking instruments and needles on it. Looking closer, I saw the cages had bunnies and mice in them.

I raced around to the front. There stood a big metal door with a red light above it. I figured the door must have had an alarm system. I fought back the urge to kick it down. Instead, I moved to the side of the door. I took a few steps back. I took a deep breath. I rushed at the wall smashing a 'me' sized hole in the wall. I turned and looked at the hole. It reminded me of something you'd see in a cartoon.

Three monkeys in lab coats came rushing in from a back room. They looked adorable. They pointed long rods at me. Okay, not so adorable. They squeezed the handles on the rods. Beams of electricity shot into me. I crackled and surged. I shook it off. I believe my behind started smoking a bit.

The three monkeys looked amazed that their shocks didn't stop me. Two of the monkeys started jumping up and down in fits. The third stayed calm. He or she turned to the other two. "The boss said she was strong."

One of the other monkeys pointed at me. "But not this strong!"

The third nodded. "Yeah, man, we hit her with everything, and all it seemed to do was tickle her!"

"It did kind of tickle a little," I told them.

The two monkeys tossed down their weapons. They threw off their lab coats. "Man, I don't need this kind of stress!" one of the monkeys said.

"Me neither," the other monkey said, rubbing his stomach. "I think I have an ulcer now."

"But we have a job to do!" the lead monkey protested.

312

The other two shook their heads. "She literally pays us in peanuts and bananas."

"But she does pay us!"

The other two each rolled their eyes. I found it to be both adorable and strange.

"But we're cute monkeys. People would feed us anyhow!" one monkey objected.

"Yeah, and without all this stress. Plus, I don't like injecting bunnies and thinking so much. I miss the days of just eating, sleeping, swinging, and throwing poop at people!" the other monkey lamented.

"We can still do all those things!" the lead monkey said. He pointed to his brain. "Only with more intelligence. Maybe we can make our poop splatter off walls and hit more people?"

The other two looked at each other. "You make a compelling point!" one said. "But you still can't beat the fact that ignorance truly is bliss!"

"Yeah, plus then we wouldn't have to deal with over-powered teens who run through walls and clobber malls with foot odor."

I cleared my throat. "Guys, you know I can hear you, right?"

"Yeah, but you can't remove your own cyber implants!" the lead monkey said, arms crossed.

The two other monkeys looked at each other. They smiled. They each reached up and pulled the other monkey's implant off. They each howled for a moment. They stopped. They contently hopped away.

The lead monkey shook his head. "So hard to get good help these days." He turned to me. "Girl, can you believe those two?"

I walked towards him and pounded my fist into my hand. The sound forced him to stagger back. "Looks like it's just you versus me now. I like those odds."

The monkey looked at me. "Yes, I understand that you would." He rolled up his lab coat sleeve, exposing a watch. "So, let me improve those odds!" He pushed a button on this watch. A cage in the middle of the room popped up. Out jumped two kangaroos.

"These guys aren't as smart as my fellow monkeys. Which means they will follow orders better!" He pointed at me. "Get her Skippy and Dundee!"

The two kangaroos, who were charming BTW, leap at me. They each kicked me in the head. Okay, that wasn't very charming. I didn't fall. But the two kangaroos landed on their feet and started pummeling me with rapid punches. Their punches didn't really hurt. But this had to stop as I couldn't concentrate on the lead lab monkey.

"Guys, I don't want to hurt you!" I told the kangaroos.

They continued to mindlessly pound me with punches and kicks. Since I didn't want to hit back, I just let them punch and kick me. I figured these animals might have been pumped up. But they were still flesh and blood and would punch themselves out.

After around two minutes, the punch speed slowed down. After about three minutes, the punches were pretty much just weak attempts. By the fourth minute, the two kangaroos just stood there panting for air. I knocked them each over with a little puff of my breath. "Enjoy your sleep!" I told them as I walked by.

I concentrated on the lab monkey. "You ready to give up now?" I asked.

He nodded and held up his hands. "Yeah, I'm smart enough to know when I can't win!"

I walked forward. "Great! Glad to see you are a smart monkey."

He waited for me to come towards him. There was something about his grin I didn't like. Just as I got right in front of him, he pushed another button on his watch. A trap door underneath me opened up. I started to plummet downwards. I landed on my feet in a small metal room. I've been in bigger closets. Yeah, this monkey was making me mad. The room went dark with a clang. I assumed that meant the trap door had closed over me. I bent down and leaped upward, extending my arm. I crashed through the trap door.

I grabbed the surprised monkey and lifted him off the ground. "Okay, buddy! You asked for it!" I said, making a fist.

"Look, please don't hit me. I'm just a poor defenseless little monkey!"

"One that has electrocuted me, sent kangaroos after me, and tried to trap me in a metal cage!" I pointed out.

He shrugged. "You must give me credit for being persistent… I also sent the pooping birds."

"Good point," I told him. I dropped him back to the ground.

"Phew, thanks!" he grinned.

"MACS! Deactivate the underarm shielding in my uniform!" I ordered.

"But Miss Lia, without that… you're…. Oh, right, I get it!"

The monkey waved his arms frantically. "Wait, wait! Stop, stop! What's going on?"

I aimed my armpit at the chump monkey. "He just basically deactivated my deodorant," I told him.

The monkey fell over, holding his throat. He was stiff as a board.

"I hope you have nightmares!" I told him.

Dear Diary: I learned I do have a bit of a nasty side when I get angry. But man, that monkey deserved that.

With Friends Like These...

With the monkeys and kangaroos out of the way or out cold on the ground, I started looking the place over. I now knew Doctor Stone was at least partially behind this. After all, she did give Greta this address. But had Doctor Stone acted alone, or was she ordered to do this by Doctor Dangerfield? After all, Stone did work for Dangerfield.

Searching through one of the draws of the lab table, I found a notebook. I opened it and read the words. It was handwritten...

I can't believe those jerks at the hospital, and the University and everywhere else are so in love with Donna Dangerfield. Yeah, sure, she was my mentor in med school and the first person to give me a job, but she's never thought big enough. She's always taken the safe and cautious road. We could have been so much further ahead with our cybernetics. We could have had our devices all over the world by now. We could have made people and animals more intelligent and more powerful. But no, she couldn't see it. She thought we needed more fail-safes. More ways to protect our patients. She didn't see that by giving them more power, it would give us the power to control them. To make the world in our image. A place where science and justice could thrive.

So, I did my own research on the side. Everything was progressing nicely, but now my mentor comes to my hospital and takes over the lead on my program!! I can't let her slow me down!

Yikes! That seemed scary! I had to face facts. Wendi's aunt wasn't an evil scientist. The evil scientist was Doctor Stone.

"Girl, don't you know it's impolite to read somebody else's diary?" the now familiar voice of Doctor Stone said to me.

317

I turned to see Doctor Stone standing there, flanked by Lori and Marie. Marie looked at me. "Sorry about this Super Teen, but Doctor Gem is making us do this!"

"Making you do what?" I asked.

Lori smiled. She stomped her foot on the ground, sending a shock through the floor. The floor shifted like a wave in the water coming at me. The force knocked me down. Lori leaped across the room on top of me. She drew back her fists. "I don't want to do this, but it feels so great!"

Lori fired a punch at my head. I darted my head to the side. The punch left a huge hole in the floor.

"Careful!" Doctor Stone shouted. "You super brats are ruining my lab! I know it's not much, but it's all I could afford!"

Lori turned to look at her. "Ah, sorry...."

I lifted my leg up and flipped Lori off me.

I jumped back to my feet.

I heard Doctor Stone tell Marie. "Get into this fight!"

Marie lowered her head. "Super Teen, you have to stop." She pointed at the disks on her temple. "These things have enhanced my brain so much I can see sense and change the structure of things...."

"Which means?"

Marie touched an old lab table. The table turned to gold. "What the?"

Marie shrugged. "When Doctor Stone did this to me, I was thinking I could use some money for college. Then poof. My touch turns things to gold." She paused. "Please don't make me touch you. I'm not sure I can reverse it. Just give up."

"You know I'm pretty fast. I can be hard to touch," I told her.

"I don't have to touch, touch you," Marie said.

"Now, what exactly does THAT mean?" I asked.

A couple of flies flew past Marie. She blew a little puff of breath on them. The flies fell to the ground and turned to solid gold.

Lori stood up behind me and locked me in a bear hug. Lori's grip was hard, but I knew I could break it. "Good, I hate flies!" Lori laughed.

Marie walked towards me slowly. I knew she didn't want to hurt me, but somehow Doctor Stone had control of her and Lori. I had to time this right, or I could end up golden and not in a good way. I didn't know if Marie's power would work on me, but I had to assume it would. I had no interest in being a gold statue.

I grabbed Lori's arm and threw her over my shoulder into Marie. When the two made contact, Lori turned into a solid gold statue that pinned Marie to the ground.

"Oh no!" Marie cried. "This is bad! Our team needs Lori!"

I ran up to Marie. "Don't worry. If you can see the structure of things like you say, I know you can reverse this!" I bent down and touched her gently on the shoulder.

Marie smiled at me. She took my hand. Much to my relief, I didn't turn to gold. "Thanks, Super Teen! Sorry, I tried to turn you into gold! It was like I was in a dream. Luckily, I seem to be me again."

"Good!" I said. I took another chance. I lifted the golden Lori off Marie. I pointed at the statue. "You turn her back while I deal with her!" I stared angrily at Doctor Gem.

Gem screamed at Marie, "I made you! Now I want you to make her into gold!"

Marie shook her head. "Sorry lady, no can do...."

Gem grit her teeth. "Fine, I'll do this myself!"

Gem squeezed her fists together and grunted. It looked like she had a bad case of constipation. Suddenly Gem started to grow and grow and grow. She crashed through the ceiling of the building, sending roofing material spiraling to the ground. I leaped back and shielded Marie and Lori.

"Thanks," Marie said.

Doctor Gem Stone now towered over us. Oh no, this was bad.

I turned to Marie. "I know you can undo what you did to Lori!"

Marie trembled. "You sure?"

I put my hands on her shoulders, "Yes, I am. Look, you broke Doctor Crazy Ladies' control on you. Now you're touching me, and I didn't turn to gold. You can turn Lori back!"

"How do you know that? You don't even know me!"

Oh right, I was still in my suit. "MACS blink off the mask...." I ordered.

"But Ms. Lia, then she will know who you are!" MACS said in my head.

"Exactly...." I said.

Maria looked at me and smiled. "I thought your voice was familiar! I told Lori you sounded like Lia, and she said that I was crazy; either that or had been sniffing my socks for too long!" She gave me a quick hug. "I knew I was right!"

I looked at her. "And I know you can fix this!"

Marie nodded. "I can do it! I can do it!"

"Great! While you're doing that, I'll find a way to stop a super-powered cybernetic giant mad scientist!"

"Be careful! She put those cybernetic disks behind her neck and all the way down her back!"

Dear Diary: I was so glad I could snap Marie out of being mind-controlled by showing her I trusted her. I knew the power of kindness would come through. Yeah, it's corny, but it's true.

The Not So Good Doctor...

Doctor Gem bent down. Her hand engulfed me. She lifted me off the ground. She stomped over the building into the street. Man, it seems like I always end up fighting giants in the street. I guess it's my thing, my niche. The problem was, last time I fought something this big, it was a non-living robot that I beat by throwing out into space. I couldn't do that to Doctor Gem. After all, she was a living, breathing person.

"So, you're Doctor Strong's little brat, Lia!" she cackled.

"I am her daughter, yes," I said.

"I'm activating your mask again!" MACS told me.

"Sweet outfit!" she said.

"Thanks!"

"Hey, how did your clothing grow with you?" I asked. Yeah, I probably should have been worrying about other things at that moment, but I was curious.

"I stole some of the technology from BM Science!" Doctor Gem said. She glared down at me. "Your mom helped bring Dangerfield here!"

Doctor Gem squeezed me harder. I pushed back with my arms, trying to squeeze out, but being a super cybernetic giant person, she squeezed with an amazing amount of force. Since I'm also a living, breathing person, I wasn't sure how long I could keep this up.

"Put the girl down, or you are fired!" I heard from below.

Looking down, I saw Jason had led Mom, Jess, and Tanya here.

"I order you to put her down!" Jess said in her commanding hypnotic voice.

Doctor Gem smiled. "Sorry, kid, my many cybernetic implants make my mind very strong!"

Tanya smirked. "You forced me to use my time powers on you!"

321

Doctor Gem laughed. She popped her foot out of her shoe. She waved her foot over my mom and friends.

Tanya's eyes rolled to the back of her head. "I really have to learn not to tell the bad guys what I'm about to do." Tanya gasped with her last breath.

They all fell to the ground.

"You're not the only one with a foot odor problem!"

"It's not a problem!" I said defensively. "My feet sweat. I'm human, just superhuman."

Doctor Gem looked down her now giant nose at me. "Okay, now can we get to our battle. Though so far, there hasn't been much of a fight."

I looked up at her. "Look, Doctor Gem, I don't think you've actually really hurt anybody. If you give up now, I'm sure they will go easy on you...."

Doctor Gem squeezed me. "So now you are a super lawyer?"

"No, I'm just saying, nothing you've done can't be undone. In fact, I think I stopped all the robberies your controlled people attempted."

She glared at me. "Thank you very much BTW. Do you have any idea how much this research costs? I was able to siphon budget money from the hospital as I'm also a computer genius. But I needed some quick cash, and you got in the way."

I shrugged. "I'm a hero. It's what I do." I accented my words with action. I zapped her hand with heat vision.

She screamed and loosened her grip. I dropped slowly to the ground. I pointed up at her. "We can do this the easy way or the hard way!"

Doctor Stone lifted a foot and tried to stomp me. I caught her foot over my head. "Figures you'd pick the hard way!"

I leaped upwards, forcing her foot to go flying backward. Doctor Stone crashed to the ground with a huge thud. In the background, I heard police sirens.

"*Your father has alerted the police and also sent BMS security cop*ters!" MACS texted me in my mind, which was kind of freaky. But when you're fighting a fifty-foot mad scientist, you get used to freaky fast.

Doctor Stone rolled over on her stomach. She started to push herself up. I blasted her in the butt with heat vision. I got a kick out of that.

The not-so-good doctor pushed to her feet. She turned and started blowing on her now smoking buns.

"Nice to see you have hot buns!" I told her.

Doctor Stone pointed at me. "You have to work on your banter!"

I put my hands on my hips. "Yeah, people keep telling me that. It's hard being witty under pressure."

"You want pressure! I'll show you pressure!"

Doctor Stone bent down then leaped at me. She landed on me with a decided thud! Now I found myself squished by those same giant buns I had just burned. She twisted her butt, trying to ground me into the ground. "Can you tell I do a lot of Pilates!" she laughed. She bounced up and down on me. "Man, I so wish I could fart now." She grinned. "Ah, here it comes."

She let out the nastiest fart.
PPPPPFFFFFFFFRRRRRAPPP!

She laughed. "Wow, all those years of grad school and med school, and I still find a fart to be hilarious!"

It did stink like about a million skunks who had eaten stinky cheese and rolled in the garbage for a week. Yet it didn't knock me out, though I kind of wish it did. Still, I went limp. My hope being, she'd get her big butt off me.

Doctor Stone stood up. She laughed. "Ha! Not so tough now, are you?"

I jumped up into the air, spun around, and gave her a punch to the jaw! The punch sent her reeling backward. I dropped back to the ground.

"Listen, Doc. I don't want to hurt you!" I said.

The police sirens drew closer.

The doctor shook her head. "Fine. If I can't finish you off, I'll deal with the police first."

I ran past her at super speed. I jumped up and hovered above her. "Doc, stop! You're a doctor. You heal people, not hurt people!" I told her.

She paused. "Yes, that's true, but sometimes you have to hurt a few people to help a world of people. I know some people will think I'm jealous of Doctor Dangerfield because she's so smart and so pretty and so good at sports."

I nodded. "I can relate."

Doctor Stone went on, "But that's not the case. My research was at least as good as hers, if not better. But she was the big famous doctor, so she got all the big bucks and the top job. I should be her boss!"

"Ah, wasn't she your teacher?" I asked.

Doctor Stone smiled. "Yes, of course, but even a silly kid like you must have heard the saying, the student surpasses the teacher."

I nodded.

Doctor Stone rambled on. "So now I'm like way smarter. And she won't listen to me. She wants to go slow with our research. I wanted to go fast. Look what I've accomplished…."

"Yep, you turned yourself into a giant cybernetic mad scientist!"

She shook a finger at me. "No! No! No! Not a mad scientist, an angry one. She got the breaks just because she's prettier and better with people than I am!"

Doctor Stone swatted at me like a fly. I dodged it. She swatted me again, and this time she hit me, knocking me to the ground. Now that hurt. I pushed myself up off the ground. I spat some dirt out of my mouth. "Oh gross."

I heard a familiar voice behind me. "Hey, Doc, crazy lady!" Lori shouted. "Stop now, or else you'll force me to stop you!"

Doctor Stone did stop for a moment. She turned to Lori and laughed. "Ha, your cybernetics are good but not nearly enough to stop me."

Lori smiled. "Yeah, I was kind of hoping you'd say that." Lori turned to Marie. "You ready, teammate?"

Marie nodded. "I'm ready."

Lori picked Marie up over her head. Lori flung Marie, arms extended out, at Doctor Stone. Marie flew through the air and touched Doctor Stone on her knee. Marie started to fall. I jumped over and caught Marie before she hit the ground.

Doctor Stone looked down at her knee. It had turned golden.

"How dare you!" she shouted. "I made you special!"

"I didn't ask for this," Marie told her. "You told Lori and me these were dummy test devices!"

"Yeah. I tested them on two dummies…." Stone smirked.

Marie pointed to Stone's knee. "Who's the dummy now?"

Doctor Stone watched in horror as the gold slowly started to creep up her leg. She lifted up her still non-golden leg. "I'm taking you down with me!"

I thought cold freezing thoughts: running outside in the winter without shoes and coat, eating ice, jumping in an ice bath. I exhaled super cold breath at Doctor Stone. Her leg froze above us. The upper half of her body froze and turned golden at the same time. The golden, frozen statue started to tip over towards Oscar Organa and his film crew, who must have just arrived on the spot.

I flew up behind the falling statue and caught it. I guided it down slowly to a safe open spot.

Chief Michaels and my father rushed up to me. "Are you okay, Super Teen?" my father asked.

"I'm fine, sir."

Chief Michaels looked at the frozen golden statue that was a scientist. "Man, I'm getting too old for this job!"

Mom, Jess, Tanya, and Jason had all snapped out of their foot odor-induced state. Dad and Mom, along with Chief Michaels, stood there trying to decide what to do with a giant golden statue.

Oscar Oranga walked up to me and flashed his mic in my face. "So, Super Teen, can you turn people into gold?"

I didn't know how to answer that. I certainly didn't want the world to know that Marie could do this and that she and Lori were cybernetic. But I didn't need the world extra scared of me either.

Doctor Dangerfield stepped forward and smiled. "Hi, I'm Doctor Donna Dangerfield. I was one of Doctor Stones' bosses. Doctor Stone turned to gold as a side effect of using too many cybernetic improvement disks. These things are only in their early stages. I'm afraid this was an unfortunate side effect. We will find a way to cure her."

Jess walked up to Oscar and his crew. *"Now get out of here!"* Jess said in her command voice.

Oscar and his crew bowed, packed up their stuff, and walked away.

"And cluck like chickens!" Jess ordered.

Oscar and his crew started clucking.

"Thanks, Jess," I said.

Jess gave me a nod. "I love doing that!"

I heard Mom, Dad, and the chief still pondering what to do. "We can't keep her like this. Can we?" Chief Michaels said. "I mean, she broke the law and has to pay for her crimes, but this seems unfair."

I huddled next to my super teen team of Jess, Tanya, Lori, Marie, and Jason. "Okay, we need a way to turn her back to a regular human," I said.

Jason looked us all over. "Now let me get this straight, Jess can control minds and do some magic, Tanya can control time, Lori is cybernetic muscle, and Marie cybernetic brain, which lets her change the structure of things."

They all nodded.

Jess looked at the statue. "I could just vanish her!" she suggested.

"Ah, let's go for something that doesn't involve vanishing," I said.

"I've always wanted to turn somebody into a toad," Jess offered.

"Still looking for other options," I laughed.

"I got it. Tanya rewinds her in time to the moment before she turned into a super cybernetic mad scientist. Jess makes everybody else believe that this was a natural occurrence," Jason said.

"Now that could work," I nodded thoughtfully.

"I've never reset somebody in time before," Tanya admitted, a little concerned.

I put my arm around her. "Well, my friend, there's a first time for everything!"

Tanya, Jess, and I walked up to the golden doctor. They looked at each other. They knew the timing would have to be perfect to stop her from pounding away again.

Tanya locked her eyes on the golden doctor and lowered her head. Doctor Stone began to shimmer. She turned back to flesh and blood. She started to shrink. "How long do you have to set her back through time?" Tanya asked.

"She inserted all those things on herself today when she panicked," Lori replied. She stuck out her tongue. "She forced us to stick some of the ones on her lower back and her butt."

Tanya took a breath. "Good, I can do that…I think."

Doctor Stone stumbled to her feet. "What's going on? What am I doing here?"

I nodded to Jess. "Okay, do your stuff!"

Jess walked forward. In her cool hypnotic voice, she uttered. *"You over-loaded yourself with those weird cybernetic enhancements. You turned into a giant mad scientist. Luckily, Super Teen was able to stop you. You exerted so much energy. You burnt out the enhancements. And now the police are taking you to jail!"*

Chief Michaels stepped forward, "Yep, that's exactly what happened." He pointed to two of his officers. "Officers, take her away!"

"But, but…I only wanted to do good." Doctor Stone whimpered. She glared at Doctor Dangerfield. "You are too cautious!"

Doctor Dangerfield pointed to all the damage Stone had done. "Look at the destruction you've created! Not to mention all the poor animals you experimented with!!"

The police took Doctor Stone away. I smiled. Things had worked out pretty well. My friends and I had teamed up to stop her.

Doctor Dangerfield walked over to me and offered me her hand. "Thanks for stopping her!"

"No problem, Doctor! I'm just glad I could help. I'm sorry you had to see your research abused like that," I told her. Yep, it looks like I misjudged Doctor Dangerfield.

Doctor Dangerfield looked around at the destruction caused by Stone. "I do owe a thank you to poor Gem. She did show me what great potential my work has!" Doctor Dangerfield gave me a weird smile.

Okay, maybe I hadn't misjudged her. I guess time would tell!

For now, though, it had been an amazing start to my summer break. I kind of hoped the rest of my summer would be a bit calmer. Of course, if it weren't, that would be cool too. After all, l am Super Teen, and now I have super friends! So mega super cool!

Dear Diary: I love the idea of having friends that are super like me. After all, some things, actually most things, are easier when you use teamwork. Good thing that I knew I could count on my family and friends to help me, no matter what.

***

Find out what happens next in
Diary of a Super Girl – Book 4

OTHER POPULAR SERIES
FREE ON KINDLE UNLIMITED

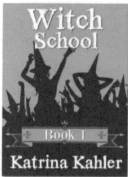

EBOOKS & PAPERBACKS

BEAUTIFUL & POSITIVE BOOKS FOR GIRLS

KIDS LOVE THESE BOOKS!

BEST SELLING BOOKS

FREE ON KINDLE UNLIMITED

KIDS LOVE THESE BOOKS!

SUPER GIRL SERIES
CHECK OUT OUR COMBO BOOKS
FREE ON KINDLE UNLIMITED

EBOOKS & PAPERBACKS